Amy & Zach

Sarah Louise Smith

First Red Line Edition, Crooked Cat Publishing Ltd. 2014

Discover us online:
www.crookedcatpublishing.com

Join us on facebook:
www.facebook.com/crookedcatpublishing

Tweet a photo of yourself holding
this book to **@crookedcatbooks**
and something nice will happen.

For Nathaniel,
because you're my best friend.
& Dad,
because you are my hero
(And I'm sorry I deleted your novel that time...)

About the Author

Sarah Louise Smith lives in Milton Keynes with her husband, two cute cats and a loopy golden retriever. She also has an extremely lovely step-daughter and a large extended family. She loves music, reading, cooking, travelling and taking long walks.

Sarah has been writing stories ever since she can remember. One day, her husband bought her a laptop out of the blue, telling her she could accept it only on the condition that she used it to write a novel, something she'd been saying she wanted to do since she left high school.

Amy & Zach is her debut novel.

Also by the same author:
Izzy's Cold Feet

Acknowledgements

Firstly, thank you, Reader. I hope you enjoy reading about Amy & Zach. Please tell all your friends if you do. Let's chat: come and find me online!

Thank you to all of my family and friends who have been so enthusiastic about my writing adventure thus far, I'm very grateful. In particular: Mum, Dad, Val, Nan, Dan, and Chloe – thank you for your constant love and support.

Thank you also to my step-sister Sarah and my mother-in-law Deborah for asking me about my writing regularly and really encouraging me to go for it.

A huge thank you to Laurence and Steph of Crooked Cat Publishing. You are a pleasure to work with.

Most of all, thank you to Nathaniel for being not only a lovely husband, but my best friend. I could never have finished this novel without your support. And I'd be seriously de-hydrated.

Sarah Louise Smith
Milton Keynes, January 2014

Amy & Zach

Chapter One

Amy

I stared out of the airplane window, taking several deep breaths. I'd told myself over and over again not to be nervous, that this was silly, that there was nothing to be afraid of, but it wasn't sinking in. I just couldn't be rational. I was surprised to find myself smile as a glimmer of green fields and a narrow road made an appearance through the clouds. We were above England. I was almost home.

"Nervous flier?" asked the guy next to me. He'd been asleep for most of the flight, and I'd been grateful for nearly seven hours of silence. I wasn't in the mood to start with the small talk now.

"No, not at all." I didn't take my eyes off of the ground below.

"You seem a little tense."

"I'm just eager to get home, that's all," I lied.

I guess many people would rejoice as their plane touched down at Heathrow after over a year away from home. They'd stand up from their seat and eagerly push their way to the exit, looking forward to seeing their families again. They'd hurry through the arrivals gate, anxious to throw their arms around their parents, to catch up with their brother and sister, to greet their friends. And yet I couldn't motivate myself to stand, to slowly shuffle out of the plane, to collect my luggage. So I waited, prolonging the inevitable, sitting in my seat, eyes closed, wishing I could open them again and realise that the past week had been a dream, a crazy stupid dream and I'd wake

3

up back in Boston, and everything would be perfect.

"Excuse me, madam," said the air steward gently. "We've landed. We're in London!"

I opened my eyes and forced a smile at the big grin bearing down on me.

"Thanks." I sighed and got up from my seat. Time to face the music.

I stood waiting for my luggage and wondered if I could get on the next plane out of there. I seriously considered it for a few minutes as I watched my suitcase coming towards me. I could grab my things, even avoid greeting my family, and just book myself on the next flight back to Boston. The thought made me feel elated and terrified at the same time. There were plenty of problems in Boston too, issues I was even less ready to deal with than a family reunion. I considered getting a flight somewhere else entirely. Maybe New York or Chicago. Or Paris. Rome. Even Afghanistan. Anywhere but here, or Boston.

I loaded up my bags and pushed my trolley to one side a little, walking slowly, letting others pass me by. I felt dizzy now that I was here, and that it was real. I needed a couple of minutes more to prepare myself. I watched my fellow passengers leaving. The girl with the cropped blonde hair who'd sat in front of me pushed a bright orange suitcase through the crowds, heading straight for the exit. A man in a suit was greeted by, I presumed, his wife. She didn't seem all that happy to see him. Who wears a suit on a seven hour flight? Another couple were hugging, crying, ecstatic to see each other. I started to move slowly out, looking around for my family.

For some reason I imagined them to look exactly as they had done when I left. Mum had been wearing a long red coat. Jack, my step-father, had an umbrella. It'd been raining all morning. My sister, Libby, had been disinterested. Just as I walked away from them she got a call on her mobile and didn't seem interested in saying goodbye at all. Ed, my twin brother, had been the only one I was sad to walk away from.

And as I saw Ed's face smiling at me, I suddenly felt a rush of emotion. His hair was longer, almost down to his shoulders in an unkempt mess. I saw he was alone and I felt a little relieved. He was walking towards me now, grinning, and wrapped his arms around me affectionately. He smelled of an expensive aftershave and felt thinner. I was pretty sure I felt fatter.

"Good to see you sis." He released me quickly and then took control of my trolley.

"Did you come alone?" I asked, trying to figure out if I was disappointed or pleased.

"Yes. Mum is preparing dinner for us. Libby and Tim are there."

Panic rose in my chest at the sound of my sister's fiancé's name. I could have done without seeing him today. We walked along chatting about the usual things, my flight, and the weather, how I was generally, how he was overall.

"Wait," he said, stopping as we reached his car, "Where's Zach?"

"He couldn't make it. He's got flu."

Zach

I tapped my credit card nervously on the counter as the clerk typed a few things into her computer.

"We have one seat available on the next flight to London," she told me. "But you'll need to board right away. I can tell them to hold the gate for you."

"Thank you." I handed over my credit card, ready to hug her for telling me this news. I'd imagined waiting hours in the airport. I glanced at my watch. Amy would be landing about now. I thought about calling her, but decided against it. She'd made it clear she didn't want to talk to me, and if I told her I was coming, she'd only tell me not to.

I ran through the departure lounge, searching for my gate, hardly able to think about what I'd say or do when I got there. I found my seat, and for the first time in two days, I slept.

Amy

Ed threw my luggage into the back of his Audi and we made our way out to the motorway. He told me about his job and his colleagues and his new place and I smiled and answered as enthusiastically as I could. I felt an overwhelming sense of nostalgia as the signs for Milton Keynes started to appear. The town I grew up in, with hundreds of roundabouts, thousands of trees and a lack of character, somehow. I loved it and hated it at the same time. Like an annoying relative, it was fine for me to complain about Milton Keynes but if someone who didn't live there had a bad word to say, then I leapt to its defence.

As we came off the motorway, I stared out of the window, barely replying to Ed's questions. It all felt rather surreal and almost like the past year hadn't happened. I thought of Zach and wondered what he was doing now. Sitting at home, alone. Or out? Out with someone else? Could I blame him if he was?

As we drove into my parent's street I felt a little emotional. So much had happened since I was last here. I knew I'd changed, grown, matured, and gone through a hell of a lot. I wondered if my family would be able to tell and then decided they probably weren't that perceptive. And then there we were, pulling up on the driveway of the house I grew up in. I looked up at my bedroom window and remembered all the happy and sad moments, the giggles and the tears I'd shed behind that glass. The house looked exactly the same; brown bricks, slate roof, ivy growing up and around the windows, flowers in pots. Memories came back to me of playing tag with Ed and Libby on the front lawn. Waving my grandparents off after a weekend visit. Eating ice creams from the van on the front step before they melted.

"That's Tim's car. He and Libby must be here already."

Despite my anger with him, I shuddered and suddenly

6

wished Zach were with me. I sighed as I took off my seatbelt.

"How do you feel?" Ed asked.

"Good. I'm great. Glad to be back." I hoped I sounded convincing.

"Well, it's great to see you."

I decided to try and be positive; perhaps this wasn't going to be as bad as I thought.

"Thank you."

The front door opened and my mum came out to give me a big hug. Jack, Libby and Tim appeared in the doorway. I thought I might be sick.

"Good to see you Amy," Mum said, holding me close to her. She looked at my face for a few minutes before stepping back and mumbled something about my being pale.

Libby hugged me next. I glanced over her shoulder and at Tim standing in the doorway, he too had turned white. He managed a small smile and I looked away. As I hugged my baby sister for the first time in a year, I almost told her. I almost blurted it out that moment in front of everyone. But I couldn't. I was a coward.

"This is my Tim," Libby was saying the next moment. "Tim, this is Amy."

I thought about the word "my" for a few moments and wondered if she knew. Like she was staking a claim on him, making it clear that despite that moment of weakness, he was hers. She was welcome to him. I smiled at them both, with their blue eyes and blonde hair. They were bound to make beautiful babies. I shook hands with Tim and we all went inside, where I was forced to drink tea, eat a homemade biscuit which was revolting, and answer a zillion questions on life in America.

"I thought you were bringing a man with you from Boston," Libby said, leaning in close to Tim who was staring at me intently.

"He couldn't make it at the last minute," I lied again. "He's ill." I glanced around the room, taking in the peach flowery wall

7

paper and the furniture that'd been there since I was nine years old. Nothing had changed, and it almost felt like I'd never been away.

"I thought he was your boyfriend."

"It's not serious." I lied yet again. They had no idea. I'd mentioned Zach only briefly in my emails.

"Tim just got back yesterday from Boston, he was there on business," Libby told us.

"Really?" I hoped I sounded normal.

"Yes," he said calmly, although he didn't look directly at me.

"Did you like it?"

We made a little conversation about Boston as if we were two perfect strangers and I started to feel a little more relaxed. Maybe we were going to pull it off.

It was strange seeing my family again. Libby had changed the most. She looked more glamorous. More make-up, stylish clothes, even her voice seemed different. She had lost at least a stone in weight. Mum was exactly the same as before, except she'd somehow put on the weight that Libby had lost. Ed seemed the most enthusiastic to talk to me and asked if I wanted to go to the pub together one night during my stay.

Mum had prepared a huge buffet, and we each grabbed a plate and filled up with lots of pre-packed supermarket-bought snacks, salad, bread and so on before gathering around the dining table to discuss Libby's last minute wedding plans. Her wedding coordinator had put together an itinerary and some information about the day. We all had a little plastic wallet each with information, informing us of everything we could possibly need to know and much more. We sat and listened to the plans, everything from cufflinks, to flowers, to food, to table decorations. I watched Mum, taking notes and being very enthusiastic.

I went out to the kitchen to make some tea, and my stepdad, Jack, followed me out.

"So how've you been?" I asked, as he squeezed my shoulders.

"Good, good, I can't complain. It's good to have you home, Amy," he said, kissing me on my forehead. I smiled. Somehow, my not being there for a year had made them all appreciate me more when I came home. I felt more loved and hugged that day than any of the days I'd spent living in that house, Mum in particular was very different. Preparing food and fussing around everyone like somehow she'd found the maternal instinct which had seemed to escape her up until now.

"Your mother is about to retire."

I was so shocked that my mouth actually fell open and I didn't know what to say.

"Why?"

"She just said it was time. She seems happier. More like the woman I fell in love with all those years ago."

I pulled a sceptical face.

"You'll see!" He told me.

We returned to the dining room. Libby was insisting she and Tim paid for all of our hotel bills. I didn't object. The rooms were over three hundred pounds a night and I had no idea if I'd return to Boston or not. If I didn't, then I didn't have a job.

Zach

I sat back and wondered what Amy's family would think of me. I tried to remember when she'd first told me about them, and realised it was actually on the night we first met. I'd asked her what her family was like and she'd frowned.

"Well, my mum's a workaholic. She wasn't around much when we were children. We're not close. I've only spoken to her a couple of times since I've been in the US."

"How many siblings do you have?"

"Two. I'm a twin, actually." She smiled at some past memory or familiar thought, "I have a twin brother, Ed and a half-sister, Libby."

"And your dad?"

9

"Well, Jack is my step-father. He's great. Very kind. Always treated me as if I were his daughter. I thought he was my real dad until I was fourteen."

"Wow. Really? How did you find out?"

"Well, my mum asked Ed and I to come into the dining room after school one day. She looked nervous, you know. I thought maybe someone had died or was critically ill or something like that."

"It must have come as a shock."

"Yeah, it did. She told us that our father was American. She'd met him when she studied at Harvard for a term. It was a brief fling, nothing serious, and they didn't keep in touch when she returned to the UK. Ed went crazy. He started yelling, demanding to know our father's name. I just sat there, staring at the dining table. I felt numb."

I saw the happy, cheerful expression disappear from her face as she told me the story.

"So have you met him? Your biological father I mean?"

"No. I know where to find him, but I haven't psyched myself up to do it yet."

"Does he know you exist?"

"Yes. Well, he knows she was pregnant. But she said he didn't want to know. He wasn't interested, wanted to get on with his life, and she hasn't spoken to him since before we were born.."

"So where is he?"

"He lives here in Boston. He doesn't know I'm here, but one day I'll get up the courage to go and meet him."

"Wow." I didn't know quite how to respond to that, and wondered if this was the reason she'd moved to Boston.

"He's a lawyer. I used to imagine he was someone famous, you know? Like an actor or something. I used to dream of someone like Bruce Willis or Al Pacino welcoming me into their arms. It's silly really."

"So when are you going to contact him?"

"I'm not sure if I will. I'm just thinking about it. What if he doesn't want to be found?"

"I'm sure he'd be proud and honoured to discover a daughter like you."

She smiled, but the sparkle had gone from her eyes. She seemed sad.

"Are you close to Jack? And your brother and sister?"

"No, not really. We email each other now and then. I guess my brother and I are close, but Libby and I...well, we are just very different people I guess."

I blinked a few times and came back to reality. A lot had changed between her telling me about her family, and this moment, when I was about to meet them. I thought I might go insane, thinking how I was going to handle this. Did I just go straight to their house, turn up on the doorstep? Should I call Amy first? Would she answer if I did? Would she be angry that I'd come?

Enough of this, I told myself. I plugged in my earphones and picked up my iPod, found a playlist Amy had made for me with all-British artists and let the music take my mind off of my troubles.

Amy

I watched Libby smiling and laughing about her wedding plans and pitied her. She was obsessed about the colour themes and flowers, the food and champagne. Every little detail was described, and all I could think about was that her fiancé had a huge secret, and she was marrying a jerk. I feigned mild interest as she passed around brochures and photos and watched my parents smile and nod. Ed seemed disinterested. I watched his hair fall across his face and realised how much this scruffy look suited him.

During a brief interlude, when Libby went to the bathroom, I moved seats and sat next to him.

11

"So how've you been, my dearest twin?" I smiled, watching him sip his tea.

"Not bad," he yawned.

"How's it going with Polly?" He'd told me in his last email that he'd met a girl.

"Well, actually. I really like her and-"

"Sorry to interrupt!" Libby grinned, obviously not sorry at all. "But we do have more stuff to share with you guys."

Ed rolled his eyes at me and I smiled. We looked up at Libby. As annoying as all this wedding talk was, she seemed happy. I decided to at least give her my full attention.

"Right," she said, sitting down and picking up her wedding planner, "the cake..."

Zach

The air steward passed me my meal and I realised how hungry I was. I hadn't really eaten much in the past few days. Call me crazy, but I love airplane food. Today I had beef stroganoff, with mushrooms, green beans, and rice followed by a chocolate brownie. It was delicious.

The guy sitting next to me smelled each item on his tray and screwed his nose up.

"I'm going to write to that Richard Branson fella." He had a gravelly voice and a Scottish accent.

"Oh yeah?" I asked.

"Yeah. Call this food? He's having a bloody laugh!"

"I think it's nice," I told him. "Try it."

The Scot leant forward and tasted a little of the beef.

"You're right, actually. Mmm." He took another mouthful.

"Zach," I said, offering my hand. He shook it.

"Greg. So where you from Zach?"

"Boston. You?"

"Well, Glasgow originally but I live in Inverness now. You know where that is?"

"Scotland?" I asked. He laughed.

"Yeah. Scotland. I'm not far from Loch Ness."

"Wow. So is it true? About the monster?"

He turned and looked me in the eye. I noticed some stroganoff sauce around his mouth.

"Yes," he replied, very seriously. I laughed. He didn't.

Amy

Libby's long list of plans eventually came to an end. Tim looked like he was about to fall asleep.

"So, when are you going back to Boston? Two weeks, right?" Mum asked as I went with her into the kitchen to clear up the dishes.

"I'm not sure Mum. I planned on two weeks, but I'm not sure if I'm going back to be honest."

I thought about telling her all about what had happened with Zach. We'd never been close and despite my warm welcome home, I didn't think we ever would be. But she smiled at me and I suddenly felt compelled to share.

"Well, don't you have commitments there? Like your job and-"

"Well, it's just that, it's complicated..." I began.

"I'm sure it'll all come out in the wash." This was her favourite saying. Her answer to problems at school, fights between her children, even when her own mother was diagnosed with terminal cancer, that was Mum's response. I wasn't even sure what it meant. It was like her way of dismissing the problem at hand, warning me not to talk about it any further. So I stopped, the one moment where I felt close to her fading away again to lurk in the shadows of our relationship.

"I'm going to bed," I told them all shortly afterward. I couldn't bear to hear another wedding detail and I was tired from the flight.

I found my old bedroom much the same as when I'd left

home, except for an exercise bike which looked brand new and dusty. Ed had put my suitcase just inside the door, and I rummaged around and found my toothbrush and slipped on my pyjamas. Tim was on the landing as I came out of the bathroom.

"Phew, this is weird isn't it?" he whispered. Again, that panic feeling.

I didn't say anything, just shot him a look of annoyance and went back to my room. We'd agreed to never speak of it again, to imagine it'd never happened. What part of that didn't he understand?

Zach

Greg spent the rest of the flight telling me about the legend of the Loch Ness Monster, or Nessie, as he preferred to call her. He told me about various sightings of something large in the water, which could not be explained. I humoured him, unsure whether he was speaking about it so seriously just to tease the ignorant American, or if he really was crazy.

"So, what do you?" I asked after a bathroom visit, hoping to change the subject.

"I run a Nessie museum," he told me. Ah, that explained it then. "Yourself?"

"I'm a web developer," I told him, watching his blank expression, "I build websites."

"I need a website!" He pulled out a card. It said 'Gregory Brown; Nessie Museum Manager.' I thought *'Gregory Brown; Delusional Lunatic'* would have sounded better. But despite the clear craziness about him, he seemed a nice enough guy so I told him I'd get in touch when I returned to Boston. I figured building a site for something unusual like that might be a little more fun than my regular clients. He started talking about photos he could send me of Nessie, and I actually started to wonder if she really *did* exist.

14

"So why were you in Boston?" I asked.

"Family wedding," he told me, "my niece married a yank. Now I'm spending a few days with an old friend in London, then back home for me. Back to Nessie. How come you're coming to the UK?"

"Same thing, a wedding. So, have you ever seen Nessie?"

"Well, actually, yes. It was my twenty-first birthday and I'd been out celebrating with my friends..."

"So you were drunk?"

"Yes, but, listen..."

Amy

I couldn't sleep; I was still on Boston time. The events of the past few days were replaying in my head. I pictured Zach's face just before I'd stormed out. I wondered what he'd be doing right now. I tried calling him but his phone was switched off. I tried the apartment and got the machine. I called back a few more times, not so much with the hope that he'd answer, but just to hear his voice.

My bed felt cold and lumpy. I suddenly had a desire to be back in Boston again. I closed my eyes and imagined I was lying in Zach's arms, snuggling under the bedding I'd helped him pick out in the sale. I smiled and decided I'd call him again in the morning, leave a message if necessary. I missed him more than I had ever thought I would.

Zach

At 8am I was in the rental car, a blue Ford Focus. I paid nearly a hundred pounds extra for a GPS, which the guy who rented it to me said the Brits called "Sat Nav." I figured it was the only way to ensure I got there. Being in the right side of the car and driving on the left was a bit weird, but not so bad once I got on the freeway. I passed green fields and towns and it seemed pretty much how I imagined it; green and rural. After an hour or so I came to the exit for Milton Keynes. Amy had told me it was full of "roundabouts" which it turned out were traffic circles. She was right. I passed over several before I came to what seemed to be the right residential area and finally found her parent's street, and then their house. It was like another world. The houses were small, again something Amy had told me, but also really close together. Kind of dainty but cute though.

I pulled up on the street outside the house and wondered if I'd done the right thing. Surely travelling all this way would show that I loved her and I was sorry.

I looked up at the ivy growing up and around the windows, and imagined Amy walking out of the front door, carrying a suitcase, about to move to a different country, all by herself. I felt proud thinking how brave and courageous she was, much more so than she ever gave herself credit for. I needed her, and knew I had to somehow win her back, make up for my mistakes and beg her to forgive me.

I took a deep breath and walked up to the door, knowing that talking this through was the only way to get past it.

Amy

I watched Tim butter Libby's toast and wondered if I'd ever be able to sit in the same room as him without feeling nauseous.

"We'll leave soon after this," Libby was telling Mum. "Amy, you should see Tim's apartment. He has a view of the Thames from his bedroom window."

"*Our* bedroom window," Tim corrected her before helping himself to bacon.

Mum had insisted we all get up at eight thirty, and come down for a huge breakfast she'd prepared including mushrooms, sausages, eggs. It was perhaps only the second or third time I'd ever seen her cook, but all the food just made me feel ill.

16

I took a bite of toast and a sip of coffee, burning my tongue. I looked out at the back garden. I remembered sitting there when my mum told us about Jack. Libby had been in the garden, playing with our dog, Camilla. I'd envied her that moment, because Jack was her real father. Her father had stuck around, when mine had not. I didn't envy her now, with that slime ball kissing her hand as she bat her eyelashes at him.

The door bell rang, and Ed went to answer it.

"Whoever could that be?" Mum wondered as Ed walked into the room, followed by our mystery guest. I thought I might faint when I saw who it was.

"This is Zach," Ed told everyone. "He's here to see Amy."

Ed looked quizzically at me and I glared at Zach, who was smiling broadly at everyone, avoiding my eyes.

"Well, it's very nice to meet you Zach," said my mum, getting up to shake his hand. He took her hand and shook it with gusto.

"You too, Mrs. Starling. I'm sorry if I'm interrupting you."

"Please, call me Maggie. No bother at all. I'm so glad you're feeling better."

He frowned for a moment and then realised what I must have told them.

"Yes, I'm all better, thank you!" He glanced at me and I glared back. Silence. I sat there, frozen, completely unaware of what to say, what to do. Tim had once again turned ghostly white. I shuddered at the thought of Zach ever finding out what had happened between us.

Jack got up next and took Zach's hand.

"I'm Jack," he said. "Amy's step-father."

"It's great to finally meet you." Zach shook his hand vigorously, looking calm and collected although I knew he must feel anything but.

"So Zach, you decided to fly all this way to be with Amy?" Mum asked him. He nodded, raised his eyebrows, and looked at me, smiling as if nothing had happened.

"That's very sweet of you." She smiled before giving a glance to tell me I was being rude for not even getting up. I was glad to see him, I realised. I wanted to rush to him, kiss him, and ask him to hold me. Then I remembered why I was here alone in the first place.

"What are you doing here?" I finally managed to say, in an angrier tone than I had planned.

"Amy!" my mum said, "that's not the way to greet someone who's flown thousands of miles to see you."

"It's okay Mrs. Starling." Zach turned to look at her with a charming smile. "I should have told her I was coming. I did call, but you didn't answer, so...well, here I am. It's great to meet you all. I've heard so much about you."

"That's strange," said Libby. "We've heard almost nothing about you."

"Really?" He looked hurt.

"Please, sit down, are you hungry?" Mum pulled out a seat but before Zach could react I stood up.

"Let's go outside and talk."

"I guess this is her boyfriend then?" whispered my mum as I led the way out.

"Actually," said Zach, "I'm her husband."

Chapter Two

One year earlier. Boston, MA, USA.

Amy

I'd been in Boston for three weeks. Twenty-one days since I'd seen my family. I admitted, I hadn't thought about them that much. Ed and I had been in touch on a weekly basis, mostly little anecdotes about our working days, I usually told him a little about people I'd met or places I'd seen.

I realised that I'd been depressed, before I'd moved across the Atlantic. I had been coasting along, smiling often enough to hide it, but really, inside, I was disappointed. Disappointed with life. I'd imagined something more exciting, somehow. I'd pictured falling in love, going on exotic holidays, hosting posh cocktail parties for my friends. I'd have a nice house with flowers in my garden and I'd wear expensive suits and...just be somebody. Somebody important.

In reality, I was living in a small one bedroom house I'd only just about managed to afford with my adorable but slightly crazy cat. I'd experienced lust, and unrequited love and stupid love when you know he's going to dump you, and I'd pretended to love because he was so lovely to me. But no one that lasted. Just before I left for Boston, I was lonely and unsure what the point of it all was. I took no pleasure in anything. I sat on my bed crying and wondering what the heck was wrong with me.

Then one day, I decided. Maybe life in America wouldn't be so mundane, surely there'd be new faces, new friends, new colleagues, perhaps even new good looking men. Maybe a change of scenery would brighten my day. And maybe I'd finally be able to find my father. And so far, I had loved it.

One of the things I liked most was the office I worked in. We were on the top floor of a tall skyscraper, not far from the harbour. My cubicle was by the window, and I could see the sea. I often stared out, watching the small white specs move in towards and then out from the harbour.

"You okay?" Harriet, my only friend since arriving in Boston, always seemed to appear a few steps in to my cubicle before I'd realise she was there.

"I've been in Boston for twenty-one days," I told her.

"Home sick?" she asked.

"No, actually I'm not at all," I told her, and I meant it too.

"You want to go out for lunch today?"

"Sure." She walked away and I smiled. She was the main reason I was happy in Boston. Harriet had made me feel comfortable. She'd helped me find an apartment online before I'd arrived, she'd picked me up at the airport, she'd taken me shopping and she'd invited me out a few times with her friends. She was fun and bubbly and exactly the sort of person I needed when she was the only person I knew.

Since arriving, I'd done some research about my father. All my mum had told me were the basic facts:

1. His name was Andrew Moore

2. He studied law at Harvard

3. He was an arsehole who was unlikely to want to meet us.

My mother had insisted for years that there was little point contacting him. He didn't want to know us as babies, and he wouldn't want to know us now. Then one day Jack said:

"It was all a long time ago and it's up to Amy and Ed to discover for themselves if he's *still* an arsehole."

Mum didn't respond to that. Ed had muttered something

20

about not being bothered anyway. Whereas I'd been inspired to finally find out who he was and where I might find him.

As it turned out, it was surprisingly easy to find Andrew Moore because he'd set up a prestigious law firm in Boston. I simply googled "Andrew Moore + Harvard lawyer." I found him and knew right away that it was definitely him; there was a photo on the website which looked like Ed, but twenty years older.

So when I saw the job advertisement for my exact same position, but in the Boston office, I saw it as some kind of sign and applied right away. Franco, my new manager, was keen to take me on since I knew so much about the company and the job, and he organised a visa and before I knew it, I was packing my stuff. I needed a change of air, scenery, new people and a new life. I'd become stagnant, bored, lifeless lately and the prospect of going somewhere new – and maybe meeting my father – was thrilling.

Between announcing my plans and actually flying to Boston, Ed, and my closest friends had warned me. It wouldn't be easy. I wouldn't know anyone. America wasn't as exciting as it might sound. My father might not want to know me; that was if this guy was even him, perhaps it was just a freakish coincidence that he looked like Ed.

I ignored all their advice, and went anyway.

Zach

My mother called.

"Hi Mom."

"Hello Zachary." She's the only person the world to call me this.

"How are you Mom?"

"I'm doing great. How are you?"

"Good. Scarlett and I broke up."

A moment of silence.

"Well, I'm sorry to hear that but you know these things are for the best sometimes."

I knew it. She didn't like her. I could tell. Mind you, she never seemed to like any of my girlfriends.

"So you didn't like her huh?"

"She was nice enough. But, you know, not your type, I don't think."

"What would my type be then Mom?"

"I don't know. I always imagined you with someone who liked going for long walks and read a lot of books, instead of having manicures and going shopping."

"Scarlett's not stupid Mom." I felt defensive about her, although I wasn't sure why, I had no feelings for Scarlett and that's why I'd broken up with her.

"I know. She's just a little…"

"Shallow?"

"Yes."

"I know."

"You'll meet a suitable girl soon enough."

By suitable, she means a) Jewish, b) intellectual, and c) fertile. She loves my brother Aaron's wife, Mel, although Mel is an atheist, she's very smart and has given Mom two grandchildren, so that's two out of three and she can't complain.

"Thanks."

"It's just…you're getting to that age, you should be settled, Zachary."

I sighed.

"How's Dad?"

"Oh, he's okay. He's working in his yard."

We spoke for a little longer and then I said I ought to get on with some work.

"I'm sorry about Scarlett, really."

"Thanks, Mom."

Amy

22

I sat at my desk and thought of Andrew Moore, the American dad I'd never met, and wished he'd taken me away when I was a baby to grow up in the US, I'd have gone to a school just like the one in Saved by the Bell, and been a cheerleader, and had an accent, and said "neat" and "awesome" a lot.

My first twenty-one days had passed very quickly, and so far I felt I'd made the right decision. I loved Boston. I loved the extremes of looking out into the Atlantic in one direction, and turning to take in the huge skyscrapers in the other. I liked the feel and buzz about the place.

That evening Harriet and I were sat on her balcony, looking out at the Boston night sky, drinking piña colada's. I noticed Harriet's face screw up with every mouthful and asked her if she liked it.

"Not really." She laughed, then carried on drinking it anyway.

The light was fading and I could only just make out the silhouette of the buildings around us. I pulled my cardigan closer around me and put my feet up on the foot rest Harriet had dragged out from her living room. The balcony was small but I loved sitting out there, feeling the cold air on my skin and just talking with my only friend on the same continent as me.

"So did you get dumped, you know, in England?" she asked.

"Well, there was a guy," I told her, taking a sip of my piña colada.

"I knew it!" She screwed up her face again after her own sip.

"But...it was a case of unrequited love..." I wasn't sure this was true, I wasn't sure if I'd actually been in love with him. I'd shed a lot of tears, but I sometimes wondered if they were tears of humiliation and rejection because he didn't want me, more than of a broken heart.

"Ah, the worst kind of love." Harriet squeezed my arm and stood up.

"More piña colada?"

"Sure." I handed her my glass. I stood up and leant against the railing. There was a couple kissing on the street below. I sighed. It'd been a long time since I'd been kissed like that. Harriet came out with another piña colada for me, and a glass of wine for herself. We sat.

"What about you?" I asked her. "What's your sorry tale?"

"Unrequited love for me as well, sadly," she said, looking down at her now empty glass.

"Crap. It's crap, isn't it?"

"Sure is."

"Actually, there's a guy at work I like. Do you know Sid?"

I knew him. He looked far too old for Harriet; at least ten years her senior.

"Not well. He's nice huh?"

"He's a lovely guy. Divorced."

"Ask him out."

"I couldn't, too shy." She was fiddling with her glass and yawned slightly.

"Have a party!" The piña colada was talking now.

"What? Why?"

"A party for your fortieth. Have it here. Just a few drinks, some snacks. Invite your friends, some people from work. Invite Sid."

"You know what; it might be a good idea."

Zach

I heard a noise in the hallway as I was locking up and peeped through the spy-hole. My neighbour, Harriet, was saying goodbye to a brunette with a drunken hug.

Amy

Towards the end of the month, I received news from Libby.

To: Amy Starling
From: Elizabeth Starling
Subject: Exciting news!

Hi Amy,
How are you? I'm sorry I haven't been in touch. You know how it is, busy, busy, busy. I have some news! I'm getting married, can you believe it! His name is Tim. His family are rich! He's got this huge apartment on the Thames! It's wonderful. He proposed to me at the Ritz! We're thinking about getting married next summer. You must come!
Libby x

Whoa. Too many exclamation marks. I re-read it. I wasn't too shocked. Libby had always been impulsive, and marrying a rich guy seemed like something she'd do.

Still. Libby, getting married. She's only known the guy for a little over a month, and she's getting married. My younger sister. Married before me.

I went out with Max, my longest ever relationship, for a year and I didn't even think about marrying him. Okay, so I did think about it a little. Quite a lot actually, but still!

I tried to imagine what sort of wedding she might have and could only picture something on the scale and grandeur of Will and Kate. Sounded like Tim had enough cash for it. Maybe he even knew some royals. I smiled at the thought of my mother posing for pictures besides Princess Anne.

On my first day in the Boston office, Harriet took me out to lunch and told me she'd always had a crush on Prince Andrew, which I found kind of odd. I later discovered that she was hoping I somehow knew him, or at least knew someone who knew him, or something. I told her I thought William was cuter, and she laughed and said he was "too young."

Snapping out of my thoughts, I stared at my screen and typed in the now all-too familiar web address to look at the photo of my father again. I still hadn't even considered how I might contact him. I was desperately curious, but I didn't feel up to the task of meeting him just yet. I needed to prepare for rejection, just in case.

Chapter Three

Zach

I'd been thinking about getting a dog. Maybe a cat. I wasn't sure which. Dogs are more loyal, but cats are less responsibility. And if I were to get a cat, would I get a kitten or a fully-grown cat? If I were getting a kitten, would it ruin the nice new furniture I'd filled my apartment with?

I'd mentioned this to one of my clients, a French woman who had two cats. She asked me why I wanted a cat and I said for company.

"You're lonely, huh?" she'd said, and I realised that yes, maybe I was just a bit lonely.

One morning, I got back from my regular run, took my shower, wiped the steam off of the mirror and stared at my reflection for a whole ten minutes. I didn't recognise myself. I even spotted a grey hair.

I decided: I'm either turning into a woman, or I'm having an early mid-life crisis.

"I'm not even thirty one years old!" I protested to my brother Aaron that evening. "Why am I getting grey hairs?"

"Ah man, look I've got a couple myself!" He lent forward towards the beer, resting on the bar, and showed me nothing but black glossy hair. It smelled like women's shampoo.

"You're nearly forty. Big deal. You're married."

"What's being married got to do with it?"

"Everything...Nothing...I don't know. You're a proper grown up. I still feel twenty-one. I haven't even had a relationship that's lasted more than a year, how can I be at the grey hair stage

27

yet?"

"You sound like a woman."

"What?"

"Your clock is ticking, huh? You're looking for a wife. You want all that? Really? Because it's way over-rated."

"I don't want that. Sure, I'd like a girlfriend. But...I don't know. I guess I thought I'd find someone I want to at least live with. Connect with. You know?"

Aaron sighed and scratched his grey-free head.

"Next you're going to say that you want someone to cuddle at night. Come on, man, you're living the dream here! You can do what you want, when you want. You can sleep with a different girl every night. I envy you. Don't be in a rush to give up on the single life. Women come along and you feel all connected and get caught up in their magic and then look what happens. You get trapped. Like me."

"Mel and the kids are great Aaron. You love them."

"It's not as peachy as it looks, Zach."

Aaron's attention was soon drawn away to the TV near the bar. The Red Sox were playing some team I didn't even know. I'm not a sports fan. I'm a nerd, geek, dork – take your pick. I read. I spend an unhealthy amount of time on the internet. I even have a blog. It's anonymous, so you won't find it if you google me. I use a pseudonym. I like movies and music and reading and running. Apart from the occasional beer with my brother or my old college buddies, I didn't get out much, but that suited me just fine.

While Aaron watched the game, I read every word on the label of my beer bottle, and then started to peel it off slowly. I glanced at my watch. 9:30. I thought about going home. Home to my cold bed, on my own. Cuddles? Yeah, I could go for some of that. I thought about calling Scarlett but thought better of it. I barely liked her, let alone wanted her for my girlfriend again.

I bid Aaron a good night, went home, got into my pyjamas,

ate some cereal and wasted some time on Facebook. As usual, there was nothing much interesting going on in the lives of my "friends", just more photos of an ex-colleague's kids. I sighed, turned my laptop off, and went to sleep.

The next morning I bumped into my neighbour, Harriet, as I came back from my run.

"Hi Zach, how's it going?" she asked me, as she locked her door.

"Good, thanks. How about you?"

"I'm good. Working hard. Hey, I'm having a party Friday night. Would you like to come?"

"Sure." I said, not intending to go and a little worried she might be asking me on a date.

"Okay, I'll see you then. Bring beer."

I decided I'd fake a cold or a headache or something. I didn't mind making small talk with my neighbours but going to a party where I didn't know anyone wasn't my ideal Friday evening.

I opened my laptop and sat down to work. I love what I do, I get to work from home, I am my own boss, and I don't have to answer to anyone. I worked that day primarily on building a website for a company that sold sex toys. It was fun, if a little surprising to discover some of the fetishes and toys some people are into.

My office is probably the best room in my apartment. I've got a really comfy couch in there which I sometimes sit or lie on when I'm feeling uninspired. I've got shelves and shelves full of books, and a huge painting of a boat at sea, which I bought on a whim when an ex-girlfriend (Shelly, we lasted three months) took me to an auction. I'm not sure I like it, but it cost me eight hundred dollars, and my sister-in-law Mel insisted it gave the room "depth."

I sat at my desk, Monday to Friday, working. I got lost in a world of code, and creativity, and email, and telephone calls and then at 6pm I made myself something to eat, usually alphabetti spaghetti, cereal, or instant noodles, and then I surfed the internet, watched a movie, and excepting the occasional night out for a few beers, I slept, I ran, and that was my life. I kind of got the feeling something was missing, and it wasn't Scarlett. I just didn't know how to fill that void. And then I met Amy.

Amy

"What if no one comes to the party?" Harriet asked me with a worried expression.

"They will. *Relax.*"

I watched her walk away. I didn't really want to go, but I couldn't let her down, especially as it was my suggestion. I figured I'd go for a few drinks, and then sneak out while Harriet was chatting to Sid.

Zach

There was a knock at my door. I opened it to Harriet, she'd never knocked on my door before.

"Hi, Zach, how're you?"

"Great. Never better. Thanks. You?"

"Great. Are you still coming to the party tonight?"

Damn it, I was going to fake an illness, but I'd forgotten about the whole thing. I hesitated for a second and then figured I'd show my face, get a drink, and then slip out.

"Of course. Happy Birthday."

"Thanks. Do you have a couple of spare chairs you could lend me?"

I passed her four of my dining chairs, which had only been sat on a couple of times since I bought them, and told her I'd see her later.

Amy

There was something about Harriet's apartment that was almost clinical. There was little colour; it was mostly black furniture, white walls. There was a lack of personality about it. Unlike me, she didn't have random books lying around, or hairclips or notes...or even a pen. I'd actually paid a fortune to ship all my books out to Boston. I knew it wouldn't feel like home until I'd lined my shelves. I wanted them on display, surrounding me, not hidden away in a storage unit.

Harriet didn't have that much music but I rifled through the CDs in her collection. I pulled out a seventies Disco compilation and put it on. Harriet came out, looking slightly apprehensive and putting her arms up in a gesture as if to say "so what do you think?"

"You look amazing." I told her. She grinned.

We spent the next twenty minutes applying her makeup. She said she wanted a chic look, which I had no idea how to achieve, especially with her very limited make up kit.

"You should have brought your make-up." She sighed, disappointed as she rummaged through, showing me the few items she had. I wasn't sure what would make her think I was a make-up expert or owned many cosmetics, seeing as my daily routine consisted of a light dusting of eye shadow, a flick of mascara and that was about it. Tonight I'd been a little more daring and actually added eye liner and a touch of lip gloss to my look.

Eventually, we decided on a silver eye shadow – this was the best choice as she only had four different colours – and a bright red lip stick, which I didn't like at all but Harriet said it made her feel glamorous and seeing as making her feel good was the overall goal, I decided to let her go ahead. I clipped her hair up at the back, letting some curly tendrils fall down at the front.

She grinned at me in the mirror and even with the blood red lips, I had to admit she looked good.

The doorbell rang and her face froze.

"Your first guest!" I said, smiling. Harriet grinned and went to answer the door.

Soon, the apartment was filling up with various different faces and getting rather crowded. A handful of other people from work came, then there were some of Harriet's ex-colleagues, college friends, and other people she'd met during her forty years on this Earth. She introduced me to every single person, none of whom I would remember by the time I got home, with one exception.

Zach

9pm came and I put on a blue shirt, dark trousers and even splashed on something nice smelling which my mother gave me for my birthday a couple of years ago,

A short balding guy with round glasses opened her door, and nodded at me before walking away. Some music I'd never heard was playing and people were standing huddled in little groups. I made my way to the kitchen which was empty, and I put a couple of bottles of beer I'd bought with me in the fridge. As I stood up, Harriet entered the room, followed by a girl with long dark hair, and the most beautiful green eyes I'd ever seen.

"Zach, thanks for coming!" Harriet kissed me on the cheek like we were old pals.

"This is Amy. She's British," she said with a British accent. "She doesn't really know many people in Boston so I'm introducing her to everyone."

"Hello, nice to meet you, Zach." She had a cute British accent which made me like her instantly.

"Nice to meet you, Amy," I said, shaking her hand. She had small, soft, petite hands. Harriet kind of bowed and left the kitchen.

"So, how long have you been on this side of the pond?" I asked, opening my beer and leaning against the counter.

"Nearly three months." Wow, I loved her voice. It was sexy. Somewhere between Mary Poppins and Baby Spice. No, really.

"You like Boston so far?"

"Yeah. I do, actually." She smiled nervously.

She opened the fridge door and bent down to get out a beer for herself, and I silently admired her cute behind. I took the opportunity to take a deep breath. Don't screw this up, I told myself. Be interesting. Be *smooth*.

She stood up, sipped her beer, and smiled nervously again. Her hair fell about her shoulders. She was wearing an amazing dress which showed me her curves. Her hair lightly brushed her breasts as she spoke and I willed myself to look at her eyes, not at her chest.

"I'm sure it's not that different, than England I mean," I said, sipping my beer.

"Oh, you'd be surprised." She smiled. "Have you ever been to the UK?"

"No." I tried to look disappointed. "I've always wanted to though." I imagined her showing me the tourist trail.

"Well, it's worth the trip, to London at least. But I like it here. Actually, I like Boston a lot."

"Great," I said, rather too eagerly.

"So, how do you know Harriet?"

"I live across the hall, actually." I nodded in the direction of my apartment. "How about you?"

"We work together," she said, smiling.

"Is she a good person to work with?" I asked, and immediately regretted it. What sort of a question was that?

Amy laughed. "Yes, she's great. Is she a good neighbour?"

"Ha. Yes, I don't know her all that well to be honest. I don't know anyone here, either. Just Harriet. And now you."

"Well, join the club, I hardly know anyone either." Her eyes were sparkling. I wanted to kiss her then and there.

I was suddenly very glad I'd come to the party.

Amy

33

As soon as I saw Zach, I knew he was my type. Dark scruffy hair, brown eyes that looked at me intently, a kind smile and, perhaps most importantly, easy to talk to. I felt like I'd known him my whole life within a few hours of meeting.

"So, tell me about yourself, Zach," I said, as we walked out through the living room and to Harriet's balcony.

We sat down on plastic chairs, looking out at the street below.

"What do you want to know?"

"Whatever you want to share. Who *are* you?" I felt myself blush, wondering if I was being too nosey or forward. He didn't seem to mind.

"Well. I'm thirty one years old. Born and raised in Massachusetts to be a good Jewish boy."

"You're Jewish?" I asked, then regretted it instantly, as if it was an issue or a problem. I was really just interested.

"Well, my family are. I'm not that religious. But, you know..."

All I could think of was his penis. I'd never slept with anyone Jewish before. He saw me glance down towards his groin and I blushed.

"Okay, and what do you do for a living?" I asked next, trying to recover from my embarrassment.

"I work for myself, I'm a website developer. I design sites for a number of clients."

"Wow. Do you enjoy it?"

"Yes. I do. Very much, actually."

"Any siblings?"

"Yes, a brother, Aaron. He's married. Two children."

I smiled. His eyes were locked on to mine while he talked and I couldn't take mine off of his. I felt a rush of excitement in my chest and blushed yet again.

"We had a blast growing up. He was always the jock, you know, the sports fan. I was the opposite. The nerdy one."

I smiled again, and asked about his parents.

"They're great, very supportive. They travel a lot. My dad was a lawyer, he's just recently retired."

"My mum's a lawyer," I told him. So is my dad, I realised, but I didn't say it out loud.

"I like the way you say 'mum' instead of 'mom'."

"We spell it with a 'u'." I was about to go on to tell him that several words were spelt differently in Britain, before wondering how that could possibly be deemed interesting. Luckily, he spoke before I had a chance to get extraordinarily dull.

"Cool. So enough about me, tell me about you."

"Erm, well..." I didn't know where to start and didn't want to bore him. "I'm twenty-nine. I work as an Account Executive for a PR firm, with Harriet."

"And you like it?"

"Sometimes, yes. I transferred here from our London office."

He nodded enthusiastically, his eyes still staring right into mine and I felt like he was really interested.

I told him about my family. As I spoke, I became aware of some sort of invisible force between us. I wanted to touch him.

"Any hobbies?" he asked, sipping his beer. I'd nearly forgotten I had hold of mine and took another swig myself.

"I'm a complete nerd I'm afraid," I admitted, allowing myself to breathe out and thanking him silently for breaking the awkward moment.

He grinned. "Don't be afraid. You can't possibly be more of a nerd than me."

"Okay," I laughed, relieved. "I read a lot, watch movies, spend an extraordinary amount of time on the internet, I watch documentaries, mostly about wildlife and that sort of thing. This is the first party I've been to in months, and to be honest, I'd rather stay at home with a good book, or a great movie, than go out to a night club, or whatever."

Zach

I'd met my perfect woman. I imagined us sitting, side by side, each on our laptops, eating cereal, writing blogs and discussing books and turning down invitations for nights out because we'd rather stay at home, together, being nerdy, discussing the mating habits of African lions. Not that I was into the Discovery Channel myself, but if Amy was, I was willing to start watching it too.

Amy

"Well, I too spend an extraordinary amount of time online," he said, smiling again, winning me over more and more each second. "What music do you like?"

It went on like this for a good few hours. We had so much in common it was almost scary. We didn't even go back for more drinks.

"What a beautiful night." I sighed, staring up at the shiny silver specs scattered high above.

"I love warm summer evenings, with clear night skies," Zach said, moving a little closer. My eyes fell from the stars to his and I realised he was about to kiss me. My heart started beating even faster.

"Well!" Harriet made us jump, she was standing in the doorway, hands on hips. "You two really hit it off, huh?" She nudged me and winked.

I looked behind her and noticed there were only a few people left. I looked at my watch, and was shocked to find it was gone 2am. The latest I'd stayed up in a long time. I blushed and said something about getting a cab home.

Harriet wandered back into the room and I looked at Zach, and smiled nervously. I felt terrified he wouldn't ask me out, or ask for my number, or something. He looked at me kind of sadly.

"I had the most amazing time," he said, and I sighed with relief.

"Me too."

"Would it be too soon if we, I mean, I don't know if you're busy tomorrow-"

Me, busy on a Saturday? Ha!

"But would you like to do something? Maybe get lunch or something?"

I grinned. Lunch. He didn't even want to wait until dinner. He wanted to see me again in a few hours.

We agreed he would come by my apartment at 1pm, and we'd walk from there to a restaurant and have something to eat.

We said a very polite good bye. I hugged Harriet, who was in heavy conversation with the only guest left – Sid. The guy she liked from work, the guy I'd suggested throwing this party for. So, I thought as I took the elevator down to the street and found a cab, the party was a success, not only for me but for Harriet too. I felt slightly smug that I'd suggested it and foolish for not looking forward to it more.

Back at my apartment, I couldn't sleep. I just lay in bed, thinking about Zach. I hadn't been prepared for this. For this fuzzy feeling.

I woke up after only a few hours sleep, but felt very awake and kind of excited, and lay there, smiling to myself about my good fortune. I had a shower and then mooched around my apartment. Four hours to waste until I met Zach for lunch. I rearranged the books on my shelf, cleaned out the kitchen, changed my outfit three times, and finally deciding on a purple long sleeve cotton top and black jeans, slouched on my sofa and started painting my nails, hoping our conversation hadn't already peaked and we'd have no more to say.

The buzzer rang and I jumped up to answer it.

"It's me, Zach. Sorry I'm a little early." I realised I'd missed his voice. Already. I had it bad.

I laughed. "Come on up."

He was carrying a brown paper bag with bread, salad, cheese, and a bottle of wine, plus a handful of DVDs.

"I'm so tired. Can we stay in and eat lunch here?"

I smiled, realising that was exactly what I needed, rather than going out, and kissed him. He dropped the bag and DVDs to the floor and wrapped his arms around me. The passion and excitement of the moment was overwhelming. I didn't care that I was ruining my still-wet nails, quite possibly leaving purple polish all over his shirt. He ran his hands through my hair, and then down my back, and up inside my top. He started undoing my bra. I'll spare you the intricate details. Suffice to say it was good. Very good.

Zach

Ditto. It was amazing. And she didn't get nail polish on my shirt, for the record.

Amy

We spent the rest of the day in bed, watching films, eating food and, well, you know. I knew I was falling, I knew it was probably way too fast, and I knew it could very well lead to heartbreak and more depression. But I didn't care. Whatever bad may come of this was in the future. Right now, only good thoughts were in my mind. After our seventh (yes, seventh!) stint in the bedroom, Zach closed his eyes and dosed off. I watched his head lying on the usually vacant pillow besides mine and sighed, a corny, girly, happy sigh.

And in case you were wondering, the circumcision thing is no big deal. If anything, I quite liked it.

Chapter Four

Zach

The next day, I kept smiling to myself thinking about Amy. Thinking about the way she spoke, hearing her British voice inside my head. Remembering the way her dark hair fell from her face as she laughed at one of my dumb jokes. Her smooth skin. Her delicate hands and the way she gestured with them as she spoke. The curve of her breasts...then I'd shake my head, snap out of it and try to get some work done.

I had finally got into the groove when my mom rang, interrupting my concentration once again.

"Zachary. How are you my dear?"

"Good, Mom. How are you?"

"I'm fine dear. So, have you met a nice girl yet?" She laughed as if she knew she was being annoying, but I knew she wanted an answer anyhow.

"Yes. Actually, I met an amazing girl called Amy."

There was a moment's silence while she took this in.

"Amazing Amy huh?"

"Yes. She's beautiful Mom, you're going to love her." I pictured myself introducing Amy to my family. She'd make a good impression, all polite and charming and cute with that accent, and I'd stand there swelling with pride that this beautiful, intelligent English rose could want to be with me. Was she with me? Did yesterday mean she was now my girlfriend? I wasn't sure. It was like we'd skipped the dating part.

"So you're going to bring her here?"

"Yes, at some point."

I'd only met her two days ago. It felt like longer.

"Well, that's wonderful Zachary. You sound...happy."

"I am."

As I ended the call my laptop made a noise to tell me I had a new email.

To: Zach Rosenberg
From: Amy Starling
Subject: Tonight

Hey Zach,
Okay, so be honest if I'm being too pushy or over-bearing. But are you free tonight?
A

To: Amy Starling
From: Zach Rosenberg
Subject: Re: Tonight

Hello Amy,
Glad you emailed. I missed you.
I'm free. You want to see a movie?
Zach

Amy

He missed me? Already? I felt my head and heart whirl into a spin. The past few days had been intense, but amazing. I had spent most of the day thinking that he'd have had his fun, and that might be it. I wondered if I could never get enough of him.

To: Zach Rosenberg
From: Amy Starling
Subject: Re: Tonight

Hi Zach
How about a movie and dinner? I want to try the Cheers restaurant, if that's not too cheesy and a bit touristy for you?
I miss you too ;)
Amy x

He replied a few minutes later.

To: Amy Starling
From: Zach Rosenberg
Subject: Re: Tonight

Amy.
Always wanted to go to the Cheers restaurant. I'll pick you up at 7.
Z
PS: That's a Zee, not a Zed. You British butcher the American language.
PPS: I love the color of your eyes.

To: Zach Rosenberg
From: Amy Starling
Subject: Tonight

Hi Zed.
By the way, it's colour not color. You Americans!
A xxxx

Zach

It was no good, I couldn't stop thinking about her. I stopped working on the website for the children's charity (yes, I'm that selfish) and looked up Amy on Facebook instead. Her profile picture didn't do her justice.

I was tempted to google her, see if she showed up anywhere,

find out if she was on Twitter, and then realised I was bordering on cyber stalker status, so I turned off my laptop to resist the temptation. Instead, I picked up my book and began to read. I managed to get absorbed for a while, then went and got ready for our date far too early. I turned up at her building at 6:45, and leant against the wall outside for ten minutes before announcing my arrival. She came out wearing a big smile and seemed to be glowing. I felt like something flowed through us when I kissed her cheek, like a surge of electricity.

The Cheers restaurant was filled with photos of Ted Danson, Kirstie Alley and the gang, we spent a few minutes taking it all in before being shown to our table. We both ordered burgers and then sat there smiling at each other. I felt like a goofy teenager again.

Amy

"Okay," I said, deciding there were a few things I'd like to know. "Let's get the horrible sob stories over with. How long have you been single?"

Zach hesitated for a moment and I added: "Oh god, you *are* single, aren't you?"

He laughed.

"Yes. I'm single. I've just broken up with someone a few weeks ago. Scarlett."

"Okay." I nodded.

"She was nice, but just not for me. I never felt that strongly about her to be honest and it just wasn't working towards the end. We had nothing in common. So, what about you?"

"I was kind of seeing someone before I came to the US. Someone at work...it wasn't serious, really. Especially not for him. And then it was awkward at work afterward, so I guess that's one of the reasons I came here."

"What was his name?" Zach asked.

"Alex. Why?"

"I must remember to send him a thank you." He grinned. I smiled. Perhaps I ought to as well, for the first time I was grateful that Alex had turned out to be an insensitive, selfish pig. I looked across at Zach and wanted to touch him. As if reading my mind, he reached forward and lightly brushed my hand with his thumb. I remembered the feel of his hands on my naked body and blushed.

Our burgers arrived. There was enough food on my plate to feed me for three days. I got stuck in.

Zach

"Have you ever been in a really serious relationship?" I asked Amy as we sat looking out at the harbour with our leftover movie popcorn.

"Closest I ever really got to a commitment was Craig Jones. He was a friend of my brothers. He was kind of dull though. He lived in London, and I went down there at weekends. At first it was fun, but not what I wanted. He asked me to move in, I deliberated for a while, then said no thank you, and that was it."

I pictured Amy walking past Big Ben hand-in-hand with Orlando Bloom.

"Did he look like Orlando Bloom. Or Hugh Grant?" I couldn't help but ask.

"No!" She laughed. "Why?"

"I don't know. I think of a British guy, I picture Hugh Grant."

Amy giggled.

"He looked a little like Leonardo DiCaprio, actually. Which is why I got Ed to set us up in the first place. I was so disappointed when I realised he didn't have any personality."

She stretched and yawned, and I said I'd walk her home.

"Do you want to do something this weekend?" I asked her as we got to her door.

"I would love to." She kissed me and then went inside without inviting me in.

I spent most of the night lying awake, imagining her looking up at Buckingham Palace with Leonardo by her side. Their two beautiful faces, like supermodels. I whispered a thank you to this Craig Jones for being so dull, and this Alex for being mean, so that Amy had eventually ended up coming to the States, and meeting me. I was glad, however that he was several thousand miles away. Just in case he grew a personality.

Amy

We didn't see each other from the Monday to the Saturday. I figured it was probably healthier not to, and didn't want to seem like I was coming on too strong anyway. However, Zach phoned me each evening, and I was rather happy when he did.

We seemed to be able to talk for hours. He'd ask me about my day, and I about his, then we'd just share little anecdotes, talk about books we'd read, movies we'd loved or hated, share opinions on a news story, or mention something we'd thought of that day. I couldn't get enough of hearing his voice, his opinion, his view of the World.

We'd decided on Thursday night that we'd spend Saturday on a little touristy tour of Boston. I hadn't seen that much of it since I'd arrived and Zach said he'd show me around; teach me a little about the city.

I got up early to shower and shave my legs. I spent more time than usual picking out my outfit, finally deciding on jeans and a comfy shirt, plus trainers for walking around. I was ready too early and sat down to look at my email.

To: Amy Starling
From: Ed Starling
Subject: American dream

Hi Amy

How're you? Good I hope and enjoying the American dream? Things here are much the same. I haven't spoken to Mum or Jack for a while and Libby seems pretty busy. I've been going out with my mates, working, and doing up an old motorbike I bought from a guy at work. Nothing much more to report, but it's been a while so thought I'd see how you are.

Have a nice day now!

Ed x

I was pleased to hear from him and touched he'd thought to make the effort.

To: Ed Starling
From: Amy Starling
Subject: Re: American dream

Hi Edward :)

Nice to hear from you. I'm great, and the American dream is quite something. I met someone, he's cute and charming. Work is good and I've been doing the same old – reading and watching movies.

Be careful on the bike!!

Speak soon

Amy x

Zach knocked on my door at 9am on the dot, and we headed out into the warm Boston air. Just as before, I felt instantly comfortable in his presence and we chat about work, Harriet's party, and then about Boston. Zach shared the following facts with me:

One: Boston is the capital of, and largest city in, Massachusetts and also one of the oldest US cities.

Two: Over four million people live in Boston, making it the tenth largest metropolitan area in the US.

Three: Local sporting teams are the Boston Red Sox (baseball), Boston Celtics (basketball) and the New England Patriots (football, not to be confused with soccer). The Bostonians were, in general, passionate about these teams. Zach however is not.

I'd already discovered the Bostonians love of sport when practically the whole office had been discussing some supposedly interesting Celtics news a few weeks earlier. Literally everyone was involved in the discussion. Plus, there seemed to be a large number of Red Sox souvenirs available everywhere I looked.

Four: Boston was the location of several important events of the American revolution, including the Boston Massacre and Boston Tea Party. For some reason during these stories, the words "British troops" made me feel a little guilty. Like it was my own ancestors who wouldn't give these people their independence.

"But, some of your ancestors were probably also those seeking independence." Zach told me. "Your father is American is he not?"

I smiled, and didn't respond. Every time I thought of my father since I'd been here, I felt strange. I was compelled to meet him on one hand, but couldn't stand the idea of him turning me away on the other. I pushed it to the back of my mind and listened to Zach's tale of the local colonists throwing the tea into the water.

I was impressed with all of Zach's knowledge, and told him so.

Zach

I accepted the compliment without telling Amy that I'd bought a guide book just yesterday and spent half of my evening learning some of these facts. I didn't want her to know that despite growing up in Massachusetts and living in Boston for the past three years, I didn't have much to say about my own city.

We walked and talked some more, with me pointing out various points of interest, some of my own merit and others recited from the book.

Eventually, we came to Faneuil Hall, one of my favourite spots in Boston. There's always a buzz and vibe about the place, different smells, different faces, and a different atmosphere depending on the time of year, whether it was Christmas or Valentines, or in this case, a humid, warm afternoon. We wandered through Quincy Market and to the food hall, stopping at various stores and eventually sitting for a coffee and lunch.

"I love it here, it reminds me a little of Covent Garden."

We were looking out at a guy juggling batons.

"Where's that?"

"London. There's various shops and so on, like this, and street entertainers."

"Sounds neat, I'd like to go there someday."

"Maybe I'll take you."

Amy

After lunch we wandered around, both buying a few books and I found some Red Sox souvenirs to send to Ed for his birthday. He was always a keen sports fan and I quite enjoyed looking around at the branded souvenirs.

Next we walked to Massachusetts State House. I'd passed it a few times but never stopped to really appreciate. The sun was shining on the golden dome and I took a photo on my phone. I sent it with a text message to my best friend at home, Taryn, when we were sitting in Boston Common, reading our new books and soaking up some sunshine.

Taryn, I love Boston! The spirit of the place is addictive. Come visit and you'll see for yourself. Amy x

There was something about sitting there with Zach that made me feel like we were a couple. I couldn't quite believe that we had only met a week ago. It felt like I'd known him my whole life.

Eventually, we walked back to Zach's apartment. I glanced at Harriet's door as he unlocked his, hoping she wouldn't come out and interrupt our romantic afternoon together.

"Wow," I said, as we walked into his immaculate living room.

"Did you decorate this yourself?"

The walls were an olive green, the black sofas had plump beige suede cushions, and there didn't seem to be a thing out of place or a speck of dirt. The kitchen was open plan, with a counter and bar stools, and a small pine dining table which looked brand new.

"Well, Mel, my sister-in-law did it, she's an interior designer, and it's not always this clean, either. I have a cleaner who came just yesterday." He threw his jacket on the sofa and told me to make myself at home while he prepared some dinner.

I wandered around, looking at his stylish furniture, and picking up books from the shelf. He'd read a variety of novels I'd never heard of but quite a few I had, too. He had a varied taste and a lot of books on art and history. I sat on the sofa and watched him cooking.

"What're you making me?" I asked.

"Pasta with goat's cheese and tomato," he told me without looking up. I loved the way he said tom-mate-o versus my tom-art-o.

"Smells delicious." And it was.

Zach

After our food, I looked through Amy's iPod. She certainly had an eclectic taste. She had boybands, and indie, and acoustic rock, sixties disco and the Beatles...she had the Grease and Hairspray soundtracks, and a whole load of stuff I had never heard of.

"Who are Take That?" I asked her.

"Only one of the best British bands ever," she told me. "I don't think they ever made it big in the US but you have to listen."

The first song was very typical cheesy boyband, but after some educational tips from Amy, I realised some of their more recent stuff was actually quite good.

We spent the rest of the day listening to British music, including a lot of Coldplay, and playing scrabble. Then we watched Notting Hill and cuddled on the sofa.

"After all this music and now this movie, don't you miss England?" I asked her.

"Not when I'm with you."

Amy

I stayed over that night. Zach has one of those mattresses that moulds to the shape of your body and I don't think I've ever slept so well. I left before breakfast, attempting to play a little hard to get and not allowing my temptation to be with him 24/7 over rule my brain telling me that most men get bored easy and there can be too much of a good thing. However, when Zach asked me as I was leaving if I wanted to go out for dinner on Tuesday evening, I instantly said yes.

Zach

"I'm snorry." Amy sniffed as I answered the phone.

"What? You sound sick."

"I've got an awful cold. I can't go out tonight."

"I'll come over."

"No, please. I look awful and I don't want you to get ill too."

"Really, I don't-"

"Please, Zach. I don't want you to see me like this. I look ghastly."

I laughed, quietly.

"Okay, well I'll call you later. Feel better soon."

Amy

I got up from the sofa and stumbled to open my door, wondering who on earth would be bothering me at 11am on a Tuesday. I looked through the peep hole and saw Zach standing there. I felt a mixture of joy and panic and smoothed my hair down on top of my head as best I could, wiped my nose and eyes on a tissue and pulled my dressing gown tighter around me. As I opened the door, he stood there smiling, holding a large brown paper bag.

"What are you doing here?" I asked, hoping I didn't look as awful as I felt.

"I had to see you," he said, holding up the bag. "I bought you some soup, and drugs, movies, and hot chocolate. I'm going to take care of you."

"That's so sweet." I moved out of the doorway to let him in.

"But what about work?"

He lifted up his other hand. "I bought my laptop."

I closed the door and smiled. Someone to take care of me. How could I say no to that when I felt so rotten?

Zach

Within twenty-four hours, I was sick too. We spent the next four days lying on Amy's sofa, with blankets over us, watching movies, sniffing and coughing. My head felt like I'd been hit with a hammer and my whole body ached, and yet somehow I felt good, being there with her. I realised it was moving fast and it was intense and maybe it'd fizzle out too quick...but I couldn't help it. Being with her, and being sick, was better than not being with her, but healthy.

"What's your most embarrassing memory?" I asked her on the second day.

"Ugh. I was fourteen," she started without hesitating, "and I was on holiday with my family in Spain."

She sneezed and I passed her a tissue.

"There was this guy I liked. His name was Tristan and he was British, he worked at the resort as some sort of summer job. He was about twenty, so a little old for me really. I couldn't take my eyes off him for the first five or so days that we were there."

"What did he do, at the resort?"

"He worked behind the hotel bar, organised pool games, that sort of thing."

"And you really liked him?"

I tried to imagine Amy at fourteen and pictured this beautiful creature, just a little shorter maybe than the one before me now.

"Yes. Totally crazy about him. He was polite and friendly to me, but unfortunately I read that to mean that he was interested. I followed him about a lot, strutting around in my bikini and trying my best to flirt."

"Young love." I passed her another tissue for her wet nose.

"So, a few nights before we were due to leave, I decided I had to tell him how I felt. I was concerned about leaving and never seeing him again and I decided I'd have sex with him before I left."

"What?! At fourteen? I was obsessed with Star Wars and riding my bike at fourteen."

"Well, I guess girls mature faster or whatever."

"So it seems. Okay, go on..."

"So, I snuck out one night, my parents thought I was sound asleep in the room I was sharing with Libby. I waited outside the bar until it closed, and then fell into walk beside Tristan as he was returning to his room. He looked surprised to see me and said something about it being late."

Amy

I told Zach the whole awful story.

"Tristan looked confused, but allowed me to come into this room. I sat on the bed, practically shaking, while he went to the bathroom and then came back.

"So, what's the problem?" he asked, starting to look a little nervous.

I took a deep breath.

"Us. This..." I said, gesturing with my hands as if to symbolise a connection between us.

"This...what?" He was standing in the bathroom doorway, frowning and turning a little pale. Struck by a sudden rush of confidence, I got up, went over to him, and leaned in to kiss him.

"Whoa!" He jumped back. I instantly felt my face flush red.

"What?" I asked, hating the sound of my innocent voice.

"What the fuck are you doing? You're a child! I'll get into trouble!"

"I'm nearly fifteen," I told him, crossing my arms and trying to seem angry.

"Do your parents know you're here?"

"Of course not. I snuck out. I can sneak back in really early in the morning-"

"You were planning to spend the night with me? To have sex with me?" He was almost shouting.

"I thought you liked me," I said, my eyes starting to fill with tears.

52

"You're a lovely girl but you're just a kid. Come on, you've got to get back to your room."

He opened his door and gestured for me to leave. We walked quickly and in silence. As we got to the door he started to knock.

I grabbed his wrist.

"What are you doing?"

"I need to speak to your parents."

"No, please, they don't need to know."

By this point, Jack had opened the door with a look of annoyance and then shock to see us both there.

Tristan told him everything, and then walked away without even looking at me. Jack gave me a stern look and took me out onto the balcony where he gave me a long talk how dangerous it was to just go to his room like that. I sat there, crying and humiliated.

The next day I stayed in the room. I said I had a headache, but I was too embarrassed to face Tristan. About 11 am he came and knocked on the door. I thought maybe I had another chance, but he told me he'd been on the phone to his girlfriend back in England – my heart sank - who told him he'd been too harsh on me. He said he was sorry for telling my dad, and that I was a nice girl but far too young for him. He was flattered, but hoped I'd realise I was too young to be having a boyfriend anyway. He said all this without much conviction or feeling and left me just as embarrassed as before.

I told Zach this story, feeling my face flush with warmth at the horrible memory.

Zach

"Crazy fool. I wouldn't have turned you out!" I said, squeezing her arm.

"Ha!" She laughed. "I'm sure I wasn't worth risking a job over, or even being arrested over, I was underage."

She got up, picking up our huge pile of used tissues. I helped her clear up. We warmed some chicken soup and settled down again on the sofa.

"What about you?" she asked. "What's your most embarrassing moment?"

I smiled. I could sit here, talking to her forever, even with my sore throat.

"On my twenty-first birthday," I told her, "my college roommate shaved off one of my eyebrows after I passed out in a drunken mess. That was pretty embarrassing."

She placed her hand over one side of my face, covering one eyebrow.

"Yes, that would look pretty strange," she said, kissing me lightly on the lips.

I picked up the pile of DVDs we'd rented.

"What shall we watch?"

Amy

On the fourth day we felt significantly better so we cleaned the bedding, ordered Chinese food and had a few glasses of wine. It felt good to be back in the land of the living but I didn't want Zach to go home so I suggested he stay one more night.

I slipped in between the sheets that night and sighed.

"What?" he asked, sliding in next to me.

"It's that fresh feeling. You know, clean sheets? It feels so good when you get into the bed."

"Mmm," he said, moving his feet around. "Like the feel of fresh new carpet on your feet. It's all soft and bouncy."

He smiled.

"Or the smell of freshly cut grass." I put my head on his chest.

"Walking along, kicking autumn leaves, hearing them crunch."

"Good one." I relaxed against him as he put his arms around me. "Standing on the edge of a cliff with the wind blowing your hair."

"Being with you."

I kissed him.

After that, we spent every night together, usually at his place.

Zach

"Dude, she's always there?" Aaron asked me during a call while Amy was at work.

"Yes, what's wrong with that?"

"It's just so fast..."

I knew he was right, it seemed like we were rushing into a very serious relationship...but I couldn't stop myself.

Amy

It was the last week of August, and we'd been seeing each other for four weeks. Practically living together for two. A movie montage of this time would include walks in the park, dinners both at his place and out in Boston. A lot of discussion with Harriet about how it was going from me...me waking up in his arms.

"It's like movie love," I told Harriet one lunch time over tuna baguettes.

"Movie love isn't real, so be careful," she said, munching on her side salad while I played with my fork.

"How isn't it real?" I asked, defensive.

"Because the movie is usually the start of the relationship. The falling in love. But then they have to get on with real life, and that's why the movie ends, because no one wants to see that part, it's boring."

"For some, maybe but I couldn't ever imagine it being boring with Zach."

"We'll see." I ignored her cynicism and changed the subject. She updated me on her progress with Sid. Things were going well, they'd been on several dates and she still seemed to really like him.

Back in the office, I handled some enquiries for a client and had a long meeting where I doodled little hearts all over my note book.

The next day was a Saturday and I was lying on my back on the sofa, my head on Zach's lap, my book in my hands above my face. He was watching a documentary on television. Every now and then he flicked my book and it fell to my nose. After about the tenth time, I sat up, grabbed the cushion next to him and bashed him around the head with it.

"I guess I deserved that." He grinned, putting the cushion on his lap. I rested my head on it.

This was pretty much how we'd spent every evening for the past few weeks. I went home from work, grabbed some things, and made my way to Zach's. By the time I arrived he'd have dinner ready. We'd eat together, often sipping some wine, talking about our day. We'd clean up, and then we'd watch a DVD, or read, or we'd sit side by side on our laptops. I still wasted an unordinary amount of time on the internet. I didn't care, and it seemed "better than mindless soaps or reality TV" – Zach's words, not mine.

I stared at the words in my book for a moment and thought about the last time I'd eaten at home. It'd been a good few weeks. We'd only known each other a month.

"Am I here too often?" I asked, resting my book open on my lap.

"No, you could be here all day, every day, it's fine. It's more than fine. It's good. It's wonderful."

"But, every night. Don't you want a break?"

"Do you?"

"No, but I don't want to crowd you."

"Amy, I-" He looked down at me and then up again at the

TV.

I sat up and turned to face him, surprised at his serious tone. "What?"

He muted the TV.

"Amy, this past month has been amazing."

"Incredible."

"Good. Glad you think so."

"But?"

"There is no but! I love having you around, I feel comfortable with you being here."

I smiled. "Me too. I was just checking."

"Well, check no more. Okay?"

"Okay."

Zach

I spent the rest of the night wishing I'd said it. It might have served to reassure her, and surely it had been a good moment.

As we lay in bed that night I stared up at the ceiling, sure it was the right thing to confess and yet still not one hundred percent sure I'd get the right answer.

"Are you awake?" I whispered.

"Amy?"

No answer.

"I'm falling in love with you," I whispered quietly, and put my arm gently around her.

She sighed happily. "And I'm falling in love with you too," she whispered back.

She turned in my arms and I kissed her hard on the lips. "I love you," I whispered as I kissed her neck. "I love you." Now, her shoulder. "I love you." Her left breast. "I love you." Her right breast. I whispered it over and over again as she pushed me onto my back.

"I love you too," she said, as she climbed on top of me.

Amy

The first time I heard the word "dick" in general conversation I was about twelve, and it came from my cousin Mary. She was talking on the phone to her best friend who had reportedly had sex with five different people by the age of sixteen.

"You sucked his dick?" Mary was saying excitedly as I walked into her room.

I felt disgusted. I thought I might be sick. The next day, I found my mum and decided I'd ask her if it were true, if this really went on. My parents were never very open about sex. It was a taboo subject. I learnt about it at school, and from friends, but I'm not sure I'd ever heard either of them even say the word "sexy" let alone give us a chat about the birds and the bees.

Mum was hanging out the washing in the garden and I just went straight up to her and said, "Mum, is it true that some girls suck men's penises?"

My mother turned to me, face as white as the cotton sheets she was hanging out to dry and told me, very firmly; "Only whores."

I sat thinking about it for a long time and vowed I'd never do that. Never sink that low. Never be a whore. No man would be worth that humiliation. How disgusting.

How things change, I thought, as I turned around on top of Zach and into the 69 position.

He groaned. "I love you!" he said again, but louder this time.

Zach

Sex was not taboo in my household. My parents sat us both down one day and told us the facts of life. They told us where babies came from, taught us about contraception, and warned us about AIDS. Even my dad was quite forthcoming and open.

"Sometimes adults have sex for pleasure," he told us. "It's not just for making babies. It feels good."

Mom had blushed but nodded her head encouragingly.

"Do you two have sex?" Aaron had asked, giggling.

"Yes. We do," Dad replied. I wish he hadn't. It wouldn't have hurt to lie. Now when I think of that memory I get a horrific mental image of my dad bending my mom over the dining table while we were in bed.

I lost my virginity when I was sixteen. Her name was Adele and she went to my high school. We dated for two weeks. I tried to persuade her to "do it" for twelve days straight. She kept saying we weren't ready. On the thirteenth day, we were in my bedroom making out, and I tried to feel her chest. She wasn't sure at first, but then she got into it and pulled off all my clothes, and we ended up doing it under the covers. It was very brief, probably only a few minutes, if that.

Afterward, we got dressed and she said it was over. I shrugged my shoulders and mumbled "whatever." Not my proudest moment.

Amy

My first time was with a boy I met on holiday in one of the Greek islands, I can't even remember which, but he was the same age as me, which was seventeen. We did it in his parent's hotel room whilst they were down at the bar. It hurt. I bled a little on the sheets. As soon as we realised this, we spent the rest of the evening looking for some spare linen. We broke into a door marked "staff only", found some and changed the bedding.

The second, third, fourth, fifth, and sixth times were on that same holiday, with the same boy. His name was Carl. We wrote to each other a handful of times after we got home, but eventually we stopped contact and I never saw him again.

To: Taryn Carmichel
From: Amy Starling
Subject: Love

Hi Taryn,
How are you? Sorry I took so long to reply to your email. How's Josh, still working hard? Happy Anniversary for tomorrow. I sent a gift, but it'll be late (so sorry). Can't believe it's five years since your aunt Doris made me trip over my bridesmaid dress :) How's little Emma? Tell her I send lots of love and cuddles. I miss her, and you, so, so much.
BUT: I confess, I am so happy here. If it weren't for the absence of you and Ed, I'd be perfectly content. Taryn: I'm in love. His name is Zach and he's so right for me, it's like he's my personal ad come to life. He's sweet and funny, caring and attentive and, perhaps most importantly given my history, he loves me back! He even told me so.
It's happening fast and that's a little scary but the whole thing has just been intense and passionate and exciting and I'm just...happy :)
So have you met Libby's fiancé? She told me she saw you at the theatre?? Small world!
Love you lots,
Amy xx

Chapter Five

Zach

It was a Saturday afternoon, and we were going out for dinner with Aaron and Mel to a new restaurant in downtown Boston that I was designing a website for.

Amy arrived at my apartment with a whole suitcase full of clothes; I'd suggested she might as well leave a supply of clothes at my place. I helped her unpack some things and hang some in my wardrobe. It was like she was unofficially moving in without even talking about it, but I didn't feel we needed to discuss it. It seemed natural.

"I don't know what to wear tonight," she said, holding a black dress up against herself and looking in the mirror.

"You look good in anything." I winked.

"Thank you. But I don't, really. And I want to give the right impression, you know?"

"What is the right impression, exactly?"

Amy

"I want to look nice and attractive, but also intellectual and mature. I want them to like me."

"They will love you, don't worry." He pulled me into his arms and I relaxed a little.

We put the rest of my clothes away and it felt a little like I was unofficially moving in. I didn't say as much but it felt a little odd. I'd left a handful of stuff at my apartment and figured

I'd suggest we went there now and then; I was paying rent after all, and had a twelve month lease so it felt like a bit of a waste. But Zach's apartment was bigger, and I felt so at home there – probably because I'd now spent more nights there than in my own apartment. As I was there so much without paying any rent I suggested he stop the cleaner coming over and I cleaned myself when he was working late.

Harriet and I met in the hallway each morning about 8am to travel to work together, and then said our goodbyes again about 5:30, and I'd let myself into Zach's apartment with a key he'd given me. Most days, he'd be working in the spare bedroom, but dinner would be prepared in some way. We'd fallen into this routine and I loved it. I loved having someone there when I got home from work. He'd always ask me about my day, and tell me about his. Still, we never tired of conversation.

"I'm looking forward to meeting Aaron and Mel," I told Zach as he made me a cup of tea and we sat on the sofa. I'd put the Discovery Channel on and left a program about dolphins on in the background.

"Good. It's a shame your family are so far away. I'd like to meet them too."

This seemed a good opportunity. "Well, I was wondering if you'd like to come to Libby's wedding? It's next June."

"Of course!" he said, squeezing my thigh. "I'd love to."

"Libby and I used to play make-believe weddings, you know, with Barbie dolls and stuffed animals. We would set up the guests and bridesmaids and everything. It seems strange that she's setting it all up for real."

"You don't speak about her very often."

"There's not much to say. We're so different. She's into fashion and celebrity magazines and shopping. We played together as kids but we slowly drifted apart as we got older."

"And Ed?"

"Ed and I are close at times and I miss him. You and Aaron seem pretty close."

Zach spoke to him every couple of days.

"Yeah, we are. We're very different though, you know. I'm the geek and he's the...complete opposite."

"You're not a geek," I said, smiling.

"I am and you are too." He smiled back.

"Okay, so what do I wear? Casual, or formal? What are you going to wear?"

Zach

We pulled up outside in my car and Amy checked her face in the mirror. She'd gone for a semi-casual look with a long skirt and frilly top. Like I'd told her, she looked beautiful no matter what she wore.

"That's them," I said, nodding my head in their direction, "the couple fighting in that BMW over there."

Amy looked over. Aaron was gesturing with his hands and Mel had her arms crossed.

"Maybe we should stay here a minute."

"No, let's go see them. They're always like this. You'll see."

The previous evening we'd had a long talk about meeting Aaron and Mel.

"What does Mel look like?" Amy had asked.

Amy

"She's tall, long blonde hair. Wears a lot of make up," Zach had replied, squinting at the paper he was reading.

"Do your parents like her?"

"They love her."

I don't know why, but I was more nervous about meeting Mel than any other member of Zach's family, and she wasn't even real family, was she? She was an in-law. But I wanted her to like me. Because I figured, if she liked me, Aaron would like me. If Aaron liked me, then that would be good. Because Zach and Aaron seemed to be close, from what I could tell. I needn't have worried.

Zach

We got out of the car and walked over to theirs. I knocked on the window and Aaron turned and smiled at me and got out. Mel got out the other side, looking a little embarrassed.

"Hey bro." Aaron gave me a quick, hard hug. I kissed Mel on the cheek and turned towards Amy, who was no longer looking nervous but just serene, calm, and beautiful.

I felt proud as I introduced her.

"It's lovely to meet you both," she said, shaking their hands.

"I didn't know you were British," Mel said. "My Grandmother comes from Maidstone, do you know it?"

She linked arms with Amy and started walking towards the restaurant.

"Wowzers. She's cute!" Aaron nudged me in the ribs as we walked slowly a few paces behind.

"I know. And she's so...smart...and fun. She's kind of moved in, actually."

"Really? Haven't you known this girl for like, two weeks? Slow down here a minute."

"Nearly two months. Slow down for what?"

"You're living the dream, man. You get to date anyone you want. See a different girl every night."

"I told you, I'm getting too old for that." And it wasn't as if I'd exactly had a different girl every night, anyway. Amy and Mel were headed towards the ladies restroom, firm friends already.

"Really. Don't do it. You know what happens, you've seen it happen to me. It's great. You go along in this dream-induced state. It's all sex and lingerie and fun and laughter. Then she starts hinting about getting married. You think 'well that's a good idea, she's a great girl' right?"

"Right," I said, wondering where this was going.

"Wrong. She's great as a girlfriend. As soon as she becomes your wife, everything changes. Mel is just a bitch."

"I'm not about to marry her...and don't say that about Mel, she's great. You two are just going through a tough time. It'll get better."

"You don't know what it's like. She is so concerned about the kids and keeping the house clean and her stupid job. She doesn't like it if I work late, but she wants me to bring home more money. She doesn't like it when I watch football, or see friends. She says I'm not around the girls enough. Nothing I do is good enough. We haven't had sex in nearly four months. Four months! Listen to me. It's not worth it."

We'd been seated at a table and he picked up the menu as the girls came back.

"What's not worth it?" Mel asked. He glared at her.

I thought about when Aaron met Mel, at college. They dated. They seemed to get on well. But when I compared it to my past two months with Amy, it was nothing like this. They didn't have anything in common. Mel was uptight but passionate. Aaron was easy-going and really only interested in sport. My mom had said on several occasions before they got married; "She's wonderful. But not right for Aaron." Over the years, they'd become less and less like a couple and they argued all the time.

I looked at Amy, who was already staring at me. I winked. She smiled and squeezed my thigh under the table. Something stirred in my chest. No. We weren't anything like Aaron and Mel were two months in. Already, we were stronger.

The restaurant was quite dark, with small studded lights and candles on the table. There was only one other couple in there, and classical music was playing very quietly in the background. I saw the owner, Ralph, giving directions to the staff. He glanced at me and waved me over. I excused myself from the table.

"Ralph!" I said, shaking his hand. "The place looks great!"

"Thank you. The website is looking good; you are doing a great job. Who are you here with?"

"That's my brother and his wife over there, and my girlfriend, Amy."

"Well, whatever you order is on the house. I insist!"

"Thank you, Ralph."

Amy

I looked at the menu and decided straight away on a chicken and asparagus risotto. I looked around the table at my companions. Mel was biting her lip and frowning at the menu. She had bleached blonde hair which was curly and down to her shoulders. She wore big earrings and brown lip gloss. She wasn't as pretty as I'd imagined. Not that I had any reason to believe she was exceptionally attractive, but I just imagined someone a little more glamorous for some reason. She sat to my right, Zach was to my left.

My eyes fell to Zach. I smiled and blushed a little, realising how obvious it must be how I felt about him. He was examining the menu and glancing up and then down. I decided he must be trying to choose between two different dishes and re-reading them over and over.

Aaron's mouth was opening and closing slightly, as if he were inaudibly mouthing whatever he was reading. He, too, didn't look anything like I'd expected. I was expecting another Zach, but a couple of years older. Maybe a different hair cut. For some reason I expected him to be very good looking in a kind of rugged, broad shoulders way. Zach had mentioned that he was into sports, I guess that's why.

The Aaron that sat before me was, however, quite different than the one in my imagination. He had dark hair like Zach's, but other than that, they were totally different. He had a small mouth and very dark, long eyelashes. I looked back to Mel and wondered what they'd been fighting about in the car.

A waitress came to our table.

"Are you guys ready to order?" she said, enthusiastically, as it seemed all Americans did.

"Sure we are." Aaron started to point at something on his menu.

"I just need a few minutes..." Mel was still staring at hers. Aaron sighed loudly. I looked down at my cutlery and glanced at Zach. He gave Aaron a look, but it wasn't noticed.

"No problem, I'll be back." The waitress walked away and silence fell on the table.

"I'm just not sure what I want," Mel said, looking a little embarrassed.

"You never are."

"Aaron. Please. Can't you just for once-"

"For once, what?"

"Be patient? Please. We've just met Amy."

"It's okay." I didn't want my presence to make him worse.

"I'm sorry Amy." Aaron smiled apologetically at me.

"No. Really, it's fine."

"Okay. I'm going to have the pasta."

"Waitress!" Aaron said, clicking his fingers.

Mel looked at me with a "I hate it when he does that" look.

The waitress took our orders and we were left to an awkward moment. I wracked my brains for something to say and finally remembered they had two kids. Zach talked about them all the time.

"So, you guys have two children?"

"Yes!" Mel brightened up. "Sophia is the eldest. She's six."

"She's really smart," Zach said, proudly. I fell for him even more.

"She's great. Then there's Lucy. She just turned four. She's a handful, you know, into everything. But adorable. She asked me how long we'd be out tonight. I said a few hours, she said "Mommy, what about us?" It was so cute. I told her the baby

67

sitter was coming. Our neighbour's daughter, Kayleigh. She's fifteen and very responsible. Lucy was so pleased. She loves Kayleigh."

I smiled. This was a woman obviously born to be a mother. Unlike myself.

"They sound great." This must have been a good choice of words. Mel beamed at me and took a sip of water.

"Thank you. They are. You guys must come round one afternoon and you can meet them."

"I'd love to," I said, smiling. I looked at Aaron.

"So how long are you in the US for, Amy?" he asked, sipping his beer.

Somehow, this had never come up with Zach. I hadn't ever thought about it. Tomorrow was another day and we seemed to be living for the moment.

"Well, my visa expires next June," I told him. Zach looked at me in amazement.

"What?"

"June," I told them again, pleased he looked so concerned and yet worried at the thought of it not being extended. That was, if he wasn't sick of me by then.

"Don't worry. He'll just have to marry you!" Mel said, winking at Zach. I felt my heart do a little somersault and hoped no one could tell.

"Well I got a twelve month visa to start with, just to see, you know, if I like it. My company are supporting a full green card application, but it's a long process."

"So, do you like it here?" Mel asked. The waitress placed our food in front of us. It smelt delicious. I picked up my fork and told her that I loved it here.

"See, nothing to worry about." Aaron teased Zach, who smiled at me but still looked worried.

The rest of the evening passed by pleasantly, everyone relaxing a little once we started eating. The food was good and I asked Aaron about his work. He sounded pretty passionate about it, considering accountancy is allegedly one of the most boring careers there is. Mel talked some more about their daughters. I asked how they met. They both told the story with a smile on their face and I got a glimpse into a happier time for them.

"It was my second year in college," Mel began.

"My third," said Aaron. "I was playing soccer with some friends in a grassy courtyard between our dorms."

"I was sitting under a tree, reading," Mel added, with a smile on her face.

"I kicked the ball a little too hard and it bounced right in her lap. She wasn't impressed."

"I yelled something about being more careful and how he could hurt someone."

"I said let me make it up to you, take you out for dinner."

"I'm not sure why I accepted, but I'm glad I did." Mel smiled at Aaron. He smiled back.

We were interrupted by Ralph, the owner, coming to ask us how the food was.

"Delicious," Mel told him, wiping her face on a napkin.

"You must be Zach's girlfriend." Ralph flash me a big smile before offering me his hand. I was pleased to hear the word "girlfriend" and grinned like someone had just given me a hundred dollars.

"Nice to meet you."

"Where are you from?" Ralph asked, releasing my hand.

"Guess!" Zach joked, before I had a chance to respond.

"Australia?"

I laughed.

"England," I told him. He smiled.

"Well, welcome to America. The food is on me, and I hope you all enjoyed yourselves."

We assured him that we had enjoyed it and left a sizeable tip. We said good night to Aaron and Mel, and the minute Zach pulled out of the car park, he asked me about my visa.

Zach

I couldn't relax after I found out that Amy might have to move back to the UK in June. I spent most of the evening thinking of ways to ensure she stayed. Firstly, making sure she wanted to. Then making sure I helped with any sort of visa renewal or extension. I decided to google all this when I got home and find out what the rules were. I'd marry her if I had to. The thought surprised me. Then I considered that I could move to England with her, if necessary.

The girls had gone to the bathroom again just before we left the restaurant.

"Stop thinking about it," Aaron said, as we waited by his car.

"What?"

"Amy leaving, next year, potentially. It's a good thing. No long-term commitment. Have some fun. Then let her go."

"What if I don't want to let her go?"

"Zach, you've been with her for, what did you say, a month?"

"Two. But Aaron...I love her."

"I think I'm going to throw up."

"I know it's early days, but..."

"Yes, exactly, very early days. It's another nine months before she leaves. That is, if she leaves. A lot can happen in that time."

Still, as soon as we left the parking lot, I asked her.

"So, are you going to apply for a green card?"

"I already have. I like it here," she said, smiling. "You want me to stay, huh?"

"Of course." She squeezed my thigh again.

"Good. That's good."

Amy

When we got home to Zach's apartment, he switched on the answering machine.

"Zach. It's your father. I am thinking, we always said we'd

70

play golf together. Let's arrange it. Aaron and I are keen to go next Sunday. Call me back."

Zach grinned.

"He's been saying he wanted to take me to play golf since I was about fifteen."

"You should go." I told him.

"Yes. I guess so."

"Really." I put the kettle on to make some tea. "It's important. He won't be here forever."

"Says she who hasn't spoken to her mother for several weeks."

"Well, yes. But if my dad was around, I'd want to spend time with him."

"But he is around somewhere isn't he? Why don't you take the plunge? You said you wanted to. Go meet him."

Zach had totally distracted me from the mission I'd set myself the day I'd decided to move to Boston. I'd been back to look at Andrew Moore's website several times, and I'd imagined meeting him time and time again. Somehow, I couldn't find the courage to face him. I sometimes wondered if the fantasy of a loving American father was better than the reality could ever be.

For a few weeks, I'd been wondering if my purpose of moving here wasn't to seek out Andrew Moore, but just to meet Zach. It was a silly, romantic notion, but really, if I was honest, I was just being a coward.

I looked at Zach now and bit my lip.

"What if he doesn't want to be found?" I admitted my biggest fear.

Zach

"I'll play golf with my dad, if you find yours."

Amy started looking angry. I was glad she was making tea. It always made her feel relaxed and calm, and I loved that she loved it. It was such a typical, stereotypical British thing to do,

71

and she looked so cute sitting there sipping her tea morning, noon, and night.

She poured out two cups and bought them over to me on the sofa.

"Don't you think it's time?" I said gently.

She sighed.

"It's not as easy as that."

"I know it's not easy. But just think of the time you are wasting. He won't be around forever, either."

Amy

To: Maggie Starling
From: Amy Starling
Subject: Parentage

Hi Mum,
How is everyone?
I know you hate this subject, but please hear me out. While I'm here in the US, I would like to look for my real father. I know you feel "nothing good can come of this" and maybe he doesn't want to be found, and maybe I'll get hurt. I know you feel rejected and bitter towards him...
But I feel I need some reassurance from you. I'm not sure why. Please, just tell me something that will make me think this is a good idea. You knew him, you liked him once – so he can't be all that bad, can he?
Love, Amy.

I considered telling her about Zach at this point but decided I needed to focus on the problem at hand. I re-read it three times and copied Jack before sending it. I kind of felt I needed him to know what I was doing. Plus, he was always more logical and reasonable than she was.

Zach

My father and I stood at the golf club, staring out at the rain which was perhaps heavier than I'd seen in my lifetime.

"Well," he said, turning away from the window, "let's get something to drink shall we? Doesn't seem like the sort of weather to be outside."

I was kind of relieved. I loved the idea of playing golf; of being outside, taking part in a relaxing pastime, spending time with the guys. But I was also pretty sure I'd suck at it.

Aaron was already ordering three beers as we approached the bar and we found a table near the window and stared out at the rain.

"So your mom tells me you have a new girlfriend." My father took a sip of beer from the bottle. I wasn't sure why Aaron had ordered beer when it was only 9am, but I sipped some of mine as well.

"Yes. Amy," I said, smiling.

"He's crazy about her," Aaron said, rolling his eyes, "he can't stop talking about her."

"Well, it's about time he found a nice girl. Settle down, buy a house."

"Whoa, let's not get carried away," Aaron said, "he's only known her a month."

I didn't bother to correct him. Two months. Eight wonderful weeks.

"Why don't you want me to be happy?" I asked him, aware of how much negatively he'd thrown at me since I'd met Amy.

"I do." Aaron sighed. "I'm sorry. Amy is great."

"Good. When do we meet her then?" Dad asked.

"Soon."

Amy

I rushed into my apartment as the phone was ringing. It'd

73

been three days since I'd been there and it was started to feel like a waste, paying the rent. I picked it up and said a breathless "hello."

"Amy. It's your mother."

"Oh, hi Mum. How're you?"

"Fine, fine. How're you?"

"Good thanks. Great, in fact."

"Glad to hear it. I tried calling yesterday but there was no answer."

"I was at my boyfriends."

"Oh, right. What's his name again?"

I wasn't sure I'd mentioned his name previously, in fact we'd hardly spoken in the time I'd know him and all she'd had to talk about was Libby and her wedding plans and just how rich Tim appeared to be.

"Zach."

"Hmm...sounds very American."

"Well, he is American."

"Of course. And how's work going?"

I didn't like the small talk. I wanted to find out if she'd read my email.

"Work's good. It's not all that different here than it was in the UK. How's work for you?"

"Fine thank you. I received your email."

"Yes, look, Mum"

"Before you say anything else, yes: he is, or was, a nice person. Things didn't go well with us, but he was young and so was I. I have no idea how he would react but if you feel this is something you need to do, then go do it."

"What, really?"

"Find him."

"Why are you telling me this now?"

"Because you'll never let up. I just hope he doesn't let you down. If you find him that is. It's Andrew Moore with an "E", and I believe Harvard is close to Boston so perhaps you could start there, but of course that was thirty years ago."

"He definitely knew were pregnant, right?"

"Of course he did. Do you really think I'd not tell him? We ceased contact while I was pregnant. Just be prepared, okay? Just in case."

"Thanks, Mum." I hung up without a goodbye. I turned my laptop on.

Zach

I drove home, without having even touched a golf club, but glad I'd spent some time with my dad. Sometimes my mom can dominate the conversation and it was good to get my dad's perspective. We'd discussed politics, sports – I had less to say on this subject of course – work, the weather, his gardening, the economy.

I called my mom when I got home and left a message saying I'd like to take her out for lunch. I couldn't encourage Amy to find her dad if I wasn't going to see my own parents at least now and then.

Amy

To: Amy Starling
From: Taryn Carmichel
Subject: RE: Love

Amy, darling, how are you?
I miss you too. There's simply no one to go out and have cocktails and pizza with, and I miss your laughter and your insane worrying and your hugs. Tell me more about this Zach. He sounds lovely but don't rush into anything you may regret. Have fun but be sensible, babe. Don't get hurt again, okay?
Josh and Emma are great, thank you for asking.
Now: what about your dad? Have you found him? I keep

looking back at that website and you're right, it must be him. But you haven't mentioned him again. Are you being shy and unsure or just waiting for the right moment? Either way, do it. You have to at least try. Remember the night in Edinburgh? Remember our conversation? You were so determined then. Have some cocktails with Zach and then go call him. If not for yourself, for me. I'm fascinated to know more about him :)

Yes, I met Tim. He's handsome, but a bit flashy and showy with his cash. Insisted on buying us a round of drinks, and then a bottle of champers when Libby introduced us. I know she's your sister and you love her but, really, she is so shallow! They seem well suited, I think.

Gotta run babes but I love you. Maybe we can chat on Skype? Josh set it up for me. I'm not sure how to use it but I'm sure I can figure it out just to hear your voice :)

Hugs,

Taryn oxoxoxo

I flicked from my email to the web page already open and then just stared at the screen, rereading the website once again. I almost knew it by heart. Andrew Moore was CEO of a law firm in Boston. I looked at his face and couldn't quite believe how much it looked like Ed. Same facial features and the same colour hair. Same colour as mine, too.

I wrote down the telephone number and email address. I wasn't sure how I was going to handle this, but at least I had a name and face to put in place of the blank spot I'd associated with the word "dad" since I was fourteen years old.

I told Harriet the next day at work.

"Wow. This is kind of exciting. And who'd have thought it'd be so easy to find him like that? Google is just...amazing."

I laughed.

"Are you sure this guy is him?"

"I'm pretty sure, yes." I showed her the website and then bought up Ed's Facebook profile to compare photos.

"Seems a pretty good bet." Harriet smiled. " All three of you have the same eyes, same hair and skin colour..."

I smiled and closed the website. I had looked at it so many times in the past few months that I was starting to wonder if we did look alike at all.

"So, what's your next move? Telephone call? Email?"

"I'm not sure. Zach suggested I call. I'm thinking email might be easier. It might come as quite a shock."

"For sure. What are you going to say?"

"I've no idea."

By the time lunch came around, I'd written and deleted about ten different drafts. I was finding it hard to concentrate on work and decided I'd have to push it out of my mind until I had some time to really consider what I needed to say.

As Harriet and I were heading into Nelson's, our favourite eatery just around the corner from work, Mel was coming out.

"Wow, Amy, hi," she said, kissing me on the cheek.

"How're you Mel?"

"Great, thank you. Just ate too much. Try the pasta, it's so good."

"I will." I smiled. "Do you work around here?"

"Yes, do you? Oh, we should have lunch together one day next week."

She gave me her card with her office number and we said our goodbyes.

"Zach's sister-in-law," I explained to Harriet as we found a table.

"So, you met the family?"

"Well, just his brother and Mel."

"So it's going well? I just knew you two would hit it off."

"Very well. I'm so glad you invited him to the party."

"Well, I'm glad someone got something good out of it. Sid turned out to be such a bore that I told him last night I didn't want to see him anymore."

This didn't surprise me. Sid seemed pretty monotone to me.

"Does Zach have any single friends?"

Actually, Zach didn't seem to have that many friends. He only really mentioned Aaron, and his friend Matt, his best friend from college. I think Matt lived about an hour away but that's all I knew about him.

"I'll ask him," I told Harriet.

That afternoon, I finally contacted Andrew Moore.

To: Andrew Moore
From: Amy Starling
Subject: Hello

Dear Andrew,
I am not sure how to start this email, so I'm going to get straight to the point.
Thirty years ago, did you know a British woman named Maggie Harrington?
If yes, then I think you can guess who I am. My name is Amy, I'm twenty-nine years old and I'm currently living in Boston. If you are the right person, I'd very much like to meet you.
If you are not the right Andrew Moore and this message makes no sense, please let me know. Or, if you simply do not want to meet me, then I understand and there will be no hard feelings.
Kind regards,
Amy Starling.

I sent it to Zach, who said it was perfect. Harriet said it seemed a little formal but I said that's exactly what I needed to be, this is a stranger after all. Judy, an intern who sat in the cubicle next to me, said she'd just go to his office and speak to him direct. That scared me half to death and I decided to hit "send" before asking anyone else.

He replied ten minutes later.

Zach

I was staring out of the window, wondering how Andrew Moore would reply when my mother called.

"Hello dear."

"How are you Mom?"

"Good. I was delighted with your lunch invitation."

"Great. Are you free tomorrow?"

"Yes I am."

"I'll pick you up at twelve."

"Wonderful. Aaron and Mel said Amy is quite something."

"She is."

"They said you are quite in love, too."

I laughed.

"Well, yes. I suppose I am."

"Good. About time you met someone who makes you feel that way. Just be careful, you know she might end up wanting to go back to the UK."

"Don't worry Mom, it's all under control."

"Okay, well I look forward to seeing you tomorrow."

Amy

I opened it with both excitement and fear.

To: Amy Starling
From: Andrew Moore
Subject: Re: Hello

Amy,
Wow.
You found the right man. I have hoped for many, many years that you'd get in touch.
Are you free for a cup of coffee? I think the sooner the better. How about straight after work today?

Andy.

I forwarded it to Zach and called him.

"Wow. So you going to go?"

"No. I'm going to suggest tomorrow."

"Why wait?"

"Because I need to think about what I'm going to wear."

"Amy, he won't care what you are wearing, trust me."

"Well, I do. I need to make a good first impression."

"Amy, this man abandoned your pregnant mother. He's the one that needs to fix first impressions."

"I also need to prepare emotionally."

"Okay, fair enough."

I emailed back to say I'd meet him at the Starbucks on the corner of the street I worked on, one week from today, at lunch time. He replied to say he couldn't wait. I thought I might be sick.

Zach

Amy played with the food on her plate. For the first time in over a month we'd decided to eat at her place as she said felt the rent was wasted if we didn't stay there once in a while. I considered suggesting she just move in with me and save the rent, seeing as she was always at my place anyway, but now didn't seem like the right time.

She'd made Moroccan lamb with cous cous, which was delicious. I'd nearly finished mine and she'd barely had a few mouthfuls.

"You okay?" I asked her after several minutes of watching her play with her food.

"What, sorry?" She looked distracted and confused.

"Stop worrying, it'll be fine."

"It's just going to be so...strange, you know?"

"Have you thought about calling your mum?" I said, taking

care to pronounce the 'u'.

"Or your brother?"

"What for? Mum is obviously a bit edgy, and I'm not sure there's a lot to report to Ed yet."

"Just a suggestion. Do you know what you're going to wear then?"

She didn't say anything and her silence made me irritated.

"Amy? You okay?"

"I'm just thinking, give me some space will you?" she snapped.

"I'm just trying to help!" I snapped back.

"How can you possibly help? You have no idea what it's like. You and your perfect parents, who are still together, in your perfect childhood. You have no idea what it's like to never know your father!

"Amy, my childhood wasn't perfect either. You can't think your family was more messed up than anyone else's." I raised my voice more than I'd intended.

"Oh yours was messed up too? Yeah, right."

"What is wrong with you?"

"What's wrong with you? You had it all, I don't even know what my father's voice sounds like!"

"I had it all, did I? Well, how's this; my mom got sick when I was sixteen and she wasn't well again until my second year in college."

"What?"

"She had cancer. She lost her hair, she was in and out of hospital, she was really, really sick for about five years."

With that I put my plate in the kitchen, and walked out.

Amy

"Hi," Zach said as he answered the phone.

"I'm sorry." I sniffed, crying a little.

"Me too."

"No, I was moody and stupid. I'm so sorry about your mum. That must have been so hard."

"It was, but that wasn't the time to get angry and shout at you. I should have been more understanding. You are tense about meeting your dad, and that's natural."

"So can we forget it now?"

"Forgotten. Our first fight."

"Yup. It feels weird being in bed without you," I admitted, shivering under my covers.

"I'll be there in ten minutes."

I smiled and put my phone down on the floor beside my bed. Harriet had commented on a number of occasions now that it seemed a little unhealthy to be practically living together when we'd only been seeing each other a few months, but it just seemed natural to me to be with Zach as much as possible.

Zach

"This is lovely," my Mom said as she placed her napkin on her lap and looked around the restaurant.

"So how have you been?" I asked, always worried at the answer. She'd been well for years but I often felt I was just waiting for bad news to come. She looked at me fondly, perhaps sensing my anxiety.

"I'm incredibly well, thank you."

I relaxed a little and the conversation moved on. She asked me a lot about my job, and told me all the family news. One of my cousin's was having a baby another had a new house. I wondered if Aaron would have sat there, listening, taking an interest and decided, no, he probably wouldn't have. We ate salmon and had a glass of wine each and I told her about the tour I gave Amy of Boston.

"I'm glad you're making such an effort," she said warmly, touching my hand.

"Well, I think this one might be worth making the effort

for."

"Wonderful. I'm very happy for you."

I smiled and squeezed her hand. I was very happy for me, too.

Chapter Six

Amy

I'd always heard that "New England in the Fall", or autumn as I prefer – was something spectacular. I wasn't disappointed. As the leaves began to turn beautiful shades of bright red, orange, yellow and gold, I really started to feel at home in Boston. It grew a little colder, but it just gave Zach and I an excuse to snuggle even more in our loved-up state.

It was the night before I was due to meet Andrew Moore. I'd decided to wear my best work clothes; a black suit with a crisp white shirt. I'd cleaned my shoes and bought some underwear which held my stomach in; since arriving in Boston I'd managed to add an inch or two to my waistline.

"You nervous?" Zach asked, giving me a squeeze as we sat down on the sofa to watch Gavin and Stacey, I'd managed to find the DVDs while wandering around a local mall with Harriet and told Zach to be prepared for a great night in.

"Yes," I said, "but isn't that normal?"

Zach

"Of course it is! It'll be fine, though."

I watched her fidget around a little before picking up the remote control and settling back to watch the DVD.

I hoped I hadn't just lied; I had no idea if it would be fine. This Andrew Moore seemed keen to meet her, but it was surely going to be awkward and perhaps not what Amy was expecting at all. I'd asked her a couple of times what sort of relationship did she see herself having with her father, once they'd met and she didn't have an answer.

I was also growing uneasy at this point because I had something I needed to tell Amy, but with all the issues with her dad, I'd chickened out. There had been a few times when I should have shared my "secret", but as she was feeling a little sensitive and emotional, I couldn't ever find the words to tell her. Only that morning, my mom had asked if she knew. I said no; that I was waiting for the right opportunity. Once again, I pushed it to the back of my mind, figuring I'd tell her later. Later never came.

Amy

I sat in Starbucks, sipping a latte and reading a history magazine I'd found lying around. My stomach was doing somersaults and my brain was going over and over again what I might say, what he might say...

"Amy?" I looked up and saw my brother, Ed, only twenty years older.

"Andrew?"

"Please, call me Andy," said my father, my real, biological father, sitting down opposite me. He didn't take his eyes from mine. I felt myself blush and there was a moment's awkward silence. So here he was, finally.

"I'm sorry, I've just wondered what you look like for a long time. Let me start again! Hi, Amy. I'm Andy. Can I get you another coffee?"

I said yes and he went off to the counter. I watched him standing there, ordering my latte and realised he looked nothing like I'd originally expected, before coming to Boston. Taking out the Bruce Willis hopes, I'd always kind of thought of my father being a little overweight, maybe balding and kind of dull. That image had slowly faded after I'd found the website, although that only contained a headshot. What I saw actually looked remarkably like me and Ed. Dark hair. Green eyes. Same build. There was no doubt that his man was our father.

He came back with our coffees.

"So, first, let me just say that whatever you know about me already, good or bad, I'm sorry that I haven't been in your life thus far."

"It's okay, I understand it was difficult." I took a deep breath, trying to calm myself.

"Yes...it was, but I should have made more effort, it's just your mother...well, she didn't give me a lot of opportunity. She was in England, I was here. I was so young and-"

"Please," I said, reaching out and putting my hand on his, "you don't have to do this. I understand. Really, there's no need to explain, I just want to get to know you now."

He sighed and squeezed my hand, which felt a little strange. We both sat back.

So this was my father, at last. I carried his genes. I had so many questions that I couldn't think where to start.

"You know, I didn't have any way of getting in touch with her after you were born. I didn't even know if you were a girl or a boy. I guess I just allowed myself to forget...but I have thought about you over the years-"

"What?" I was shocked.

"I have thought about you," he said, smiling.

"I have a twin brother," I told him, "Edward. Ed."

He sat back for a moment, his jaw open.

"I have a son as well?"

My mother could have prepared me for this.

"Yes."

He shook his head and whistled in astonishment.

"I wish she'd told me. But you're hear now."

"I'm sorry that she didn't. I'm so angry with her."

"Don't be. It was a long time ago."

We smiled at each other while I had an imaginary argument with my mum in my head.

"Well, you have a half-sister. Jemma. She's twenty three."

Another sister? It hadn't even occurred to me that he might have more children. Jemma. An American sister. I'd imagined just finding a father, and now I realised, I was finding a whole new family. Did I have grandparents and aunts and uncles, cousins?

I tried to imagine what Jemma might look like.

"Tell me about yourself." He sipped his coffee and sat back, relaxing a little.

I filled him in on the last twenty nine years. How Ed and I didn't know Jack wasn't our father at first (he showed sympathy but didn't seem surprised or angry). How I'd been creative at school, gone on to work in public relations. I owned a little house, I told him, which I was renting out. He raised his eyebrows occasionally, nodded in all the right places. Then I told him how I'd come to the US for work, and a bit about my job.

"Amy, can I just say, you're remarkably beautiful."

I couldn't help but smile from ear to ear. My father thought I was beautiful! Suddenly a rush of emotion filled my whole body. More than anything else, I wanted to earn this man's respect. I wanted him to be proud of me. He would be the parent my mum never was. He'd encourage me and inspire me and show off my photo to his buddies.

"Thank you." I smiled.

"Any boyfriend?" he asked next.

"Yes. Zach. He designs websites and he lives here in Boston."

"Great, well I'd like to meet him. Do you have any questions for me? I still feel like I owe some sort of explanation-"

"How did it happen?"

"What?"

"How did we happen, I mean Ed and I? How did you meet, and how did she end up pregnant?"

He sighed. "Your mother hasn't told you this stuff?"

"Nope."

"You really want to know?"

"Yes. I don't want the gory details, but the basics."

I wanted to know if I was born out of love or lust. I wasn't sure which was better, but I wanted to know.

"Maggie had won a scholarship to come to Harvard for a couple of terms. I liked her right away, she was so intelligent, really smart and took her studies very seriously. But she had a fun side too. She made me laugh a lot. She had never been to the US, and I showed her around. She really liked it here and I thought at the start of our relationship that there was a chance she might stay, although we never really discussed it."

This sounded a little too similar to Zach and I.

"You were conceived on a weekend break to Chicago. Your mother had always wanted to go there, and I took her away for a short break. We were just friends, really, but we ended up in bed, with no contraception, and I thought 'it won't matter, this one time' after that weekend, she told me she was going back to the UK. I tried to persuade her to stay but she said she didn't feel as strongly as I did. I was hurt, but I dealt with it and we were friends for the few weeks before she left."

I made a mental note to ensure I took my contraceptive pill every day so that history didn't repeat itself.

"It was as simple as that. Neither lust nor love, just something in between; a casual relationship that didn't work out."

I nodded, trying to picture my mum back then, with this man. Good friends who kind of started a relationship that didn't have any future. Creating two new lives by accident.

"Then, she called me a month or so after she'd got home and she told me she was pregnant. My whole world turned upside down...I didn't know what to do. I wanted to be a politician back then. Thought I might even make president one day – ridiculous, I know – I didn't want to go to England. She wasn't prepared to come back to the US, and told me she didn't want a relationship. I tried to keep in touch, we wrote to each other for a few months. She sent me the pregnancy test result, with a smiley face. It just felt surreal for me. Then she stopped responding. I called but she changed her number. I didn't even know one hundred percent for sure that she hadn't had an abortion. I guess I could have done more. I could have flown over, but it was like the problem had gone away. So I didn't think about it too much. It's only since Jemma was born that I started to wonder about you. I'm sorry. I was young, and stupid."

"It's okay," I said, touching his arm, "it's not your fault."

He smiled sadly.

"I wish it'd been different, but I'm glad you're here now. What about Ed, what does he do?"

I filled him in. We joked. We sipped our coffee and a few more after that. He told me about himself. He graduated Harvard and went on to become a lawyer in Boston. He had a wife, Yvonne, who he'd met and wed within a few months, and then they'd had a daughter, Jemma. I still couldn't quite believe I had another sister, why hadn't it occurred to me before? Of course he'd have gone on and had a family. They lived "upstate" and also had an apartment in the city, and a boat. He liked golf and was a basketball fan.

This couldn't have gone more perfectly. We sat there for a couple of hours and I had to text Harriet to cover for me at work. I wasn't ready to leave the conversation. Only one question was nagging at the back of my mind.

"Do Yvonne and Jemma know about me?"

"Yes. Yvonne does, but Jemma doesn't. I think she'll be surprised but excited. I'll find a way to tell her. You'll get on great, I'm sure."

"I'm sorry I missed all those years, and I realise it's too late to be your father, but I'd like to be your friend. Do you think we can manage that?"

"It's not too late to be my father."

He put his arm around me and for the first time, my father

was giving me a hug. It felt good.

"Come for dinner on Saturday," he said. "Jemma will be home too. Yvonne actually was the one who suggested you come. Bring that boyfriend of yours, if you like, and stay the night."

I left Starbucks smiling, and on a bit of a high.

Zach

I sat waiting for Matt, my best friend, wondering why it'd been so long since I'd made the effort to spend any time with him. I hadn't intended to be a crap friend; it just sort of happened. Matt had been travelling a lot for work and I had been spending all my free time with Amy. I just didn't make any plans to see him. So I called, apologised, and we agreed to meet for lunch.

"Hello stranger," he said, picking up the menu. "I'm starving, what are we eating?"

We both ordered clam chowder – a sure sign of the colder weather and a bit of a tradition. "So what's new with you?" I asked after the waitress had taken our order.

"I've got a new job, actually, working in Providence. Less travel, which is nice, and more money."

"Sounds good."

"What about you? You've been hard to get in touch with lately. I left you a bunch of messages. I don't think I've seen you since you ditched Scarlett."

"I met someone."

"Oh yeah, that's great. What's her name?"

"Amy. She's British. She's amazing, seriously. She's smart and fun and beautiful...I'm just feeling so...happy, man."

"Still talking like a woman, I see."

The waitress bought our drinks and smiled, obviously overhearing our conversation.

"Seriously, she's great. I can't wait for you to meet her."

"Good, I'm pleased for you. How did you meet?"

I told him the story of Harriet's party. He told me a bit more about his new job. We talked about some other college friends.

"So, this Amy then, what's so great about her?"

"It's like...she's a reflection of myself. We're on the same wavelength, we think the same way, and we want the same things. She is so...interesting to talk to and be around."

"What are you doing this weekend, I'll come by and meet her."

"We're going to meet her father."

"Meeting the parents, that's fast."

I didn't tell him it was only Amy's second time meeting her father, but it dawned on me that I was privileged to be a part of such a big, historical event in her life. Which made me incredibly nervous about the whole thing.

I told Matt we'd arrange a meet another time soon. It was good to catch up though and I realised I should have made more effort. How had my relationship with Amy taken over my life, made me neglect my other friendships?

Amy

We pulled into the driveway of my father's house and I gasped at how lovely it looked. All American houses seemed big to me, and this was no exception. There were flowers outside and a huge tree on the front lawn.

Even Zach said it was a "nice place" as we looked up at it..

Zach parked next to Andy's BMW and another car pulled up besides us. I swallowed hard. I was nervous to meet them, especially Jemma, who might not have had a great reaction when she heard about me. I had no idea what to expect.

As if reading my mind, Zach squeezed my hand.

"Relax Amy."

I took a deep breath.

As I stepped out of the car, I saw my new sister. I knew it

was her because she looked so much like me. Long, dark hair. Thinner than me. Same eyes. Same nose. Andy had been right, she could have been my twin, if I didn't already have one.

"Hello, you must be Jemma," I said, smiling as she opened her car door. She frowned.

"Hi," she replied, taking me in.

"I'm Amy," I said, offering my hand. She shook it, still looking confused. Zach offered his hand, and I introduced him. She was still looking puzzled and I realised she didn't know who we were. She was about to ask when Andy and a petite blonde woman who looked a little like Hilary Clinton appeared at the front door and swooped in.

"Jemma, this is-"

"Amy, yes we met." She was friendly, but a little uneasy.

"You're late," said Yvonne, to Jemma.

"Sorry Mom, there was a hold up, and- sorry, but who is Amy?"

Ignoring her, Andy introduced us to Yvonne who smiled politely and shook our hands.

"Jemma, can I have a word with you in the back yard?" She followed our father round to the back of the house and I took a deep breath.

"I'm sorry," Yvonne apologised.

"It wasn't supposed to be like this. Andy wanted to tell her before you got here. Bad timing, that's all. I'm so happy to meet you; you really are all Andy has spoken of since you met."

I swelled with pride and we went inside. The hall was bigger than my mum and Jack's living room at home. They had black and white tiles and a huge sweeping staircase. Yvonne showed us into an even bigger living room, with cream walls and brown leather sofas. There was a vase of lilies on a large oak coffee table.

"You have a beautiful home Mrs. Moore." Zach smiled, taking in the room.

"Thank you, Zach, please, call me Yvonne." She gestured

towards the seats and we sat. I glanced back at the windows to the back garden and saw Jemma and my father talking.

"Don't worry, I'm sure she'll handle it okay," Yvonne smiled. "Can I get you something to drink? Some ice tea maybe?"

We both accepted and she went off to the kitchen.

"Well, this is awkward," I admitted, straightening my hair with my hand and fidgeting nervously.

"I can't believe how much she looks like you," Zach said, glancing out of the window.

Jemma walked in.

"I've always wanted a sister!" she practically screamed. I stood up and she hugged me. "I can't believe it!"

Andy was standing in the doorway, smiling.

"Zach," he said, "it's wonderful to meet you. I'm sorry we didn't get off to the best start. I'm Andy."

"Nice to meet you." Zach stood up to shake his hand.

Zach

Jemma insisted she and Amy take a walk around the block to talk alone. Amy seemed a little apprehensive but managed to hide it quite well. Yvonne was preparing dinner which left me alone with Andy.

"Well, that went better than expected," he said, settling down opposite me.

"I wanted to tell her in person, but she's been off at medical school. I didn't get the opportunity. I asked her to arrive a few hours earlier than you, so I could tell her, but then she comes late and my plan went to hell."

I immediately liked Andy. He was natural, confident, and honest. I could see that Amy had a lot of him in her, despite having been bought up several thousand miles away. I sipped my ice tea and watched his green eyes taking me in.

"Seems Jemma took it well, though?"

"Yes, she was a little hurt I'd never told her before. But, you know, there seemed little point. I didn't really expect to ever hear from Amy. Or Ed. I didn't even know they were twins, or that they existed for sure! I thought there was just one, didn't have a name or anything to go on. Anyway, I'm glad she's here now."

"I have to say, it's great of you to invite us both here like this, and to welcome Amy into your family."

"Least I can do. She's my daughter, it's about time I behaved like a father. Now, tell me about yourself."

"Well, I run my own business," I began, feeling a little intimidated.

"Awesome! What do you do?"

"I'm a web developer."

"Great. I may have some clients I could maybe send your way, actually if you're interested? And where do you live, in Boston?"

"That'd be great, thank you. Yes. I bought my apartment a few years ago."

"Property owner, that's good."

I almost felt I was being interviewed as a potential son-in-law, which seemed a bit early, but also a bit odd considering I'd known Amy longer than he had. However, there was something about him which made him completely likeable. He was genuinely interested and just easy to talk to. Much like Amy.

Amy

Jemma and I stepped outside of the house and she linked her arm in mine. She was wearing a knee-length white dress with small poppies embroidered all over it. Her silver bangles fell to her wrists and jangled as we began walking.

"I know this probably seems so over the top and tell me to back off if you want," she began, "but I'm just so psyched. A little pissed with my dad – our dad! Wow! – but oh my god, I've always wanted a sister. Seriously. And now, just like that, I have one!"

I smiled. "Thank you, I'm very flattered Jemma, I was worried how you'd react."

"Well, I'm a little angry with Daddy. He could have pre-warned me, but within a few minutes of it settling in, all I could think of was: I have a sister and a brother!"

"Well, that's good, I'm glad."

"I just love your accent!"

I smiled. I was used to American's saying they loved my accent. They often asked me to quote Shakespeare or talk about the Queen.

"So you're going to be a doctor?"

"Yes. A paediatrician. It's hard work, but I love it. What do you do? I want to know everything!"

Her enthusiasm was a little overwhelming. I told her a bit about my job and living in Boston. A little about Zach.

"Your mother, she's in London?"

"Near London, yes. She's married to a guy called Jack and had another child, Libby, my sister."

"Bet you miss them."

"We're not close. Libby and I are very different. I miss Ed, though."

"I can't wait to meet him. Does he know about me?"

"Not yet."

I know it might seem odd, but I hadn't told Ed about meeting our father yet. I wanted to keep it to myself, just for now. All my life I'd shared everything with him; toys, relative's attention, friends at school, birthdays...I just wanted to keep our father to myself, for now.

We'd come back to the house.

"I don't want to seem scary or come on too strong, but I so want to get to know you better."

I smiled.

"Me too." Her excitement was infectious.

Zach

I sat and listened to Andy telling me about his boat, and realised just how much like her father Amy was. It was astonishing. Not only did they look alike, but the way he spoke, too. They both used their hands a lot when they were speaking, and had a very similar laugh. Amy and Jemma returned, smiling, and I was glad to see her looking more relaxed.

We spent the evening drinking, telling stories, eating lobster and cheesecake, and then we played a few games of cards. Amy seemed so relaxed with Andy, you'd never be able to tell that they'd only just met. He had a way of making you feel relaxed around him. They were welcoming, friendly people.

Around midnight, Jemma and Yvonne had both gone up to bed and the three of us were sitting and talking.

"So, are you here to stay Amy?" Andy asked after a while.

She glanced at me and bit her lip. We still hadn't talked that much more about the future, what might happen. I waited for her response.

"Your hesitation tells me you don't know for sure." "Well, I'm happy here," she begun, looking at me again.

"Depends on this one, does it?" Andy laughed, taking a sip of his wine.

"Don't worry," I said, "I won't let her go anywhere." I got up and kissed Amy on the forehead.

"Excuse me," I told them, sensing they might like to be alone. "I'm going to bed."

"Let us know if you need anything," Andy told me as I left the room.

Amy

My father smiled at me as Zach walked away.

"I'm so glad you're here." He held out his wine glass.

I clinked mine against his and finished what was left in my

glass. My head was swirling a little and I felt incredibly tired, but I wasn't ready for the night to end just yet. I stared at him for a few seconds. I could have sworn I'd travelled in time and was sat looking at Ed as a fifty year old.

"I think mentioning me, on your green card application, should help. You know, because I'm your father. I don't think you'll have a problem if you want to stay here permanently."

"I do...I hope to," I told him.

"You're not close to your mother?"

"Not really. We have our moments. We haven't been in touch much, since I've been here."

"And Ed?"

"Ed and I were close growing up. Now, not quite so much."

"Have you told him about me?"

"Not yet. I will."

"I'd like to meet him too."

"I think he'd like to meet you, especially when I tell him everything you've told me. And he'd like to meet Jemma too, I'm sure."

"Good. Well, tell him to come over. As soon as he can."

I nodded. I wasn't sure Ed would rush over here. Andy yawned and got up.

"Let's hit the sack," he said, taking my wine glass. We walked out to the hall.

"Zach is great."

"He really is," I said, yawning and realising how tired I was.

"Do you love him?"

"Yes," I answered, without hesitation.

"Good, glad to hear it. Now, let's get some sleep!"

He kissed my forehead, and then took our glasses out to the kitchen.

Zach

The guest room was quite something, with pine furniture, a

huge bed, and framed photos of various different cats and dogs, who I imagined were family pets. A love of animals was obviously another trait Amy had inherited from her father. She had mentioned she missed her cat, who she had given to her friend Taryn, at least once a week since we'd met.

As I came back from the bathroom, I heard Amy and Andy talking.

"Do you love him?" My heart stopped for a second.

"Yes," she said simply, without hesitation. I grinned.

Amy

The next morning Yvonne cooked us all French toast which she served with blueberries. I felt so relaxed in their presence, it was as if I'd been around since the beginning. The kitchen and dining area was open plan, with solid oak worktops, a huge island with pots and pans and utensils hanging from the ceiling. The dining area had large windows running down the rest of the room, flooding the whole space with sunlight. French doors opened up to the garden.

"Yvonne used to be a chef," Andy told us.

"Really, I'm not surprised, this is so good," Zach said, tucking into his breakfast.

"Your father met me when he tried to complain about the food!" Yvonne laughed. "I never thought we'd end up married."

"Twenty five years and still going strong," Andy said with a mouthful of eggs.

Jemma tapped her fork against her glass of orange juice and stood up.

"I'd just like to say, that, despite the years of deceit from Dad," - this was directed at Andy and then she turned to me, "I am so glad you found us Amy, and I look forward to getting to know you better."

I felt a little overwhelmed as we clinked our orange juice. I swallowed hard to avoid tears.

Zach

"Well that really could not have gone better, huh?" Amy said as we drove away.

"They are very welcoming and they seem very fond of you, you must be pleased."

"I am. It just feels a little overwhelming and almost too perfect."

Amy plugged her iPod into the car stereo and put Boston's "More Than A Feeling" on. We sang along as she found more classic hits all the way home.

Amy

"I can't believe how well it's gone," Taryn said on a Skype call, after I'd filled her in on all the activity with my father.

"I know, it's amazing isn't it?"

"How's it going with Zach?"

"Great. We just click, you know?"

"Yes, I do know...wish I could meet him though. I don't suppose you'll be rushing home now that he's on the scene and you have this whole new family."

"We'll be coming home for two weeks in June," I told her. "Libby's wedding."

"Oh yes of course. That's still too long way. I miss you."

An idea dawned on me.

"Come and visit!"

"Really?"

"Yes, really, why not?"

"Could Josh and Emma come as well? We have some time off work soon, I wonder how much the flights would be. Are you serious?"

"Yes of course!"

"I'll talk to Josh."

I loved Josh. Even though he'd stolen my flatmate and best

friend, I loved him for loving her. He was romantic and kind, he treated her like the princess she was, and when he proposed I was almost as delighted as she was. When baby Emma was born I acted the aunt, and loved every minute. But somehow I'd gone from being number one in Taryn's life to number three. I was happy for her, it was right and natural. I just felt a little lost for a while. Just another reason to move to Boston, one less thing holding me back.

But I'd missed her. I'd missed her direct honesty and her colourful clothes. She was obsessed with Wuthering Heights and would quote it at me relentlessly. I missed the look on her face when Emma tottered into the room and I missed having someone in my life who knew me so completely.

Yet somehow, I realised, now Zach was getting to know me even better than Taryn did. My phone calls to her had been less frequent and we were in danger of drifting apart even further. I missed her and honestly hoped she'd make the trip. She emailed me three days later.

To: Amy Starling
From: Taryn Carmichael
Subject: Boston trip

Hello Amy,
Flight is booked! Would have called but if I've calculated right, it's 4am there. So excited! We arrive on 15 November, for two weeks. Are you sure there's enough room for us to stay?
Emma will seem so much bigger to you. I just hope she's okay on a seven hour flight!
Can't wait to meet Zach.
Love you girl!
Taryn x

To: Taryn Carmichael
From: Amy Starling

Subject: Re: Boston trip

Taryn,
How exciting! Can't wait to see you all. Plenty of room.
Love you,
Amy x

It had been three weeks since we'd spent the weekend at Andy's house and I still hadn't told Ed about him. Jemma had called me a couple of times to chat, and suggested we meet up at "our dad's house" again soon. Yvonne had also called a couple of times and Andy and I had met for lunch once a week. They'd become the family I felt I'd never had and I felt more comfortable with them than I ever had with Mum, Jack, Libby...it was strange, but I liked it.

"So, you told your brother yet?" Andy asked one lunchtime as we sat outside a small Mexican restaurant, eating fajitas and tortilla chips.

I wiped some salsa from my lip.

"No, I haven't spoken to him to be honest," I lied. I had emailed him. But our emails were always short and sweet, and I wasn't sure emailing was the best way to communicate this news anyway.

"I'd have thought you'd deliberately have called him, just to tell him the news," Andy said, looking a little hurt.

"I mean, I don't flatter myself that I'm a great subject of conversation...but, is there something you haven't told me? If he doesn't want to know me, it's okay. Just tell me so."

"It's not that," I admitted, "it's just that- well, this will probably sound really immature, but..."

I told him a little about my childhood. About sharing everything with Ed from birthdays to my mother's love. That I'd never felt she'd loved me as much as him.

"I'm sure that's not the case," Andy said. "But even if it is, that's not the situation here. I don't know him. I would like to know him, but what I have right now is a beautiful, intelligent, wonderful daughter and while it might sound odd to say it, I really do feel a fatherly affection for you. It's crazy to think that the bond we've built up could be damaged by my meeting or being in touch with Ed. And, anyway, he's thousands of miles away. So, let go of your hang-ups. Call him. He's your brother."

So, the next morning, I called. I picked up the phone and curled up on the arm chair. Zach sat on the sofa, typing something into his laptop, pretending not to listen although he kept glancing up at me.

"Hi Ed," I said, trying to sound a little more upbeat than I felt.

"Amy-Wamy!" He sounded genuinely pleased to hear from me.

"How are you?"

"I'm good thanks. You?"

"Not bad."

"How's work going?" I asked. He told me a little about his new boss, about the girl he was seeing who worked with him as well. He asked the same question and I told him a little about my work.

"You like still it, then, in America?"

"Loving it, yes."

"You always loved America. Remember that year you tried to get us all to celebrate Thanksgiving?"

I remembered it well. I was a little obsessive about the US, partly because I knew my father was American. I was about seventeen, and I persuaded my mum to buy napkins with the stars and stripes on them, and cook a turkey. I made a pumpkin pie, which I burnt. We had to all list things we were "thankful for." It was a semi-success. The following summer, I'd suggested we celebrate July 4 – Independence Day. Jack told me it'd be unpatriotic, so I had a little celebration of my own, which basically involved me and Taryn going to an American burger bar for dinner. I drank too much Budweiser and was sick in the taxi on the way home. Not a fond memory.

"Of course I remember," I said, laughing. "I didn't imagine living here though."

"Well, now you are. Living the dream, huh?" He laughed.

"Ed. I found him."

Silence.

"Who?" He knew who. He was just testing. Making sure.

"Our father. His name is Andy."

"Okay, how did you find him, how do you know it's definitely him?"

"Mum gave me some information."

"She knew where he was?"

"Only that he studied law at Harvard. I found him. I googled him."

"Wow. So are you going to meet him?"

"I already have, Ed. I've had lunch with him and met his family, he's great, really great, and he can't wait to meet you, too."

"Why didn't you tell me sooner?"

"I don't know, I wanted to see what would happen, I guess. And I wasn't sure if you even wanted to know."

I explained how we'd met the first time. The story Andy had told me about him and our mother. About Yvonne and Jemma.

"What does he look like?"

"Like you. Just like you, only older."

"I'd like to meet him, but this is a lot to take in...you know what, can you just give him my email address? Maybe we should start with an email."

"Sure. What about Jemma?"

"Let's just start with him, then I'll see about Jemma."

"Okay, fair enough."

I called Andy a little while later and suggested he email Ed.

"Thank you," he said. He hung up the phone before I could respond.

Chapter Seven

Amy

I felt a rush of emotion as I saw Taryn walking through the arrivals gate at Logan airport. I let the tears fill up in my eyes and realised how much I'd missed my best friend. She didn't say a word, just walked up to me and put her arms around me tight. We stayed like that for a minute or two.

"I missed you," I whispered.

"Ditto," she said.

I greeted Josh and Emma, who was walking and talking – a toddler, completely different to the baby I'd left behind.

I was fourteen when I met Taryn. Her family moved into a house in the same street as us. I'd seen her sitting on her front lawn one morning in the summer holidays and had gone over to say hello and we hit it off straight away. She was the first person I'd gone to when I'd found out what Jack wasn't my father.

We were best friends throughout the rest of secondary school, through the sixth form, and then we both got jobs working as administrators for a manufacturer of party goods. Balloons, candles, banners, invitations, streamers, wedding favours and that sort of thing. We both applied, and I secretly hoped I'd get the position of course, it sounded like a fun company to work for (I was wrong) and I was desperate to start earning money. My mother was desperately disappointed that I didn't want to go to university and kept throwing suggestions and hints and prospectuses at me, but I needed to escape and get my own place. It wasn't that I didn't want to study any further, I just didn't know what to study. So I looked for any job I could get that seemed to pay enough for me to be independent.

It so happened that this company needed two junior administrators and we were both in. We mostly answered phones, typed letters, filed paperwork, put together mailings and helped out which ever department needed it. I think the term "dogs body" would also have been an appropriate job title.

However, it meant that I had seven hundred pounds a month, and so did Taryn, so we saved up, and we found a tiny one bedroom flat to move into, which was a few miles from our parents houses and close to work. We had to share a double bed, but it didn't bother us as we were both single. Taryn had a couple of casual boyfriends during the two years we lived there, but she stayed at their houses if she wanted to spend the night with them. So, we shared a bed, ate together, worked together, and spent all our free time together. Sometimes we'd have a little falling out, of course. But we always got over it pretty quick. I was happy, during those two years. I was away from my parents, and only saw them and Libby when absolutely necessary. Ed was at university in Hull, so I rarely saw him. He emailed me occasionally but we were leading such different lives that anything we'd had in common seemed to have disappeared.

Then, my cousin Mary announced she and her boyfriend Johnny were engaged. They were going to get married two months later in Devon, and she wanted Libby and I as bridesmaids, along with a couple of friends. It was going to be a huge wedding, over two hundred guests, and Johnny's parents were paying for most of it. His dad was a Lord, or Earl, or something. They had a lot of money, and my aunt Sandra, Mary's mum, was obviously thrilled. So, the wedding went off without a hitch. I had to wear this hideous orange dress - who looks good in orange? I think Mary chose it to ensure that her bridesmaids had no chance of looking better than her, which isn't usually in her nature, but with that number of important people staring at her, I guess she needed to impress.

It was a four day event, and we arrived on the Thursday evening. Friday morning we were taken by coach to a picnic lunch and while we all enjoyed strawberries and champagne, sitting on thick tartan blankets and squinting in the sun, Johnny's uncle stood up and made a speech. I don't remember what he said exactly, but it was something about finding your one true love. I sat there, a little dizzy from the champagne and suddenly realised, I believed in love at first sight.

When I say uncle, please don't imagine a fifty year old man with a thinning grey hairline and pot belly. Johnny's youngest uncle was only thirty-five. I was twenty, so he was still fifteen years older than me. But he was just gorgeous, and his speech was funny yet sentimental and by the end of it, I was mush.

I spent the rest of the day trying to find a way to go over to him, start a conversation. We stayed at the picnic site most of the afternoon, a round of cricket was set up and Mary, and Libby to my surprise, joined in and were actually pretty good. Ben, the uncle, was obviously multi-talented. He was good at speeches, he was popular with his family and every time I looked for him (about every five or ten minutes), he was chatting to someone different. From what I could tell, he seemed good at cricket, too.

While everyone was sitting around eating gourmet BBQ food, I looked from face to face and couldn't find him anywhere. Eventually, I saw, he was sitting on a small mound a hundred metres or so away from everyone else. I stood up, brushing crumbs from my dress, and noticing I was a little tipsy from all the champagne. I wandered slowly away from the group and towards where he sat. I casually glanced towards him and smiled as I got nearer, trying to look as if I was just getting a breather from the crowd and happened to spot him, rather than had intentionally come over.

"Hello!"

"Hi," I said, back, holding out my hand. He shook it.

"I'm Amy, Mary's cousin."

"Ben," he told me, "I'm Johnny's uncle."

I smiled as if I didn't already know.

"It's a bit much, isn't it, all these people?"

"Yeah, that's why I came up here, to get away."

"Oh, I'm sorry." I started turning to walk away.

"No really," he said and I turned back. He was looking at me intently, smiling. I thought I might just fall on to him and have sex with him right there, in front of everyone.

"Take a seat." He patted the grass next to him. So I did.

We sat talking for a while, mostly about the wedding and the size of the thing. I realised right away that he wasn't like any other man I'd met (which wasn't that many, though, to be fair). He was a grown up. He was divorced, he had a mortgage, and a career. I asked him about it all, about his life, and his house, and his work. I guess it was pretty obvious I was interested and when it was time to go back to the hotel, he asked me innocently if I'd like to come back to his room for a drink from the mini bar. That night was the first night I enjoyed sex. Previously, it'd been over very quickly, nothing special, and I hadn't even had an orgasm. Ben, being older and more experienced I guess, made sure I enjoyed it. It was passionate and intense and even now when I think about it, I grin a little, and a tingle runs down my body. He knew how to make a woman feel good. So, we spent the next three days together. We were all over each other, and I was completely besotted, convinced this was true love. In the few instances that we weren't side by side, I called Taryn to tell her all about him, but she never answered the phone and I figured she was just out and about, busy.

The wedding went well, and despite a word of warning from my mother about behaving appropriately and remembering how old Ben was, I had the best few days. We walked about hand in hand, spent hours making love (we didn't sleep much), and when anything formal was happening, like the wedding ceremony, or the reception, when we were sat at different tables, we spent most of the time just staring at each other with a grin.

Then, Monday came.

I woke up and stretched, in Ben's bed, where I'd woken the morning before, and the morning before that, but this time I had a sense of panic. We were leaving today. He lived in Manchester. I lived in Milton Keynes. What were we going to do?

Ben came out of his bathroom and smiled at me.

"So, we're leaving today," I said, trying to seem calm and cool.

"Yes, and I just want to thank you," he said, sitting on the bed and squeezing my leg.

"The past few days have been...amazing." He looked a little nervous too, which I took as a sign that he was about to ask me something. Maybe to move to Manchester, or even elope.

But, instead, he got up and walked to the wardrobe, dropping his towel to reveal his perfect bottom, and grabbing some clothes. I, too, got up, pulled on my clothes and said something about did he have a pen so that I could give him my number.

He spun around, looking even more nervous than before.

"Well, you know Amy, there's probably not much point, is there?"

I gulped.

"Why not?" I heard my voice quiver and swallowed hard.

"Well, you know, you live in Milton Keynes. I'm up in Manchester. It'd never work out, would it?"

"But..." I hesitated. This could not be happening. Don't say it. We stood there, staring at each other. Ben looked like he just wanted me to leave.

"I love you." I heard the words coming out of my mouth and instantly regretted them.

He laughed. He actually laughed! I wish I could go back to my twenty year old self now and I tell her it's okay, this guy is a prick. He'll be forty in five years time and when you next see him, you'll wonder what you ever saw in him. Incidentally, the next time I saw him when Mary's first baby was christened. He was greying and looked like he'd aged more than several years...he smiled at me like he wanted to strike up a conversation. I didn't smile back and walked past him as if I didn't know him. But back in the hotel room, I felt devastated.

"You don't love me, Amy, you don't even know me."

I didn't know what to say, so I just grabbed my things and headed for the door. He ran and stood in front of it, blocking my way.

"I'm sorry, but I thought you knew. This was just for this weekend. Some fun. You're young, I didn't expect you to be looking for something serious."

"I wasn't looking for anything," I said, a tear running down my face and my voice cracking, "I just thought the last few days meant something."

"They did! It was great, but, you know, you're only twenty."

I felt about five inches tall.

"So? What difference does my age make?"

The tears started flowing now, and I hated myself. I felt like a child.

"Listen, you'll thank me one day, honestly." He put an arm on my shoulder which I shrugged off, "you can do better than me, really. I'm a messed up guy."

He moved aside and I left the room, practically ran all the way to my own, locked the door and fell on to the bed in hysterical fits of crying and, embarrassingly, wailing. I eventually calmed down and rang Taryn to tell her, but she still didn't pick up. So, I returned home, sitting beside Ed in his beat up green Metro, staring out of the window, feeling heart-broken, humiliated, and depressed.

"He might get in touch," Ed said, obviously uncomfortable.

"He won't." I turned the radio on. We didn't talk the rest of the journey.

I knew something was wrong as I unlocked the door to the flat and smelt something strange. Mustiness. Like nothing had moved or been out of the flat for several days. I figured Taryn had spent the weekend with her latest boyfriend, Josh. I walked into our bedroom to find them naked, in a compromising position. Taryn yelped, and kind of laughed. Josh pulled away from her, pulled the covers over himself and I stood there for several seconds, shocked. I felt the tears coming again and walked back out, into our living room, or should I say living area, as it was just one big room really that acted as a kitchen, dining room and living room in one. This was against the rules. We'd agreed; we won't have sex in the flat. It might seem strange, but we were sharing that bed. I didn't want to get into it knowing Taryn had had sex in it. The rule had been her idea.

Now, looking back, maybe it wasn't a big deal. I'd been away all weekend and, I assume she'd have washed the sheets and everything.

Taryn came out into the living room, giggling, pulling her dressing gown on.

"I'm sorry Amy," she said, laughing, then stopping instantly.

"What's wrong?"

I sat on the sofa, wondering how I could possibly cry any more. Where had all the tears come from?

"What's wrong?" she asked again.

"You promised," I said, "we agreed we wouldn't ever do that. That's my bed, Taryn."

"You weren't here. I didn't think you'd be back until later."

"That's not the point, that I came home early. Where have you been all weekend? I tried calling."

"We didn't answer the phone, we've been in there all weekend."

"Oh, nice. I'm glad you were having constant sex when I needed you most. Thanks a lot. In my bed!"

"Our bed!" she corrected me.

I stared at the floor, and pictured Ben and I in bed in the

hotel. I started crying harder.

"What's wrong?"

I mumbled something about love.

"Josh told me he loves me!" Taryn burst out, unable to keep it in, despite my obvious depressed state.

"That's great." I said, managing to smile.

"He wants me to move in with him."

And that was when I lost her. Taryn moved in with Josh a few weeks later, leaving me to pay for the rent on our tiny flat by myself. I managed, just about. Taryn bought me a new bed even though I insisted that she didn't need to, and they got engaged a few weeks after that. I never told her about Ben. She was so happy and loved up, I didn't see the need. It was the first time I'd ever not told her something, in all our years of best friendship. After a few months, I got a new job, and I saved up, and a year later I managed to buy my own little house.

Taryn and Josh spent all their time together after that, and I was lucky if I saw her once a week. So, when I look back on Mary's wedding, I kind of view it as losing two things – the first man I ever loved (and I still believe I loved him...maybe it was because he was the first person to give me an orgasm) and my best friend. Because, although we were, and still are, friends... Josh was her best friend now, which was fair enough. It wasn't until I met Zach though, that I really understood.

Still, I realised as we sat in the taxi, I was still very important to Taryn.

"You look so well," she said, taking my hand as we sat on the backseat.

"Good!" I said, laughing.

"Yes, it's very good. You look...healthy and happy."

"I am."

"Good, that's great. I'm glad you are so settled here," she said, although I detected a hint of disappointment. I was pleased to know I'd been missed.

"I'm also happy we're here," she continued, "the flight

seemed to take forever!"

She leaned back and stared out of the window, still holding my hand.

Josh told me she'd been counting down the days with Emma until the trip.

"She's been so excited to see Aunty Amy."

I smiled and Emma and ticked her tummy. She giggled and tickled me back, under my chin.

When we reached my brownstone apartment building, Taryn gazed up at it with a grin.

"It's just like I imagined." She laughed.

She said pretty much the same thing when we got inside. I made them cups of tea, and we crashed on my sofa, which had hardly been sat on.

"You sure you'll be okay here?" I asked.

The plan was they'd sleep at my place and I'd stay with Zach. I hadn't mentioned that I stayed with him every night anyway. Until the day before, I'd not been home for two weeks. I'd only come to clean and set it up for their stay.

"It's great, thank you so much," Josh said, sipping his tea and taking in the view from the window. Emma had crashed on the sofa and fallen asleep.

"So, when do you think you're coming home?"

I frowned.

"I'm not. I love it here. I've applied for a green card."

Taryn laughed. "What? With all the "have a nice days" and the cheesy enthusiasm and the size of everything?"

"I'm serious Taryn. I like all that. Americans seem so much more genuine than the British. They're not as sarcastic or cynical."

"I thought you liked sarcasm and cynicism!"

"I did too. But I feel I fit in here. I know it's hard to understand, but I'm really happy."

"Well, you do seem very happy in your emails and on the phone. So I guess I'm happy for you. I bet your family miss you though."

"You think? They don't call or email very often."

"I saw your mum in Sainsbury's. She told me you were doing well. She seemed proud."

I somehow couldn't imagine this. My mum being proud of me.

"I can't wait for you to meet Zach."

"He's the reason you want to be here. Right?"

"He helps, of course. I've also enjoyed building a relationship with my dad."

"Have you and Zach talked about the future?"

"Not really. We haven't been together that long."

"But it seems very serious already."

"Yes, well. I think he's probably the best boyfriend I've had." I couldn't help but grin.

I missed this. Harriet was great, but I couldn't be as comfortable with her as Taryn, who I've known since I was at school. We were kindred spirits. Our mutual love of boybands, and in particular Take That, bonded us together and we'd seen each other through a fair amount of boys, men, concerts, parties, hangovers, fights with our parents, different jobs, and then Taryn's wedding, pregnancy, and Emma's birth. Josh had held her left hand, I'd held her right.

"That's great, we're happy for you," Josh said, nudging Taryn.

"Very happy," Taryn smiled, "but you better come visit regularly."

I nodded and got up to make more tea. I had vivid memories of their wedding; they got married on a beautiful sunny day. Amber, Taryn's sister, and I both wore pale blue dresses with silver boleros. Taryn looked radiant and Josh handsome. Everything had been perfect and beautiful. For a second, as I waited for the tea to brew, I wondered what I'd want my own wedding to be like. Would I want to get married in England? I blushed, realising how far my mind was racing ahead. But no, I would be happy to get married here. I'd invite everyone over, it'd be like a holiday for them. I wondered if my whole family would come. I couldn't see my aunt Grace making the trip, with her dodgy hip and grumpy attitude. Even more reason to get married in the US.

"We can't wait to meet Zach," Taryn said, looking at a small framed photo of us together as I bought the tea in.

I drew them a detailed map of the walk from my apartment to Zach's, told them to make themselves at home, freshen up, and come round for about 6pm. Zach was cooking us a feast.

Zach

Although I'd met Amy's "new family" as we called them, it was quite a different experience preparing to meet someone from her life in Britain. Someone who really knew her well, and could quite possibly think I was just an annoying American.

Therefore, I went all-out on the meal. I bought expensive wine – both red and white, I bought crab meat and fresh salad as an appetiser and then prepared lamb with a sauce my mother used to make for me every birthday. I'd made a bakewell tart, which I'd found the recipe for when I googled "British desserts."

I had a feeling Taryn's opinion of me would be important to Amy.

"Wow, it smells delish!" Amy called as she came home. I kissed her forehead as she leaned in to smell the pan I was stirring.

"Did they have a good flight?"

"Yes, thank you. It was good to see them. They'll be here for six." She stood behind me as I was washing the salad in the sink and wrapped her arms around me.

"Great."

"Do we have time for, you know..." she said, kissing my neck and running her hands downwards.

"There's always time for that," I said, turning and pushing her up against the fridge.

Amy

Taryn, Josh, and Emma arrived at six on the dot.

"Punctual, I like that." Zach winked at me as they knocked on the door.

I opened it and welcomed them in, hoping my post-coital flush had gone.

"This is Zach," I said, wondering if they could tell by the way I looked at him that he meant more to me than any previous boyfriends had.

Taryn threw her arms around him.

"Any man Amy loves, I love too." She kissed him on the cheek. He looked a little surprised.

"Thank you, any friend of Amy's..." He kind of laughed and shook Josh's hand.

"Josh, nice to meet you."

The evening was a huge success. Zach showed off his cooking skills;

"Believe it or not, I lived on cereal and pop tarts before Amy came along," he'd joked.

Taryn told him all about my youth. Josh and Zach talked about websites, Josh worked in marketing and had a lot to say on the subject. Emma played with the new toys I'd bought her. We drunk wine, we laughed, and for the first time I realised I had in fact been missing out on something from the UK.

Zach

"I bought these to show you!" Taryn said, pulling a photo album out of her bag.

"Oh no!" Amy put her head in her hands.

I flicked through and saw photos of Taryn, Amy, and their friends from high school age right through to Taryn's wedding. Amy looked happy and colourful in all of them. There were photos in school uniform, others in bars, drinking martinis.

One of a group of them with cucumbers on their eyes.

"We were having facials!" Taryn giggled. Amy quickly turned the page. The next photo was of them dressed up for a night out. The Leonardo DiCaprio look-a-like had his arm draped around Amy's shoulder. I sneered at him before moving on.

"It's great to see some of your history," I told Amy.

"Some of it is greater than others!" She laughed.

I liked Taryn and Josh right away and instantly found myself wishing they didn't live in another country so that we could have seen more of them. They were obviously very fond of Amy and their little girl was incredibly cute.

The next day, Amy set out to her apartment. She was planning on taking them on a tour of Boston.

"Just like our date, do you remember?" she asked before she left.

"Of course. Doesn't that seem like a long time ago now?"

"Yes, funny isn't it?"

It did kind of feel like we'd been together forever already, like life before she came along was just a dream which I couldn't really remember all that well. I said as much to Aaron during a brief phone call. He'd asked if I wanted to play pool that night, and I'd declined as we had plans for more entertaining with Taryn, Josh and Emma.

"You're not going to propose, are you?"

The thought had crossed my mind, but I didn't see the need to rush into it.

"No. Not yet. But, someday, yes."

He sighed.

"I'm not you, and Amy isn't Mel."

He didn't respond, but asked me if I wanted to play pool another night that week instead. We organised to meet on Thursday.

"Zach, have you told Amy about-"

"No," I admitted, feeling guilty and knowing I needed to tell her, but also aware it was a little late now. I didn't know how I'd say the words, or how she'd react. I had a feeling it wouldn't be good.

"Well you need to."

"I know." I sighed.

"Okay well, I'll speak to you later."

"Maybe you should talk to Mel," I said, hoping he wouldn't get mad with me.

"And say what?"

"That you're unhappy. Talk about why."

"I think she knows I'm not happy. She isn't happy either."

"Then talk about it, find a way to improve it."

"I'll see you Thursday."

I sighed and said goodbye.

Amy

I was quite proud, showing my friends all around Boston. We got tickets for a tour bus and I pointed out various places I'd been, including restaurants I'd eaten at, my office, the Starbucks where I'd met my dad, and so on. Josh bought us all lunch.

The next week was just like old times. We hang out every day, I bonded with Emma, and Zach and Josh really hit it off.

The day before Thanksgiving, Andy called me.

"How are you getting on with your friend?" he asked.

"Great. It's really good to see her."

"That's nice. Are you doing anything tomorrow?"

I hadn't really given it a lot of thought, stupidly with hindsight as it was a big US holiday and it might have been nice to celebrate with Taryn, Josh and Emma. Zach's parents always went to visit his aunt in California for Thanksgiving, and Aaron and Mel were always with her parents, so apparently he never made much effort to celebrate it on his own.

"No, not really."

"Well then we absolutely insist you all come for dinner. We

have enough food to feed an army. Really."

I wasn't sure what Taryn would think but she admitted she was curious to meet the "man who knocked up your mother," and we all agreed a turkey dinner with pumpkin pie would be pretty appetising, so off we went.

"It's wonderful," Taryn said as we pulled up outside the house.

"This is my dad," I said, feeling a little weird. "This is my best friend, Taryn."

Andy gave her a hug and Jemma greeted her much the same way she did me; bounded into my arms and kissed me on the cheek.

Zach

I loved the way Andy and Yvonne had made Amy a part of their family so easily, and so fast. We were welcomed as generously as ever, and Taryn, Josh and especially Emma were made a big fuss of.

Yvonne cooked a great meal and we all munched away on turkey, and potatoes, and pumpkin pie. Jemma sat and showed Emma a kids book, teaching her all about Thanksgiving and Andy laughed and joked with us all.

After a fun day, everyone had gone up to bed except for myself, Andy, and Josh.

"Taryn and I were saying we've never seen Amy so happy, mate," Josh said as Andy poured us each a glass of whisky.

"Well, it's not all down to me," I said. It had a lot to do with Andy, too.

"Whatever it's down to, she's happy, and you're a big, big part of that," Andy said, a little drunk. "I know it's not perhaps my place, but you better not hurt her."

"No intention to," I said, shuddering a little at the aftertaste from my drink.

"You going to marry her?" Josh asked.

"Probably. You okay with that?" I turned to Andy.

"Sounds like a good plan to me." He pat me on the back.

"You've got the father's permission now!" Josh joked.

I pictured Amy in a white dress, walking towards me on Andy's arm and smiled to myself.

Amy

Zach took Josh and Emma to the New England Aquarium, down near the harbour, so that Taryn and I could have some girl's time. We wandered around the shops, Taryn particularly excited by Bloomingdales and Macy's, and chat about old times, and newer times, and future times.

"What's your boss like, you never mention him?" Taryn asked.

"Franco? He's nice, except he sometimes spits when he speaks..."

"Oh, lovely!"

"But overall, he's great. He really did help me out, by asking Harriet to sort me out with a place."

"Which you no longer stay in."

"Well, yes, rarely! Also, Franco sorted out my visa, and has been incredibly supportive and helpful with the green card application."

"You know, before I came here, I figured this was just a phase. That you wanted to find your dad, and once you'd done that, you'd be coming home. All the talk of green cards and so on, well I thought it was just talk. But I see you with Zach..."

"Yes?"

"Well you're just so smitten aren't you?"

I laughed.

"You remember when you fell in love with Josh? You told me there's nowhere else in the world you'd rather be, than in his arms?"

"Yes. I do remember that. I still feel that way. But, it's so fast

119

isn't it? I mean, practically living together after only a few months. Just be careful, okay? You don't want it to fizzle out before you're even a year into the relationship."

"I know, don't worry, I'm being sensible."

"I'm worn out, shall we get a coffee?"

When Taryn and I were young and first allowed out to our local shopping centre alone for the first time, we found a little café and each ordered a coffee. It was revolting and we'd both declared we'd never drink that stuff again. I had so many memories like this of her, it was kind of strange to think that all my Boston memories up until now hadn't included her.

She told me all the details I'd missed on Emma since my departure; her first steps and her first words. How she liked a night light on at bedtime, and how Josh always read stories to her before she went to sleep. I watched her face light up as she recalled each memory, each detail.

"It's funny how we used to talk about where our lives would end up," I said.

"We'd talk about who would be the first to have children, and what our husbands would be like." Taryn laughed.

"I always thought you might marry an American." She laughed again. "But I figured he'd move to UK, not the other way around."

"We're not married," I reminded her.

"Not yet. I miss that part of the relationship, where it's all fresh and new and exciting. You wonder where it's going, then you realise it's just going along as it should."

"You and Josh seem happy though, as happy as ever."

"We are. It's just a bit more of a routine since we had Emma, that's all."

"Hi Amy!" Mel appeared, carrying a bunch of carrier bags.

"Mel, hi." I stood up and gave her a brief hug.

"This is Taryn, my best friend from England."

"Oh wow, how nice to meet you."

We invited her to join us and soon Taryn and Mel were in

full conversation about their kids, comparing anecdotes. It seemed strange to see my two worlds mixing; my oldest friends versus my newest. Two completely different people, from different countries, sharing the one thing they had in common, and the one thing they both liked to talk about best; their children.

Mel suggested we bring Taryn and co. over to meet Sophia and Lucy before they left, which only really left the next day. I was a little reluctant to miss out on my last day of Taryn to myself, but Taryn eagerly agreed and it was all set.

Zach

"Fish!" Emma said for about the tenth time, inside the aquarium.

"Clever girl," Josh rewarded her yet again.

"You guys will have to come and stay with us in the UK."

"We'd love to. We'll be in England soon for Amy's sister's wedding."

"Oh yes. Well, we can get together then. Shame it's so far, really."

"Yes, Amy misses Taryn a lot."

"We should get them set up with webcams."

"Good idea."

This was about the longest conversation Josh and I had without interruptions from Emma. Cute as she was, it was hard to get much adult talk in, and she kept grabbing either one of our hands and dragging us to the next exhibit.

My cell started singing *Blame it on the Boogie*. It was Aaron.

"Hello," I said, watching Josh lift Emma up for a better look.

"Mel's just seen Amy and her friend, and she invited them around tomorrow. Tomorrow! I'm going to miss the game. You think you can find a way to get out of it?"

"Not really, just be honest with Mel."

"No chance she'll understand. See you tomorrow, then."

Amy

I woke up at 3am and ran to the bathroom to be sick. Same thing at 4am, and 5:30am. There was no doubt about it; I was ill. Zach insisted I wasn't well enough to come to Aaron and Mel's for the day, and left to collect our trio without me. Taryn text me a little later with a sad face.

I slept until about noon and then lay on the sofa most of the afternoon, watching mindless TV. It had occurred to me that Taryn would see their house and meet Sophia and Lucy before I did, which felt a little weird.

Another text came in from Taryn, asking if I was any better. I replied to say no. Next text said:

You're not preggers are you, love?

I panicked, trying to remember my last period. I couldn't remember, between spending time with Zach, working, and spending yet more time with Zach, I hadn't really been bothered about recording such things. I pulled on some dirty clothes, tied my hair in a knot, brushed my teeth and headed out to the nearest pharmacy.

Zach

It didn't feel quite right without Amy. While she'd never been to Aaron and Mel's house, she was planning to join us and it was odd being with Taryn and not her.

Still, the day was a success. Sophia and Lucy loved Emma and played with her before, during and after lunch. Mel and Taryn chat like they were life-long friends, and us guys made small talk and watched a bit of the game on TV.

I dropped Taryn, Josh, and a sleepy Emma off at Amy's apartment and came home to find her holding a pregnancy test in her hand. I felt a bolt of electricity shoot through me; unsure if it was excitement or pure fear.

"Don't worry," said Amy. "I'm not pregnant. It's just a sickness bug."

Relief flooded through me. No, we weren't ready for all that, despite all this talk from everyone else about marriage and the future. Suddenly the realty of a serious relationship hit me. One day would I stand there, hoping it was positive? I couldn't imagine that. Maybe I wasn't quite ready to propose, just yet.

Amy

"Send me a text when you're home safe," I told Taryn as I hugged her at the airport.

"You take care of yourself. And you take care of her too," Taryn told Zach.

After lots of hugs and a few tears, we watched them walk away.

"You okay?" Zach asked me.

"Yes, just sad to see them go."

He gave me a hug and I remembered why I wanted to be here, in Boston.

Chapter Eight

Amy

Jemma and I were having lunch at a little restaurant around the corner from her apartment. This was the first time we'd been alone together, apart from our little walk around the block, and I'd been a little apprehensive. Yvonne had admitted to me on the phone that Jemma was a little sensitive; she'd gone from being daddy's only girl to having to share the attention and I was wary of her feelings.

We both ordered seafood salads, and a bottle of white wine to share.

"Look Jemma," I begun, "I just want to you to know-"

"What did my mother say?" She interrupted right away.

"Nothing. I'm just aware that, you know, you were the only child, and..."

"Come on, I'm an adult. Seriously, what did she say? I'm fine with it. I'm psyched to have a sister. It doesn't change my relationship with Dad."

I noticed the way she said "Dad" and not "my dad." It felt strange.

"Great. I just wanted to be sure you're okay," I told her. "So, tell me about more about yourself. Like how you came to go to medical school."

She told me that she'd always wanted to be a doctor, since her Grandma, our Grandma, had been really sick when she was about ten. She wanted to fix her.

"She was a wonderful lady," Jemma said with misty eyes. "I wish you could have known her. She was eccentric, she liked to eat candy all day long and she always, always wore odd socks. She had her hair long, down to her hips, and she gave me tips about everything; homework, boys, makeup."

"She sounds like a fun Grandmother."

"She was. I was devastated when she died, but I've been on a mission to help people beat illness ever since. Hence, medical school..."

The waitress bought our salads and we both started eating.

"Do you have a boyfriend?"

"Nope," she smiled. "I have so little time right now."

I imagined her running around like one of the interns in E.R. or Grey's Anatomy and felt honoured she even had time to come and have lunch with me.

"Zach seems great."

"Yeah, we have a lot of fun together." I could feel the excitement radiating from within.

"You seem..." she hesitated.

"What?"

"So at home here. I can't imagine moving to another country and finding all that you have; friends, a boyfriend you're crazy about and even a new family."

"Yes, it's been a rather overwhelming year to be honest."

"Well, I'm glad you are here. Really. Yes, there have been some adjustments and it was a little strange. After the initial excitement, I wasn't sure how I felt about it, but I think everyone makes mistakes, and in our father's case, it was not telling me, and not finding you himself, rather than actually conceiving you."

As I walked home, it started to snow lightly and I tried to remember what I'd been doing this time last year. Fretting over my disastrous love life. Pondering Christmas alone as my mum, Jack, Ed and Libby were going to Iceland. I'd been invited and declined; I didn't want to spend a whole week away with them.

What a lot had changed. Now I couldn't wait to spend Christmas with Zach, and my new family.

Zach

There was an eighties show on the radio, so we turned up the volume and sang along as we drove to my parent's house. I was a little nervous, but didn't want Amy to know. They'd met a few college girlfriends, and Scarlett a couple of times, but that was about it. This time it was serious. This time I was introducing a potential daughter-in-law. I smiled at the thought and glanced at Amy who was singing along to the radio and dancing about in her seat.

"You nervous?" I asked her.

"Yes. Very," she said, sliding her hand up my thigh, giving me a rush from my chest into my groin.

"They're going to love you," I told her. I believed it too. How could anyone not love Amy?

"I hope so." She checked her face in the mirror.

We turned into my parents drive and she whispered "Wow" under her breath. I was glad she was impressed. I felt proud of my parents. They'd both had quite hard lives as children but had done well and built good lives for themselves as adults.

I jumped out of the car and ran round to open Amy's door.

"My lady," I said, in my best British accent.

"Why, thank you sir," she responded, kissing my cheek.

The front door opened and my parents stood before us, no doubt ready to judge and ridicule. But I knew what the final verdict would be. I just hoped it wasn't too painful for Amy to get there.

Amy

The Rosenberg's house was huge. At least four times the size of Andy and Yvonne's, which I'd considered reasonably big. In British terms, this was a mansion. But it was beautiful. White exterior, with pale blue shutters at every window. Grey slate roof. The front lawn was immaculate, and there were rose bushes lining the driveway, which was long and swept from the road.

"Zachary! Happy Hanukkah!" his mum was the first to say. She was a pleasant looking woman, a little overweight, with dark hair cut to her shoulders. She wore little make-up, but had a kind of natural radiance. She flung her arms around him and winked at me over his shoulder. I smiled and glanced at his dad, who was tall like Zach, but with lighter hair.

I was suddenly glad I'd done a little internet research on Hanukkah, so that I wasn't completely ignorant of the holiday, but a little panic raised in me as I worried that something I might say or do could offend, or make them hate me from the minute I opened my mouth.

Zach shook his father's hand in a rather business-like fashion and then turned to me.

"Mom, Dad, this is Amy."

"It's so lovely to meet you both," I said, holding out my hand.

His dad shook it, but his mum gave me a hug and kissed me on the cheek, and I felt more comfortable straight away.

"Welcome to our home Amy. I'm delighted to meet you. Zach, you didn't tell me she was British! How wonderful!"

I smiled. "Mrs. Rosenberg, you have a beautiful house."

"Please. Call me Annie. And this is Nate." She gestured to her husband.

"Come inside and we'll get you all settled."

The house was even more spectacular on the inside, with real dark wooden floors and expensive looking furniture. Zach got our bags and led me upstairs to his bedroom. I heard his mum whisper something about how beautiful I was as we reached the landing and I blushed but felt pleased that I'd managed to pass the first hurdle at least.

Zach's old bedroom was huge. It was bigger than the room I'd shared with Libby. He had a double bed, and dark blue curtains. There was a cork board on the wall, with photos pinned to it. I stopped to look at it and Zach pointed out a few old school friends.

"That's Ray Fisher," he said, pointing to a tall red-haired kid. "He saved my life once. I nearly drowned in the local pool when I passed out."

I wrapped my arms around Zach's neck.

"Well, I'm very grateful," I said, kissing him.

We were shortly called down for dinner and gathered around a huge dining table.

I was introduced to Aaron and Mel's children, Sophia and Lucy.

"Nice to meet you. I've heard so much about you both."

"We have heard about you, too," Sophia told me.

"Really? Well, I hope it was good things."

"Yes, all good. Zach loves you, everyone can tell."

Mel laughed a little and Aaron tapped Sophia on the shoulder.

"What have I told you about listening to our conversations and repeating them?"

"Sorry Daddy. Sorry Amy."

She was so cute I thought I might have to steal her.

"It's fine," I said, tapping her on the other shoulder, "what you said was really sweet."

Nate picked up a menorah, which already had the first five candles lit, and lit the sixth. The rest of us stood in a semi-circle around him. To my surprise they all started reciting a blessing in Hebrew. I put my head down, watching their feet. I stole a glance at Mel, who was also silent like me. Sophia was kind of joining in, but she obviously didn't know all the words. Lucy was playing with her doll. I noticed Zach had his eyes closed. It had never occurred to me that he knew Hebrew, or even took any of this seriously. He opened his eyes and winked at me, and I smiled back.

"Do you know The Queen of England?" Sophia asked as we started eating. I had no idea what it was, some sort of casserole.

It was delicious.

I laughed. I'd been asked this a few times since I moved to Boston, by adults too. Britain is so tiny compared to the US that I think they all think we all know each other.

"No. I saw her once though, outside Buckingham Palace."

"Wow, really? Was she wearing her crown?"

"No. She had a nice hat on though."

"Sophia loves your royal family," Mel told me.

"I'd love to visit London," Annie interjected.

"Have you ever been to Europe?" I asked, and glanced at Zach who was smiling at me, obviously pleased that I was getting along with everybody. So far.

"I went to Paris once. But we've been saying for years that we'd like to tour Europe. See Dublin, Edinburgh, London, Rome, Venice maybe. We just never get around to organising it, do we Nate?"

"No, dear," he said. He seemed to be a man of few words.

"You should plan a trip then," I said encouragingly.

"We really should. I'd very much like to go to Israel, too. I haven't been since my great grandmother died, which was over thirty years ago," Annie said nostalgically. Nate smiled at me. I realised there was so much I still had to learn about Zach, not only was he reciting Hebrew but he had Israeli ancestry.

"Have you seen Prince William?" Sophia asked next.

"Oh he's just too cute!" – this from Mel.

"No, I've never seen him."

"Oh, what happened to that poor boy's mother? She was such an angel, and we were so devastated for your loss." Annie looked at me with real feeling and put her hand lightly on my arm. I was tempted to point out that I didn't know Diana personally so there was no need to give me any sympathy, but thought better of it.

"Thank you," I said, and turned back to my soup. Zach squeezed my thigh under the table and I stole at glance at him. He was trying not to laugh.

Zach

"So, what do you think?" I asked Mom as I helped her clear away the dinner plates.

"Zach, she's great. If she were Jewish I'd even say she was perfect."

I laughed. "Mom, you know that doesn't matter. Not to me."

"I know, dear. She seems very polite though and friendly, and smart. Beautiful, too."

"I know. She's great. I'm really happy."

"Then I'm happy for you my dear. You know, the most important part of keeping a relationship going is communication. You must be honest, open, and brutally truthful at all times."

I was a little taken aback with the relationship advice. My father was a quiet man to many, but he did open up a lot when alone with my mom, that much had always been obvious. I just didn't expect her to be telling me that talking was important, when she was married to someone so un-talkative.

I hesitated. "We do talk. A lot."

"Does she know about-"

"Not yet. It's complicated, and I'll tell you why later. I will tell her, I promise. We do talk about everything else."

"Good. Don't change that. Always communicate. I've never seen you look at anyone like you look at her," she said, squeezing my cheek. "You really like this girl huh?"

"I love her."

She looked happy, and passed me some dessert bowls to carry into the dining room.

"Just don't leave it too long," she advised, "before you tell her. She might be shocked."

I sighed. She was right, I should have told her by now.

Amy

"You want to come up to my room and watch High School Musical?" Sophia asked.

"It's not your room, Sophia, it's a guest room." Mel scolded her.

"Well all my stuff is in it."

"Just for this week."

"Well, do you want to come up to the guest bedroom and watch High School Musical?"

"No, she doesn't. Leave Amy alone." Aaron warned her.

"Actually, I'd love to," I told her, and was led away by Sophia.

"Come down whenever you're bored!" shouted Mel.

"Which will be about ten minutes!" yelled Aaron.

Aaron obviously had no idea how much I love musicals.

I could see why Sophia called it her room. There was a sign on the door saying "Grandchildren" and it was decorated in pink, obviously for when Sophia and Lucy came to stay. I had a weird moment where I imagined bringing my own daughter here to stay and quickly snapped out of it. Taryn and Harriet had both commented on my ability to get carried away with my daydreaming, and I was attempting to keep it in check.

Sophia found the DVD and put it into the pink TV they'd set up for them to watch.

There was a double bed with lots of white blankets and pink cushions and we sat up on it. Sophia leaned against me, just as Lucy came in. Without saying a word she climbed up and leaned on the other side.

"Have you seen it before?" Sophia asked.

"No. Is it good?"

"It's the best movie ever made," she said. I smiled. I didn't think it could beat Dirty Dancing but I was willing to give it a go.

"The main characters fall in love," said Lucy.

"Really"? I said. "That sounds very romantic."

"It's fake though," said Sophia.

Surprised, I didn't respond. Lucy asked her why.

"People don't really fall in love. It's make believe, silly."

"Yes they do!" Lucy said, leaning across me to poke her sister.

"People do fall in love," I said. "Your mommy and daddy are in love."

"No, I don't think so," said Sophia. I paused the start of the film.

I wasn't sure how to react.

"But I guess Grandma and Grandpa are in love," she continued.

"Well, I know that's true. Grandma loves Grandpa even though they're old." Lucy giggled.

I laughed.

"And Uncle Zach loves you," said Sophia.

"You think so, huh?"

"Oh yeah. He looks at you like you're a Princess or something." I smiled. I hoped so.

"Your mum and dad do love each other," I said.

"I like the way you say mum, instead of mom."

"That's how we say it in England."

"Do your mommy and daddy love each other?" asked Sophia.

"No, but they used to." I didn't know if that were true but probably not.

"Mine used to as well maybe. But they don't now. They fight all the time and Daddy sometimes makes Mommy cry. And sometimes she even makes him cry and then they both cry."

My heart went out to her. At least they were crying. My parents didn't even stay together long enough to see me and Ed born.

"That happens sometimes with adults. It's nothing to worry about. I'm sure they love each other just as much as these High School Musical folks." I pointed at the DVD case.

Lucy smiled, satisfied but Sophia just shrugged her

132

shoulders.

"Do you want to watch now?" I asked.

"Yes please."

So we did. It was excellent. I told Sophia we'd have to watch the sequel next time I saw her. She held out her little pinkie and I put mine around it.

"I promise," she said.

"Me too."

"Amy?"

"Yes?"

"You're my best friend."

This kid really was too cute.

"You're mine too," I said.

I opened the bedroom door and saw Mel coming towards us.

"Bedtime," she said, smiling. "Thanks for sitting through that with them."

"I enjoyed it," I told her truthfully, and went downstairs to join the grownups.

I woke up the following morning to see snow falling outside the window. Zach had gone and I stretched out in his old bed and looked at the clock. It was only six thirty. Thank goodness. I'd had a horrible feeling it was really late and I'd slept in while the whole family were eating breakfast downstairs.

I smiled to myself and stared dreamily into space. The past six months had been the best of my life. I felt complete, and whole. I couldn't imagine ever being interested in anyone else. Brad Pitt could have knocked on the door and proposed marriage, and I would have turned him down. I stretched again, sat up on the bed and looked around me.

There were some trophies on a shelf, being used as book ends. I got up and looked at them. Science awards. I looked at the books. Physics, mostly. A couple of computer and website design books, presumably from college. There was a photo tucked in between the books. I pulled it out to reveal a small boy, who was definitely Zach. I tucked it back where I found it. I liked the fact that his room had been preserved, just the way he left it, even though he'd moved out years ago.

I went over to the window. The few flakes of snow I'd seen from the bed had stopped falling, and none of it had settled. I saw Zach stretching below me. He got up and started running down the driveway.

"I love you," I whispered.

Zach

It was good to be back in my old neighbourhood. This was the first time in a long time I'd come to my parents, and the first time in a very long time that I'd spent the night. I was glad to be here for a weekend, especially since Amy seemed so comfortable here.

I ran past the houses in our street, glancing at each one to see if they'd changed. They hadn't, really. Some had been painted. Some had a new tree or something like that. I saw a couple of people getting into their cars, ready for Friday morning at work. A lot of them I didn't recognise.

I ran past the playground, where I'd broken my arm when I was eight. Aaron had laughed at me as I fell down, and only when he saw the tears in my eyes did he run and get help. I kept running, thinking about Amy. I smiled to myself.

I came to my junior high school and I stopped and looked across the school yard. The building looked so much smaller than I remembered it.

I smiled again. I felt like a love-sick teenager. It felt good.

Then I remembered my mom's words from the night before and knew I had to tell Amy, the longer I left it, the more mad she'd probably be that I'd kept it from her this long. I just hoped it wouldn't change the way she felt.

Amy

Zach had his own bathroom at his parents. His own bathroom! We'd had two to share between all of us. They had one each. I took a shower and pulled on a long dark skirt and a white long-sleeve top. I figured a skirt was the way to go. Annie seemed the skirt-wearing type. Not that I still felt the need to impress her, but wanted her to approve of me and I wasn't one hundred per cent sure I'd quite managed it yet. I tied my hair into pigtails, which made me look five years younger according to Harriet, and cute according to Zach.

I quietly walked downstairs and helped myself to a glass of juice from the fridge. Annie had insisted the night before that I make myself at home.

I sat at the dining table, admiring once again the solid, thick oak, and opened up the book I'd bought down with me. I'd barely read two paragraphs when Aaron walked in, wearing a dressing gown and yawning.

"Good morning," he said, pulling his robe tighter.

"Morning." I smiled

"So you and Zach are both early risers then. That's one thing you've got in common."

I smiled. "Yes. There are plenty more, I can assure you."

"I'm sure there are." He walked through to the kitchen and I heard him making coffee. A couple of minutes later he walked back in.

"Do you mind?" he asked, gesturing to a seat opposite mine.

"Not at all."

Since I'd last seen him he'd grown a sort of half-beard.

"So you and Zach seem to be great together," he said, leaning back in his chair and revealing a little more chest hair than I needed to see.

"Thanks. We're having a good time."

"Well, maybe he wouldn't appreciate me telling you this, but I've never seen him like this before. He's never spoken about a girl the way he does you."

I smiled. Good.

"Well, I feel the same way."

"Good. Glad to hear it."

I smiled. I wondered if he was going to start saying something about not hurting him, or treating him right. I realised how my first boyfriend, Lee Williams must have felt when I bought him home for the first time and Jack gave him a talk about how to treat women. Lee was only ten years old.

"So where in the UK are you from?"

"Milton Keynes. It's about fifty miles north of London."

"And what made you move to Boston?"

"I think I moved to find myself," I said, "if that makes sense?"

"It does. Have you found yourself, then?" He smiled and got up from his seat.

"Yeah, I think so."

I'd found Zach, and my father. I think they'd both allowed me to somehow be myself.

"You want some coffee?"

"Sure . White no sugar, please."

I watched him walk back into the kitchen. I picked up a couple of coasters from a side cabinet and put them out on the table. He bought back two hot mugs and handed me one. It had a photo of a baby on it.

"Who's this?" I asked "Sophia?"

"Yes. Cute, wasn't she?"

"She still is," I told him. He nodded and sipped his drink.

"I love Europe," he said. "I've been to various places, including London a couple of times. For business."

I nodded and was about to reply when he said, "Zach's a sensitive soul, you know?"

I nodded again, realising this was indeed an opportunity for me to be warned not to hurt his baby brother. I thought it was quite sweet really, that he cared enough to say it.

"He's loyal. Very loyal. I can see that he's serious about you. So please, not that I think you will, but just in case, don't hurt him, okay? If you're not as serious about him, then get out now."

"I am. Don't worry. I'm not going to hurt him," I promised. I meant it too, at the time.

He smiled. "I'm sorry. It's just, there's something you should know, something he should have told you, and you mustn't get angry when he does tell you because-"

Zach walked in, and looked surprised to find us both there.

"You're up early Aaron," he said, coming round and kissing me on the forehead.

"Morning beautiful." He smelt good, slightly of sweat but also fresh from the snow outside.

"Couldn't sleep in that god awful old bed of mine." Aaron sighed and took his coffee out to the kitchen.

"I better take some of this up to Mel."

I thought for a few seconds about what Zach could have to tell me that'd make me angry, and then he started talking about something else, I forgot all about it.

Zach

I left Amy reading and went and took a shower, then grabbed a cup of coffee and sat opposite her. She looked so cute with her hair braided either side of her face.

"So, you want a tour of the neighbourhood?"

About half an inch of snow had settled, but it was clear skies as we headed out again and I took her on a similar route to where I'd run just an hour or so earlier. She seemed genuinely interested and we wandered from street to street, I showed her a few of my old haunts, and we held hands.

"I love the crunch of the snow under our shoes," Amy said.

"Me too. So what was Aaron saying, when I came in?" I asked.

"He told me not to hurt you."

"Oh no, really? I'm sorry."

"No, it was sweet. He cares about you."

Amy

Later that day, Zach, Aaron and Nate went out to play pool. Sophia and Lucy were playing out in the snow and I joined Annie and Mel in the kitchen. We were making some sort of traditional Hanukkah dish with potatoes, onions, and eggs. I was peeling potatoes, Mel was grating them, and Annie was preparing some sort of dessert.

"Well, I have to say Amy, you've made quite an impression on my Zach," Annie said, smiling. "I hope you don't mind me saying so."

I felt myself blush but was honoured by the compliment.

"Thank you, Annie. He's made quite a mark on me, too."

"I'm glad to hear it. You seem perfectly suited."

"I agree," chimed in Mel. "I have never seen him so happy."

I couldn't help but grin. I felt more relaxed here than I did even in my own family's house.

Two years ago at Christmas, we'd all arrived at my parents about the same time. Ed was hung over and hardly said a word to anyone all day, before leaving early to hang out with some friends. Libby had been talking about her job, and her friends, and various dramas and crises going in her life.

We did the same thing every year, swapped the same gifts – socks, toiletries, maybe a CD. Then we'd eat a traditional dinner which my mum had bought mostly ready-made from a caterer friend of hers. Then we'd sit around, watching television. I'd get bored and read a book. When my grandparents were alive we used to sing carols around the tree. I'd always hated it.

So when they went off to Iceland I'd made excuses about work and stayed home. I'd eaten chocolate all day and had a Pride and Prejudice DVD marathon, drooling over Colin Firth.

I never felt liked I quite belonged in my family and I'm not sure why. Was I any different than Ed? I wondered if maybe I just had more of my father in me than he did. Maybe that's why I felt out of place, distant from them all.

"Do you want anything to drink?" Annie asked me. "You must make yourself at home, you're one of the family, okay?"

Zach

The pool table had been damaged by two guys fighting in the bar a few nights previously, so we just sat drinking beer. Dad and Aaron were talking baseball, then football. I just sat staring at my beer bottle, wondering if Amy was okay with my mom.

Despite my lack of interest in the sports conversations, I liked coming out with my dad, without Mom being there. He opened up a little more and I could have a decent conversation with him.

"Amy is great," Aaron said, all of a sudden.

"She is." I nodded

"I like her too." This was the first time I'd heard my dad pass any comment over a girl I was dating. "Try to hold on to her."

"I intend to."

"You haven't told her about Ellie, have you?" Aaron asked

"No," I admitted. I was surprised he had bought it up again. My dad looked down. We never discussed Ellie any more.

"You should. Sooner the better," Aaron said, getting up to get more beers.

I nodded. "Mom said the same thing."

My dad changed the subject.

Amy

Nate lit the candle and a similar ritual took place.

"It's a family tradition," Annie told me, "to get together at Hanukkah and recite some of our favourite Hebrew poems."

"I think it's lovely," I told her. And I genuinely did.

"Zach and myself were forced to go to Hebrew school every weekend," Aaron told me.

"It was for your own good," Annie responded. "They learnt a lot there."

Zach later told me that it was the worst few hours of their week, Aaron in particular hating it. Neither of them felt very religious but they enjoyed getting together to celebrate Hanukkah each year.

The food was delicious. I tried all sorts of things that I had never had before, my favourite being the potato pancakes Mel and I had prepared.

After dinner we settled down in the living room – big comfy cream sofas with huge cushions and a real fire place. It was perhaps the cosiest living room I'd ever sat in.

"Anyone for a game of 'Who Am I'?" Nate spoke for the first time in at least an hour. Sophia and Lucy got excited.

Zach

"Who Am I" is a long-standing game played at our house. When I was younger, my grandparents, aunts, uncles, and cousins would all get together and play after my mother's potato pancakes.

Each player has a post-it stuck to their head, with the name of a famous celebrity. We take it in turns to go around the circle asking questions, attempting to figure out which celebrity's name is on our heads. One year, Aaron had thought it funny to put "Jesus" on my Grandmother's head, and "Hitler" on my Grandfathers. There were a few arguments that year. Now, since Sophia and Lucy were born, it was usually quite tame and we all laughed each year as it took my mom longest to discover which celebrity she was.

This year, she had Oprah written on her head.

"Am I a cartoon?" asked Sophia, starting off. She was in fact Minnie Mouse, so we answered yes.

"Am I male or female?" My father, whose head said Elvis, went next.

Mel was Will Smith, Aaron was President Obama, Amy had John Lennon and Lucy had Snow White.

We all went around asking the questions. We laughed. Amy helped the children.

It was down to myself and Mom/Oprah. I knew I'd be reminded of this moment every Hanukkah in the future if I didn't beat my mother.

"Am I black?" she asked.

"Yes," Mel told her. Mom is Oprah's biggest fan so this was easy for her, or at least it should've been.

I considered the facts I'd learnt so far; I was male, older than thirty, still alive, white, and in the movie business. I decided to take a wild guess.

"Am I Dustin Hoffman?" I knew mom was a big fan of his, too and she'd written my post-it.

"No!" they all said together.

"Oprah!" exclaimed Mom.

It took me another four guesses. I was Al Pacino.

Amy

"Your family are lovely," I told Zach as we got into bed that night.

"Thank you. I like yours too."

"You have only met the new family," I said. "Just you wait. The British contingent are a whole different story."

"You don't have to be close to your mom, or your sister...but you know, don't hate them. Don't dread seeing them. They are still your family."

I was a little taken aback.

"I don't hate them. I guess I just don't enjoy their company."

"Still, you love them, right? And they love you. They'd be there for you, if you needed them."

"I guess I know what you're saying, but really, Zach, just you wait."

"Okay, I will make up my mind after I've met them."

"Sophia and Lucy are so cute."

"I know. Aaron and Mel, though. They seem so...distant these days."

I'd noticed Mel and Aaron barely spoke to each other. I told him about what Sophia and Lucy had said when we watched High School Musical.

"I hate that it's affecting the girls," Zach said, sighing.

"You think they'll work it out?"

"I don't know. I hope so."

Zach

The next day we all prepared to leave. Mom was disappointed, but packed us all some food to take and kept mentioning that we should visit more often.

"Amy, it was so good to finally meet you," she said, giving her a long hug.

"You too, thank you for a wonderful weekend."

"She's so polite!" Mom beamed a huge smile as she turned and hugged me.

Dad shook hands, and gave Amy a brief hug.

"Can we go out for a few beers one night this week?" Aaron asked me.

"Sure."

"I'll call you."

Mel and the girls gave us hugs and then we were off. I'd had a nice weekend but it was also good to be alone with Amy again.

"I enjoyed that so much," she said, waving to the girls as we drove off.

"Good. Get used to it. That happens every year."

"I didn't know you knew any Hebrew."

142

"We had to learn it, it wasn't much fun. I join in more for tradition than anything, and to keep Mom and Dad happy."

"Is it a problem, that I'm not Jewish?"

"They loved you, there's no problem at all, really. Mel isn't religious either."

We chat the rest of the way back about Christmas. Andy and Yvonne had invited us for a couple of days and Amy seemed excited.

Amy

I spent the next week buying Christmas presents. I bought light things for my family in Blighty; scarves for Mum and Libby, a couple more Red Sox souvenirs for Ed and a nice pen for Jack. I found books for Jemma and some expensive champagne and other little things for Andy and Yvonne. Harriet and I were wandering around in Macy's after work one evening, looking for a present for her mother when she asked me again about setting her up with one of Zach's friends.

"Matt is the only person I know is single." I took out my phone and found his Facebook picture.

"Here he is. You want me to find out if he's interested?"

"Cute. So, yes. No. Well, yes."

"You keep asking me, but you're actually quite nervous aren't you?"

"Yes."

"I'll see what Zach says."

Zach

Aaron looked miserable as I entered the bar. He was peeling the label off his bottle of Budweiser, not even looking up at the sports on TV.

I got a beer and joined him.

"So; what's up dude?" I said, sitting down. Dude was a word

143

used much more frequently by Aaron than myself, and I wasn't sure I could carry it off, but it kind of felt like a dude moment.

"It's Mel. Shit, Zach, I don't think we're going to work out."

"Come on, do you really think that? Every relationship has its bad times, surely?"

"I've met someone."

He took me by surprise then. I couldn't picture him cheating, even though I knew he was unhappy.

"Oh, no, come on Aaron. You haven't been screwing around?" I almost raised my voice. Mel didn't deserve that.

"No, I haven't been screwing around, or screwing anything or anyone. I just like this woman, that's all."

"Who is it?"

"Someone I work with. She flirts with me. She's not that smart, but she's cute and I know I could get some, if only I didn't have a conscious."

"She's not that smart? Surely if anyone is going to be worth ruining your marriage over, splitting up your family, then it should be someone you're madly in love with. Not just some random hot girl."

"I know, I know. But Mel and I haven't had sex in months. Seriously. Before you met Amy. Imagine going that long without having sex."

"Then seduce her! Take her out, buy her flowers, be nice to her."

"What's the point?"

"Seriously, you can't just give up on Mel. Don't you think you could be making more effort to get along?"

"I guess. She just irritates me."

"I bet you irritate her too."

Aaron shrugged his shoulders.

"You know it's the right thing," I told him, "you have to make more effort. For Sophia and Lucy's sake."

"I guess."

"You don't guess. You know it, and that's why you asked me

to meet you here. You knew what I'd say."

Aaron nodded and glanced up at the game.

When we were in high school, everyone knew me as the younger brother of the captain of the football team. Despite my obvious geekiness, and the fact that I excelled at the academic subjects but wasn't so hot on the sports field, great things were expected of me. The coach insisted I tried out for football, and then basketball. The girls wanted to get to know me with the hope of being introduced to Aaron. He was funny and popular, and everyone knew him, everyone looked up to him. He was a star.

To see him like this, miserable and unhappy with his life didn't seem right somehow. Surely my brother was supposed to be destined for better things.

Later, I told Amy what he'd said.

"It's so sad."

"I know."

"I hope they can work it out."

I wasn't sure if Aaron had it in him to make any effort.

"I know it takes two," Amy said with a little hesitation, "but Aaron's so..."

"Annoying? Arrogant? Immature?"

"Well, yes! I hate to be rude about your brother, but I can't say he seems a decent husband."

I sighed. "I know."

"So, do you think Matt might be up for a blind date?"

I was glad of the change of subject.

"With who?"

"Harriet."

I thought about it for a minute. She was a little older than him but he had always gone for older women, and he'd been single for a while.

"Yes, probably, shall we set something up?"

"That would be fantastic, thank you."

Amy

I lied to my mother on Christmas eve.

"What are you doing tomorrow?" she asked.

"Nothing much. Seeing some friends."

I hated lying but I didn't want to tell the truth. I'd only briefly mentioned to her so far that I'd met my dad, and she'd asked no questions about him at all. I thanked her for my gifts, she'd sent me a box of presents that I hadn't opened yet and wished her a Merry Christmas.

I took the box and headed over to Zach's, where we packed up his car and drove out to my dad and Yvonne's house. It was decorated tastefully outside, with a holly reef and a few twinkling lights. Andy appeared in the doorway and I leapt out of the car to hug him.

"Merry Christmas," he said, giving me a tight hug.

"And to you, Dad."

It slipped out. I hadn't intended it, but that's how I thought of him inside my head. Up until now, I'd only called him Andy, but Dad seemed right somehow. Still, I felt my face turn to bright red.

"I'm sorry, it just-"

"It's fine. It's wonderful."

I looked at him, he seemed happy and we went inside without saying anything more. The house smelt of cinnamon and spices, candles were lit and a huge pile of presents were under a big shimmering tree.

I saw a woman, with dark hair and a kind smile stand up in the living room as we entered. A man with a bald head and a big green jumper covering a huge belly also stood up, grinning. Next to him was a young man with red hair, about twenty, who looked a little unsure of himself.

"This is my sister, Elsa."

"Elsa, meet your niece."

It turned out that the bald guy was Elsa's husband, Richard, and the young guy was my cousin, Neil. They were friendly and welcoming and I introduced them to Zach. Yvonne came in with a big hug for us both and an hour later Jemma turned up with the same warm welcome she always gave me.

Elsa asked me all about myself; about growing up in England, about Ed, and about my job.

"What does PR actually mean?" she asked, stroking Yvonne's cat who had settled on her lap.

"Public relations," I told her.

"I see," she said, although she looked none the wiser.

I asked her about my dad as a child. She told me stories about growing up on a farm, about picking apples from an orchard and riding ponies. It sounded idyllic.

"What were my grandparents like?" I asked her.

"Modern-thinking, for their generation," she said, smiling at me. She had kind eyes. She pulled at her cardigan sleeve for a moment, thinking.

"They were very angry about not getting to know you. Andy told them about your mother and they wanted him to go after her, find out if she'd had the baby, and persuade her to come back here. They wanted to see you. Find out about you. It's a shame they didn't get the chance."

"I'm sorry I didn't turn up sooner," I said sadly.

"But you're here now." She smiled and squeezed my arm. "Better late than never."

I also tried to make conversation with my cousin, Neil, but he didn't have a lot to say. He spoke in a monotone voice looking at the carpet while answering my questions about himself. He asked nothing about me. Soon I moved on to chat to Jemma, who was as enthusiastic and charming as ever. She had read a book I'd recommended and we discussed it for a while. Somehow, I felt closer to her than Libby already, and I wasn't sure why. We didn't have much more in common. Maybe it was just because we were both making so much effort to get to know each other, to be friends. I realised that maybe Libby and I had just taken each other for granted. Maybe Ed and I, too.

I took out my phone sent him a text message.

Merry Crimbo from Boston. Hope Uncle Nigel isn't driving you crazy. I'm at our father's house. Don't tell Mum. Just met our Aunt Elsa and cousin Neil. It's crazy but nice. Speak to you soon. Aims x

Then I sent one to Libby, too.

Happy Christmas Sis. Hope you're having a lovely time, I hear you're with Tim's family. Speak to you soon? Love Amy x

Ed replied ten minutes later:

Merry Christmas Sis. It's late here and everyone's gone to bed. Uncle Nigel usual idiot self but otherwise had a nice day. Missed you. Aunts and uncles and dads and sisters. It's all a bit surreal, but tell them I said hello. Spk soon. E x

I passed on Ed's hello and everyone seemed pleased.

Amy! Happy Christmas! Having a fab time drinking champagne with Tim's fam! Call me when you can! Love Libby! X

Still over-using the exclamation marks, I noticed. But I was happy I'd got in touch.

Zach

Amy handed out home-made sweet mince pies, a tradition where she came from apparently. Everyone loved them.

I was sat next to Richard, who was balding and a little

arrogant. He told me a few sexist jokes and ate noisily. I helped Andy to clear the plates.

"What did you think of Richard?" Andy asked. "I saw you sitting next to him."

"He's-"

"Pompous? A bigot? Chews with his mouth open?"

"Well, yes..." I laughed.

"No one likes him, I'm not even sure Elsa does to be honest."

"Families, huh?"

"Yes. Exactly. Can't choose them."

The rest of Christmas passed by quietly. Elsa and family left on Christmas eve, thankfully for me as Richard seemed to have taken quite a liking to me and kept singling me out for his rude jokes and loud eating.

Yvonne made a Christmas dinner the following day and we all exchanged presents. Amy and I were a little overwhelmed by their generosity, Andy and Yvonne had spent as much on Amy, and even me, as they had done Jemma, who was also very generous.

We drunk some wine, and watched an old movie, and it was calm, and peaceful and a great way to further tighten the bond with Amy and her father, and sister.

My only concern was that the closer she got to her dad, the further she drifted from her mom, back home in England. I tried to picture her and wondered if she was missing her daughter.

Amy

"So what did your mother say, about you meeting me?" my dad asked as I cooked on boxing day. Boxing day doesn't exist in the US, but I'd told them all about it and insisted on cooking them all my family's traditional bubble and squeak with a little leftover turkey and a tin of baked beans.

"Not much," I replied. "I didn't give her all the details."

"Fair enough. Was she surprised you were spending the holidays here?"

"I didn't tell her, to be honest."

"Can I ask you something?"

"Yes?"

"What happened between you two? I'm sad you don't feel closer to her."

I sighed.

"She's just...wrapped up in her career. And Libby. Libby is her baby, and she's far more interested in her than in me. She lied to me, as well. All those years. I think I never forgave her for that."

"I'm sure she was just trying to protect you."

"Perhaps."

"Well, I know it's not easy, but don't let it eat away at you. I'm sure she's not all bad, and if she's anything like the young woman I knew, she's passionate about what she does, that's all. It doesn't mean she doesn't care about you, and I think she'd be disappointed to think you were unhappy with her."

I nodded my head and bit my lip to stop my emotion showing. Without another word I carried on cooking and for the first time, I thought about calling my mum without the prior feeling of dread.

However, by the time I did call, to wish her a Happy New Year one week later, I still dreaded it, and I still resented her as she told me all about her latest work projects and told me about Libby's wedding plans, and asked nothing about what was going on in my life.

Chapter Nine

Amy

I stood in Harriet's living room, smiling and remembering meeting Zach for the first time. I could have kissed her and thanked her a thousand times for having that party.

"Almost ready!" she called out from her bedroom.

I straightened my dress and glanced at my face in the mirror above her fireplace. There was a tiny smudge of mascara under my right eye and I dabbed it away with my finger.

"What do you think? Too revealing?"

"Oh Harriet, you look lovely."

She was wearing a long black dress. It was quite low cut and showed off her cleavage, she did a little spin and giggled. She'd informed me about twenty times already that she was very nervous about tonight. She'd been constantly asking me questions about Matt, most of which I was unable to answer as we'd never met.

"Where does he live?"

"Rhode Island, I think."

"What does he do?"

"I'm not actually sure."

"What does he look like?"

"I don't know, I've only seen the Facebook photo, same as you. Perhaps we should have found some of this out before we set up the blind date."

"How old is he?"

"About the same age as Zach I guess."

"How long as he been single?"

"No clue. A while, according to Zach."

"How long has Zach known him?"

"Since college."

She'd also talked about several different outfits she might wear and we agreed a simple black dress was the way to go. I just hoped she and Matt hit it off, as I'd done all the arranging and I didn't want her to be disappointed.

She grabbed an ankle length white coat and her purse.

"Let's go," she said, linking her arm in mine.

Zach

"So, what's this Harriet like?" Matt asked.

"She's nice."

"Great."

That was the extent of the conversation Matt and I had before the double date begun.

Amy

"Hi." Zach kissed me on the cheek as we entered the room. "You look great."

"Hi Zach!" said Harriet nervously.

"Wow, Harriet, you look great too."

"Thanks."

"Matt, this is Amy."

Matt shook my hand very enthusiastically.

"At last we meet! Zach has told me a lot about you." I smiled, pleased.

Actually, as my conversation with Harriet proved, Zach had told me little more than a few stories of their "fun" in college. He wasn't at all like I'd expected him. I'd seen a few old photos of a red-headed, tall, chubby guy with a slight acne problem and a kind of goofy grin.

What stood before me was a red-headed, tall, slim guy, with a clear complexion and a winning smile. He had very white, straight teeth and was quite cute. I turned toward Harriet, and Zach introduced them. They seemed impressed enough with each other and we headed downstairs and into a cab.

Matt immediately started asking Zach how business was and I smiled at Harriet. She looked more nervous now than ever.

"Do you like him?" I whispered.

She nodded her head, and gulped nervously. I squeezed her hand.

"Relax."

She smiled, gulped again, and looked out of the window. For the next twenty minutes I listened to Zach tell Matt about his clients, his increasing workload, and his increasing fees. I became mesmerized by his voice and sat staring at the back of his head, remembering what it felt like to run my hands through his hair and kiss his neck. He had a little curl of hair resting on his shirt collar.

Once inside the restaurant, we were shown to a little table by the window, which looked out onto the road. On the other side there was a neon sign which flashed something about the Red Sox.

"So, what do you do, Matt?" Harriet asked, forcing herself, I suspected, to get over her nerves and make conversation.

"I work in IT. How about you?"

They fell into easy conversation and I looked at Zach, he smiled at me and squeezed my hand, which was resting on the table. I could melt into his eyes. It was like looking at him, we had this unspoken bond which no one else understood. The look meant so many things, including "I'm happy."

We stared at each other for several minutes, with his hand resting on mine. After those few minutes, I licked my lips and he raised his eyebrows and grinned.

"...isn't that right, Amy? Amy?"

The trance was broken.

"Ah, look at these two! You've found someone special huh?" Matt laughed and nudged Zach with his elbow.

I looked down at my place setting and then back up at Zach.

"Sure have," Zach said, still looking at me.

"Wow, I've never seen you like this Zach," Matt said, nudging him again.

Now pretty much everyone close to him had told me this.

Zach looked away and blushed a little, while I beamed a huge smile.

We picked up our menu's, and examined the various Chinese dishes on offer.

"Why, when ordering Chinese food, do most people always have the same thing, time and time again?" asked Matt.

"That's true," I said.

"I think we should all have something different tonight," Harriet suggested, obviously feeling very daring.

"Deal. Let's all pick something we've never had before," said Matt.

Zach

A couple of hours later and Harriet and Matt were still in full conversation. Amy and I joined in with the occasional anecdote, joke, or contribution, but mostly they were both so eager to talk, to get to know each other. It reminded me of Amy and I, the first night we met. I had a feeling this was going to work out well for them.

Matt and I met at college. His roommate, a guy called Stan who we'd both lost touch with, needed a website building for a small business he was setting up. Stan had introduced us at a party and Matt and I got talking, and hit it off right away. Mostly, I think, because we were both huge Star Wars fans and quite possibly the uncoolest guys in our freshman year.

Now, I'm no Romeo. Before Amy, I went out with my fair share of women. I tried to charm them when it was worth

154

making some effort. Some girls seemed to find me cute. I've no idea why. One girl, Candice, who I dated for three months when I was a freshman, told me I was cute in a "Jewish kinda way", whatever that meant. I guess that's better than not being cute in any kind of way.

But Matt didn't know how to speak to women and had never been in a serious relationship, despite being almost thirty-two. I'd seen him stammer and trip over his words and say stupid things, and fail time after time to get a woman interested.

I watched him talking to Harriet and thought how great it'd be if he could fall in love with someone. If he could feel for someone, the way I felt about Amy.

Oh no, I realised: I really am starting to think like a girl.

Amy

Zach and I were laying in bed the following morning, him on his back with my head on his chest and his arm around me. Snuggling in bed is, to me, the best feeling in the world. Zach reached and pulled open his curtains a little, big heavy flakes of snow were falling gracefully.

"I love staring out at the snow," I said.

"Me too. Always better if you're warm indoors than trying to drive or get someplace."

"Harriet and Matt hit it off."

"Sure did."

We left them chatting in a bar around 2am. I think they barely acknowledged our leaving; they were so deep in their conversation.

"The snow is stopping already," Zach observed.

Zach

I reached over to my bedside unit and picked up my cell

phone. Aaron had sent me a text last night which I showed to Amy:

I'm not sure I can take anymore of this crazy bitch!

"Oh dear."
"I wish I could help in some way."
"Me too. It's sad, really."
"I know."
I replied:

Made up now?

He quickly came back with:

Yes. But it's not going to work out. I can't see how it can.

I sighed. Aaron and Mel were a mystery to me. Sure, she was a bit uptight, and yes, he was a bit lazy when it came to being a husband and father. But I couldn't think of a defined point where they had stopped getting along, they just had. Slowly, it had crept up on them and now we could all see that there was a problem.

"We'd better get up," I told Amy. "We need to leave for my parents in an hour."

Amy

"This much snow would cause chaos in Britain," I told Zach. I was amazed; about four inches had fallen, but the roads were ploughed and everyone was going about their business as normal. In the UK, we'd all be stuck in doors for days.

We drove up to his parents in silence. I was nursing a slight hangover from the night before, but I wasn't sure what Zach's excuse was.

"Anything wrong?" I asked after a while.

"Just thinking about Aaron and Mel."

Annie came out to greet us, with the same enthusiasm and big hug that we received at Hanukkah. She ushered us inside and told us Nate had gone out to get some bread.

"I'm very forgetful these days," she told us.

"Something smells wonderful," I said.

"I'm making soup." She waved her hand in the direction of the kitchen.

Zach helped her make coffee and we sat in the living room.

"So, how are you both?"

"We're good thanks Mom, how're you doing?"

"I'm very well. Aaron tells me you are living together?"

I felt a little nervous on this subject; we'd never officially said we were living together, it just sort of happened that I was always at Zach's place.

"Well..." Zach started, glancing at me.

"Kind of." I put my hand on his.

"I see." Annie got up. "I'll just check on my soup."

"I'm sorry," Zach said the moment she was out of the room.

"Don't be."

"We should have spoken about this; made it a little more romantic or official, rather than at my parents house, but I keep thinking that when your lease is up, you might as well officially move in – I mean, move the rest of your stuff over. What do you think?"

I kissed him. Annie came back in.

"Yes Mom," said Zach, grinning. "We are living together."

"That's wonderful! I'm very happy for you both."

Zach

My dad came home and asked if I wanted to come out and see what he was doing in the back yard. I pulled on my coat and wandered outside with him and he showed me a large crate

157

full of seeds he'd bought to start growing vegetables. Previously, he'd been a fruit and flowers man. He grew strawberries, plums and apples...as well as a variety of flowers. The garden was always a frenzy of colour, from yellow to blue, red, pink, purple and plenty of green in between.

"This year, I'm going to try potatoes, tomatoes, lettuce, onions..."

He handed me several packs of seeds and I had a look through them.

"Wow, good for you, Dad."

My dad always looked at home in the back yard. It was his space, he'd done all the hard work, designed it, made it what it was, as opposed to the house which had been decorated and furnished by my mom. He would work hard out here, whatever the weather, in his own little world.

"Just as soon as the snow is gone, I'm starting work. Come and see the new tools I've got."

I followed him through the snow and into the garage, eager to show an interest, just to get some time alone with him.

Amy

I watched Zach listening to his dad and nodding his head from the kitchen window.

"He's going to grow some vegetables," Annie told me before turning away and back to her soup.

"Lovely," I said.

"Yes, it's nice that he has a hobby to be honest, keeps him busy."

"Can I help with anything?"

"No, but thank you for asking."

"I adore your house," I said, unsure if I was repeating something I'd stated already.

"Thank you, that's very kind of you to say so. So, you're moving in with Zach officially?"

"Yes," I said, taken a little off guard.

"That is really is wonderful. You make a great couple."

"Thank you. You've got a wonderful son."

She laughed.

"I think so too."

She soon called Zach and Nate in for lunch; which was delicious and I told Annie so.

"Would you like the recipe?"

"Oh yes please," I said, without wishing to tell her that her son did most of the cooking.

Just before we left Annie asked if I'd like to come with her for a facial she was having in the city the following week.

"I'd love to!" I said, giving her a hug goodbye.

"I've never had a daughter," she said sadly. "But if you become my daughter-in-law, I won't mind that one bit."

"That's so very sweet of you."

Zach

Amy received a phone call from Harriet on the way home.

"Really? Oh, wow...really?...then what happened?" This seemed to be repeated over and over again. Every detail was being discussed. They were still chatting when we pulled up outside.

"I'm home now, I'll just come in and see you, okay..."

"Everything went well?"

"Yes. I'm just going to pop into Harriet's for the rest of the details."

Obviously half an hour's conversation hadn't been enough.

Amy went into Harriet's and I called Matt.

"Hey, how was it?" I asked.

"Great. I really like her. I stayed the night at her place."

"Cool. You going to see her again?"

"Definitely."

"See you next week?"

"Sure."

Amy was gone for over an hour. And that's the difference between men and women.

Amy

I noticed Harriet was positively glowing as she made me a cup of tea and came to settle down on the sofa opposite me.

"So what happened this morning, when you woke up?" I asked.

"Well, I woke up and he wasn't there. I panicked for a second, but heard him in the kitchen. He came in with cups of coffee and we just grinned at each other. I felt like the cat who got the cream."

"Ah, I'm so happy for you."

"I made us some toast, but it got cold because when I bought it back to bed, he just grabbed me and we made love again; this time more passionate, and we were less drunk of course. It was wonderful..."

She sighed.

"Thank you so much for setting us up. We're going out again on Wednesday evening."

"You are very welcome, it's the least I can do; I wouldn't have met Zach if it weren't for you."

I told Zach all the details when I got home.

"Well, I didn't expect such a success!" Zach said over dinner.

"Me either. I hope it works out for them, Harriet is really keen on him."

Zach smiled and took another mouthful of food. His cooking really was good.

"So what have you got planned for tomorrow, busy day?" I asked him.

"Yes, I'm starting a new project for a helicopter company. They fly tourists over the Grand Canyon. They sent me a bunch of photos, you want to see?"

We went to his laptop and I was amazed.

"I've always wanted to go," I told him.

"Well, let's arrange a trip when we get back from England."

England. My sister's wedding. It was coming around fast now and I was dreading it... I wasn't sure I could face my mum and Jack in the same way after all the time I'd spent with my dad, and Libby's wedding didn't particularly appeal to me either. During our last short email conversation, she'd told me that it was going to be a big affair, lots of guests and a fancy hotel, no expense spared. I wanted to be happy for her but I got the feeling she was more enthusiastic about the wedding than about Tim.

"It's a special, important day and I think people should spend whatever they are comfortable with, or can afford," Taryn told me when I told her how astonished I was about the amount it must be costing.

I supposed she was right. I still didn't want to go, though.

"Amy, can you look through the press release archive and find me these files?" Franco gave me a list of reference numbers to look up the next day.

"Sure."

"I had a call from the guys dealing with your green card on Friday," he said, distracted by some other thought.

"Oh yes?" I hadn't given it a lot of thought but my whole future here depended on that application going through.

"Yes, seems there'll be no problem. Your father being American, and you're working for us, and everything else seems to fall into place."

I couldn't help but smile to myself for the rest of the day. An email came in from Ed.

To: Amy Starling
From: Ed Starling
Subject: Happy New Year Sis

Hi Amy,

Long time no speak! Happy New Year! How are you?

Libby seems to be on a permanent high arranging her wedding. Tim seems cool, but I'm not sure he knows what he's letting himself in for with Libby, ha ha!

I've got a new girlfriend, her name is Polly. Met her at a pub near my office.

Also, just wanted to say thanks for giving Andy my email address. We've sent quite a few back and forth. Seems a nice guy. I haven't told Mum, FYI. I will do, just didn't want to bring it up yet. Not sure how to handle it to be honest.

Hope everything is going well with you.

Love, Ed.

Harriet popped her head in my cubicle.

"Matt just text me," she said excitedly. "He's so sweet!"

She was gone again before I could respond.

To: Ed Starling
From: Amy Starling
Subject: Re: Happy New Year Sis

Hello Ed,

Happy New Year to you too. I'm great thanks. Work is going well, and I'm still seeing Zach.

I'm not sure why I hadn't told him, or anyone in my family back home how serious Zach and I were. I knew my mum would say it sounded as if it was moving too fast, and Libby wouldn't be that interested. Ed would feign a little interest, but I didn't see the point in sharing too much; they could see for themselves that we were serious when I came home for the wedding.

Sounds like the wedding is going to be rather fancy.

Yes, Andy is fantastic. He can't wait to meet you. Maybe later in the year, you could come and stay with me and we can go over together? Also, Jemma, our sister, can't wait to get in touch either. She's so sweet and charming, they both are. She looks like us. I'll take a photo to send over next time I see her.

Hope you are well too. Tell me more about this new girlfriend of yours.

Amy x x

Zach

I was with my brother. We'd just been to see a new band play; the drummer was someone Aaron knew at college. They were awful. We got beers at a bar just around the corner and discussed just how crap they were for a while.

"So, what's Amy up to tonight?"

"She's with her friend Harriet. And Mel?"

"I don't know, actually. Probably just home with the kids," he sighed. I was about to start the conversation I'd been planning in my head for days; it was going to begin with a vague question about how he was feeling about Mel and end with a serious and frank suggestion that he start acting like a husband and father and make more effort. I took a deep breath and was just about to start when I glanced at the door and saw Scarlett walking into the bar.

"Oh no. Look who it is." I nodded in her direction.

"Man, she is hot! What did you do that for?"

"Well, she was hardly the one, was she?"

"Why look for the one? How about love the one you're with?"

"She was shallow, Aaron, and you know Amy is much better for me."

"True, true. You could have seen them both, though."

I rolled my eyes.

"Scarlett asked me if she could move in. The night we broke

up."

"Oh, now I see. Good move. Never let them move in should have been my rule. Although now you've let a girl move in who you hardly know, been seeing her even less time than you were dating Scarlett. But, look at me and Mel. Happy as anything, then she wants to move in, then she wants to get married. Buy a house. Have kids. Now, look at us."

"Aaron, give it a rest, will you? Stop complaining about Mel. She's great. She's a good person, she's a great mother. You're just bored and behaving badly, and you know it. You know she has good reason to moan and complain at you."

He looked taken aback for a moment. It wasn't how I'd planned it, but there it was.

"You think I'm being an arsehole?"

"Yes."

I picked up my beer and waited for his reaction.

"Maybe you're right. But back to you and Amy. You're going to end up getting married to her, and one day you'll be bored and start being less loving and attentive, and she'll get mad at you and change and be more demanding and then you'll realise; it was better before and Aaron was right."

I rolled my eyes and accidentally caught Scarlett's eye. She came over. I braced myself. Just before she spoke, I noticed one of her nails was broken, so I knew she wasn't in the best of moods before the conversation even begun. She was always obsessed with her fingernails. She had a manicure once a week. You'd never believe anyone could have as much to say about fingernails as she did. She could talk to you for at least an hour about cuticles. Seriously.

"Hello Scarlett."

"Zach. How are you?"

She sounded a little drunk.

"I'm good. How are you?"

"I'm a wreck, Zach. I miss you."

I didn't say anything. My mind went blank. I couldn't say I

164

missed her.

"Scarlett, hi," Aaron said, grinning.

"Oh, hi Aaron."

"She'll be lucky," she stated, turning back to me.

"Who?"

"The girl you end up with. You just have to give her a chance."

"Thank you for the advice Scarlett."

"He's met someone," said Aaron, the jerk.

"Really?"

"Yes, she's moved in. He's finally fallen in love."

"Oh right, well, good for you Zach." Her face crumbled and she walked away.

"What did you tell her that for?"

"I thought it might help her move on."

An hour later, we saw her kissing a guy in a corner.

"See," said Aaron, "she's moving on already."

We didn't talk about Mel or their marriage for the rest of the evening. I didn't know what else I could do to help. I thought about telling him to grow up, take some responsibility, show Mel a good time, be a better father, and just stop complaining. But I didn't, because I knew it would make no difference.

Amy

"So has Matt said much to Zach about me?" Harriet passed me a glass of wine, sat down on the sofa and put her feet up on her coffee table.

"Not a lot. You know what men are like, they only exchange the basic details."

"Yes, that's true. Did I ever tell you about the only man I've ever loved?"

"No. Do I know him? Is it someone at work?"

"No, his name is Brendon. He was a good friend of mine. Still is. He's gay."

"Oh no, really?"

"Really. He's two years older than me. Our mum's were best friends before we were born. We played together as children. All through-out high school, we were close. I never thought of him romantically, you know...then he went to college and I missed him more than I thought possible. I realised I was crazy about him."

"Wow, so did you tell him?"

"No. The next time I saw him, he told me he was gay."

"Wow. That sucks."

"Yeah."

"So he went on to say he was sorry he'd never told me, yadda yadda."

"So what happened next?"

"Nothing. We're still really good friends. He's my best friend, really."

"And there's been no one else?"

"I've dated many, many men, believe me, but no one has ever been as good as him, you know?"

"And Matt?"

"He's pretty close." She grinned.

"Well, I'm glad things are going well."

"And how's it going with Zach?"

"He asked if I want to officially move in!"

"Wow...although you are kind of living there already."

"Yes, but officially..."

"Look at us, all loved up and happy!"

I raised a toast to the four of us. But somehow, it all seemed a little too perfect. Zach and I hardly ever fell out, we got on so well...but it had all happened so fast. There was a cynical, glass is half empty little part of my brain that thought something bad was going to happen to wreck it all. Unfortunately, I was right.

Zach

I watched Amy getting ready to go out and have a facial with my mother. She seemed relaxed, happy and looking forward to it. No longer nervous about spending time with my family. It was nice. She kissed me good bye and off she went.

I went to my computer quickly and re-read the last email from Ellie. I'd been meaning to reply for weeks, but I'd always wanted to do it when Amy wasn't around. I didn't want her to come in and ask who I was talking to.

Just as I started typing, I felt the guilt waft over me again and wondered if I'd ever be able to tell Amy.

Amy

Annie was waiting for me outside the day spa she'd booked for us. She smiled and gave me a quick hug before we went in.

"I insist on paying," she said, winking at me as I got my purse out.

"Really, Annie, you don't need to," I said, embarrassed.

"I insist!" She handed her credit card to the girl behind the counter.

It was lovely spending time with Zach's mother. She talked about when he was little, about his difficult teen years and some of the girl's he dated.

"I sometimes thought he'd never settle, you know. No one ever seemed good enough for him."

The facials were heavenly. I lay there with my eyes closed, letting the beautician massage lotion smelling of lavender into my skin. Afterwards, Annie bought me a coffee and cake in Starbucks and we talked some more about Nate, and how they'd met at a wedding. She told me about Mel and Aaron and how worried she was about them.

"This is lovely," I said, "you know, I've never had a conversation like this with my mum. We don't talk. Not like this."

"That's a shame." Annie looked a little surprised at my

sudden observation.

"She's just so busy with her job," I told her, not sure why I was opening up. "She's so focused and doesn't seem interested in talking about much else."

"Well, don't be too harsh on her. Being a parent isn't easy, you know Amy. If I've learned anything in this life, it's that we're all different and some folks will never be the way you'd like them to be. You can't change people, so you just have to accept them for who they are, and not let it bother you too much."

As I walked home afterward, I kept thinking about Annie's words. Part of me thought they were wise and I shouldn't let my mother's apparent lack of interest bother me. Part of me felt, as her daughter, I deserved more. I tried to picture her here, as a young woman, barely an adult, walking these streets with Andy and looking forward to a great career ahead of her. Had Ed and I stalled all of that? We must have. When I thought of it like that, I think I started to understand her a little better.

Chapter Ten

Amy

As I stepped into Zach's apartment, or our apartment as he kept telling me, I saw something tiny and brown scurry behind his sofa. I grinned, hoping it was what I thought it was.

"Happy Valentine's Day." Zach gave me a kiss on the cheek.

"And to you."

"I got us a kitten, baby!" He pulled away and looked more than a little excited.

"Oh wow, let me see!" I walked over to where the kitten was hiding.

"He's two months old."

"He's gorgeous."

Looking up at me was a tiny tabby kitten. I held out my hand for him to sniff. He cautiously leant forward, sniffed my fingers and then rubbed his face on my hand. I scooped him up and rubbed his head. He purred.

"His fur is so soft."

"I'm glad you like him. A client of mine asked if I knew anyone who'd like a kitten. I know how much you've missed your cat, and how much you love animals, so..."

"Oh, Zach, really. That's so sweet, I'm so chuffed, thank you. He's lovely."

"I think we should call him Alvin," he told me.

"Alvin?"

"Yes. Is that okay?"

"Like the chipmunk?"

Zach thought for a moment.

"Yes. Like the chipmunk."

Silence. I smiled.

"Okay... Hello Alvin." I said, snuggling my face into his tiny head and then placing him on the floor.

Zach already had a few toys for him and he instantly began playing with them, battling them around the room and pouncing. We sat for a while just watching him and I felt like a momentous milestone had been passed. This was serious. How long did cats live? Twenty years? Zach was in this for the long-term.

From then on, we would constantly use phrases such as:

"Ah, look at him now."

"Quick, look at Alvin!"

And:

"Aww, look, he's sleeping again."

"We're two proud parents," I told Mel when I met her for lunch a few weeks later.

"You're too cute, both of you, and little Alvin," she said, passing me back my phone which already contained over a hundred photos.

We were both eating sandwiches and sipping coffees, sitting by a window and watching the world go by.

"Has Aaron said to Zach, or has Zach said to you...anything about our...our marriage?"

I didn't know what to say.

"A little," I admitted.

"Good. I'm glad Aaron is talking to someone about it. It's all so frustrating. Some days I think I adore him. Others I wish he'd grow up. Occasionally I just wish he'd leave."

"Mel, I'm sorry."

"Thank you. I know we're both to blame, I just don't know where to go from here. We fight over such stupid things. I don't remember the last time we had any time to ourselves, went on a date, or did something romantic, you know?"

I had an idea.

"Why don't the girls come and stay with us one weekend? You guys could go off for a romantic break. Buy some new lingerie, take some candles. Remember what it's like to be a couple, rather than two parents."

Mel was smiling at the idea.

"You really wouldn't mind having the girls?"

"We'd love to. I bet they'd like to meet Alvin too," I said, thinking about making cookies and taking them to the park and setting them out a little sleeping area in Zach's office.

"Thank you, Amy. Let me speak to Aaron."

"Make it sound appealing. Sexy. Romantic."

Mel smiled and I felt I'd done my good deed for the day.

Zach

We had been planning a night out for my birthday but as neither of us wanted to leave "poor little Alvin" on his own all evening we decided to stay in. I cooked us some Indian food while Amy played with him.

"Isn't he just the cutest kitty you ever did see?" she said.

Alvin had finally worn himself out from the toys and was curled up in a tiny ball on her lap.

"Can you pass me my book?"

"Can't you get it? I'm cooking."

"I can't disturb him. Look how sweet he is!"

I looked, and she was right. I found her book and passed it to her.

"Thank you. I adore him already."

I had to admit it, I did too.

Luckily, Alvin woke up and went for a sniff around, leaving

171

Amy with enough time to come and eat her dinner. I lit candles and we opened some wine.

"Here's to you, my lover. Happy Birthday." Amy raised her glass and gave me a sexy smile.

"And here's to you, Amy. And to the most amazing time I've had in my life."

"To us!" Amy raised her glass. "Thank you."

Poor Alvin had been shut out of the bedroom up until that night, but he managed to get a spot on the bed the next, and the one after that, and then every night from then on.

Amy

It was a Saturday morning and I was just zipping my coat up outside the apartment, when Harriet opened her door, and Matt stepped out.

"Well, good morning!" I said, grinning.

"Hi Amy," said Matt, looking a little embarrassed.

"Good date last night?"

"Yes, thank you." He kissed Harriet on the cheek.

"Still on for tonight?" We had been planning a wine and cheese evening; Aaron and Mel were coming as well.

"Yes, see you then."

Matt walked off down the corridor.

"How's you?" I asked Harriet, who was still in her dressing gown.

"Great, thank you. Where's Zach?"

"He's running. I'm just popping out for a few bits."

"Wait a minute, I'll come with you."

I waited for about two minutes and she reappeared wearing sweats and a big warm coat. We went down to street level and walked along to the local store, where we stocked up on several bottles of red and white wine and some crackers. Mel was bringing the cheese.

"Matt's so much fun," Harriet told me on the way back.

"I'm glad you like each other," I said. "I didn't want to be responsible for any failed romance."

Harriet laughed.

"Me either, I'm glad you and Zach are so loved up."

"You didn't set us up though, did you?"

"Well, I kinda did scheme a little. I didn't expect you to hit it off quite so, well, quite so fast though!"

"Harriet! You little sneaky match maker!"

"Aren't you glad though?"

"Well...yes."

Zach

Matt and Aaron were in full conversation about some sporting event which I didn't care about. Mel and Amy were preparing the cheese and crackers.

"So, Harriet," I said, trying to think of some conversation, "this is the first time you've been in my apartment. It's weird, isn't it, the rooms being the other way around?"

She frowned for a moment, glanced around, and said something like, "I guess so."

I looked around to see if Amy and Mel were about done with the cheese. This was the longest conversation I'd had with Harriet and I'm a little uncomfortable with silences. They looked like they were about ready. Phew.

Amy

Mel had selected a good variety of cheese, but it didn't occur to me until she arrived that you're supposed to eat particular cheeses with particular wines.

"Oh it'll all be yum," Mel said when I told her this.

We laid out all the different cheese, including soft creamy ones, hard ones, blue ones, ones with holes and a couple I'd never seen or heard of before, on a big wooden bread board and put the crackers in a dish. I handed out glasses of wine and side plates to all and we got stuck in.

"Mmm..." Harriet took her first bite, "this is wonderful."

We all agreed, and continued trying different cheeses and slowly got sloshed on the wine.

Mel and Harriet seemed to hit it off, Mel was giving Harriet decorating advice. I decided to take some time to get to know Matt a little better.

"Tell me Matt," I said, sitting next to him on the sofa, "what was Zach like in college?"

"He was such a geek, you wouldn't believe it. I know he's not exactly Mr. Cool now, but he was even worse back then. His hair cut had no style, and he wore t-shirts with slogans such as "I heart Pi". But, I came along and made him a little cooler. So you've got me to thank for that."

"That's so not true," Zach interjected taking a pause from his conversation with Aaron.

"What about you, Amy? What do you do?"

I filled him in on the basics and poured everyone another glass of wine.

"What about you, Matt?"

"I'm a software developer. Just started at a new firm, actually. I was travelling a lot with the old one, but this new position keeps me at home much more, which is great."

"You live in Providence, right?"

"Yes. Rhode Island. You been to Rhode Island yet?"

"Nope."

"Zach will have to bring you some time. It's another US state to add to your list!"

I wasn't really writing a list as so far I'd only been to Massachusetts but it did occur to me that seeing more of the US should be on my "To Do" list. Zach and I were always talking about all the places we wanted to travel to. I decided I'd write a list the next time we were lazing in bed on a Sunday morning. If it was in writing, we were more likely to get around to actually going to these places.

"So how long is it until your sister's wedding Amy?" asked Mel.

"About four months," I told her.

"Oh don't get her started on that subject," Harriet said. I gave a half-laugh.

"Are you excited?" Mel asked.

"I guess it'll be nice to see all my family." I wasn't sure if I meant that, or not.

"My mum doesn't call very often," I told Mel. Actually, she may have called but as I was never at my apartment, she'd never get through. She had my work number though, and my email address.

"I doubt she misses me that much."

"I'm sure it's more than you realise. She's probably just busy with this wedding."

I nodded my head. Zach gave me a gentle thigh squeeze.

"So wine and cheese evenings are all the rage in England are they?" Matt asked.

"Oh yes." I laughed and hiccupped. "More wine anyone?"

"Zach had a real thing for Posh Spice when he was about twenty one. He must like British women!" Matt said.

"Really?" said Harriet. We were all laughing. Everything is funny when you've had four glasses of wine, or was it five now?

"Oh yes, I forgot about that!" Aaron was laughing so hard he was almost keeled over.

"I just like the accent," said Zach, flushing a little red.

"Aaron likes the French accent," Mel said, very seriously. She picked up Alvin and gave him a cuddle.

"What?" Zach asked, laughing.

"Where did you get that idea from?" Aaron asked, looking confused.

"Let's just say I found some of your special DVD's. He has a fetish for French blondes it seems."

"Oooh!" Harriet said, and we all laughed. It didn't occur to

175

me until the morning that in fact, Mel wasn't laughing.

Zach

"That went well, didn't it?" I said as we closed the door on our guests.

"Lovely evening," Amy replied, walking to the fridge. "But why is the room spinning?"

I picked up the empty wine glasses and bought them out to the sink.

"Drink this." She passed me a tall glass of water.

"Why?"

"Trust me."

Despite the re-hydration, I woke up the following morning feeling like someone had hit me over the head with a hammer. I turned to face Amy who was already awake.

"Morning babe."

"Morning. I've got that queasy sicky feeling and at the same time I'm starving," she said.

"You want some breakfast?"

"Mmm yes please. A bacon sandwich would go down a treat."

"I'll join you in that. Just don't tell my mother."

My head hurt even more when I sat up.

"I don't think I've drunk that much since Aaron's bachelor party." I groaned and made my way to the kitchen.

"Duvet day?" Amy shouted.

"What?"

"Duvet day! Let's stay in our jammys, watch DVD's and cuddle up under the duvet."

Sounded good to me, and Alvin seemed to agree that a day of being lazy was in order. I came back to bed with bacon sandwiches and coffee.

"Mmm," Amy said, inhaling the coffee. "Feeling better already."

176

She produced a notebook.

"Let's write down all the places we want to go someday."

"Okay," I said. "Let's start with Japan."

"Ooh good one."

Amy

We watched Love Actually next. Zach had never seen it and I insisted it was an all-time great. He didn't agree. Next, he chose Top Gun, which we both enjoyed. Just at the bit where Goose dies, Alvin walked in front of the TV and made a cute little meow, making us both laugh.

"His first words!" I said, grabbing him and giving him yet another cuddle.

"You do know he's a cat, not a baby?" Zach said, pausing the DVD so that we could both give him an inordinate amount of fuss.

After Top Gun, we both decided we needed a shower. Zach got in first and I decided to join him half way through.

Next, it was Gladiator, and after that we watched The Proposal with Sandra Bullock.

"I have enjoyed today," Zach said, coming back from the door with the pizza we'd had delivered.

"Me too."

"We watched four movies!"

"That, my darling, is what we call a duvet day."

Zach

The next Saturday we collected Sophia and Lucy and took them back to my apartment. They'd not visited me there very often and they were delighted with Alvin and played with him for a while before cuddling up either side of Amy to watch High School Musical 2.

"Will you be our aunt one day?" Lucy asked her. I was

looking at a magazine but kept staring at the page, without reading.

"Maybe," Amy told them.

"I think you should marry Uncle Zach," Sophia said, giggling. "Then you'd be our aunt."

"Maybe one day," Amy said, and I glanced up. She smiled at me and I smiled back. It seemed hard to believe that a year ago we hadn't met, and now here she was, entertaining my nieces and contemplating becoming their aunt.

And I still hadn't told her about Ellie. *Damn.*

Amy

I loved having Sophia and Lucy to stay. It was a gloriously sunny day, when you finally start to feel that winter is turning into spring. We baked cookies and went down to the harbour to watch the boats and ate our baked goodies in the sunshine. Zach made spaghetti and meatballs and then we watched High School Musical 3 in our bedclothes before tucking them into sleep in his office under a bundle of blankets and pillows.

"They're so sweet," I said to Zach. "Have you heard from Aaron?"

I picked up my phone, I hadn't looked at it all day. I had a text from Mel:

So far so good. Romantic and relaxing. Tonight we're going to do some role play – meet in the bar and pretend we don't know each other. I'm not sure why, it is Aaron's idea and he seems excited. Thank you for this. Mel

Zach was holding his phone, too.

"He text me. He said it's going well."

"Good."

"How do you think a couple gets like that?"

"Lack of communication. Growing in different directions.

Priorities changing."

Zach nodded.

"Amy," he said. "I need to tell you something-"

"Uncle Zach!" Sophie called. He went to her. She'd had a bad dream. I fell asleep on the sofa before we had a chance to finish the conversation.

Zach

"Did you vote for Barack Obama?" Amy asked me the following weekend as we were making pancakes for breakfast.

Apparently, a few weeks previously, it had been Pancake Day; something I'd never heard of, and suspected Amy was making up. She said it's a tradition in Britain.

"Yes," I told her, searching the kitchen for maple syrup.

"Good." She smiled. "I like him, his book was quite inspiring."

I laughed. "I agree."

After enjoying our pancakes, Amy took a shower and I went straight to my computer and googled pancake day, and sure enough, it was a real British tradition, and is even celebrated in a few places in America, but more commonly known over here as "Mardi Gras." I apologised to Amy for being suspicious. I figured she just wanted pancakes. My cell beeped.

It was Aaron:

The fucking bitch says she's leaving me.

Before I even had time to digest this, there was a knock at my door. I looked through the peephole. It was Mel, with Lucy and Sophia.

"Hey girls, everything okay?" I opened the door. Mel's eyes looked red.

"Hi Zach. I'm sorry to just turn up like this, can I ask you for a huge favour?"

"Sure. What is it?"

"Would you mind looking after the girls for a couple of hours?"

"Sure, of course."

"Aaron and I have some talking to do, and he said you wouldn't mind."

"Of course, come in girls," I said.

"I'll call you in a little while. Thanks Zach."

Amy

I came out of the shower to find Sophia and Lucy playing with Alvin on our bed.

"Hello ladies," I said, pulling my towel a little tighter. "Back to visit Alvin again?"

"Hi Amy, isn't Alvin so cute?" said Lucy. I nodded.

"Amy, in here!" called Zach.

"Aaron and Mel need some time to talk," he explained. "Sorry it's interrupted our Saturday again."

"No worries."

"I think this is serious. Look at this text."

I read what Aaron had sent.

"Maybe they just need to talk through a few things."

"Yeah. Maybe."

I lowered my voice. "He needs to grow up a bit and realise he's not a young single guy anymore. He needs to stop being selfish."

"Yeah, I know," said Zach.

"Okay, I'll get dressed and perhaps we can play a game or something?"

"Great, thank you."

I ushered Sophia and Lucy into the living room and shut the door. Poor kids.

Half an hour later we were enjoying a game of eye spy, subjects of which had included my foot, the TV, Alvin, a table, and a bowl of peanuts.

"Do you know the alphabet?" Lucy asked me.

"Yes. Do you?"

"Yes, I've been learning it at kindergarten."

"Hey, you and Zach are like the alphabet," said Sophia.

"How so?" asked Zach.

"Well, from A to Z," she said, pointing at me and then at Zach. She said "zee" rather than "zed."

"Oh yes, so we are." I smiled at Zach.

"I know a game using the alphabet, I used to play it with my brother and sister, do you want to give it a go?" I asked them.

"Yes!"

"Okay, well you have to go through each letter of the alphabet and think of a word beginning with that letter. But you have categories, so for example we could start with animals."

"Ant!" said Sophia, putting her hand in the air.

"That's it. Now, Lucy, you have to think of an animal beginning with B."

"Bee."

"Well done, now I have C, so I'm going to say cat."

"Uncle Zach, you have to think of one beginning with D," said Lucy.

"Erm...snake?" The girls fell about laughing. "No D silly."

"Okay, donkey."

"Elephant!"

We carried on with the game all the way through to "zee," Zach and I giving Lucy help on the trickier letters. Then we gave them pizza for lunch, before putting the Lion King on and they sat and watched for a while as Zach did some work and I read my book. They were such sweet girls, and I just hoped Aaron and Mel were getting somewhere, for their sakes.

Mel picked them up at 5pm, she looked tired and kind of sad.

"How did it go?" I asked.

"Not well. I'm sure Aaron will fill Zach in. I'm just not sure there's anything left to fight for anymore."

"I'm sorry Mel." I gave her a hug.

"Thank you so much for looking after the girls. Again."

"No problem, we enjoyed it."

She said she'd call us in a few days. Zach tried calling Aaron, but he didn't answer.

Zach

"We're getting a divorce," Aaron told me after turning up at my apartment on Monday. Amy was at work. I'd just been on the phone to a client and had to end the call in order to let him in.

"What? Just like that?"

"It's not that shocking, is it, really? Have you got any beer?"

He opened my fridge and helped himself. I muttered something about it only being eleven in the morning but he shrugged and slouched down on my sofa.

"Do you really want it to end?"

"I don't know. We had fun last weekend and things seemed better but...I cheated. I screwed that girl at work. So I felt guilty, and I told her, on Saturday morning." He looked pale.

"You're an idiot Aaron."

"I know. I just...with Mel and I... There's no love there. I love the girls so much," he almost looked emotional, but only for a second "and it's better for them if we're apart and happy, than together and fighting every day."

I nodded. I tried to imagine Aaron being single again, or even with someone else and couldn't quite picture it.

"So are you moving out?"

"Yes. That's why I'm here, in the city. Looking for an apartment. She's going to stay in the house for now, with the girls."

I thought about Aaron and Mel's wedding. Mel had worn

182

what my mum called an "odd" dress, and Aaron drank too much the night before and had a headache all day. Even then, I couldn't remember them seeming totally in love or passionate about each other the way I felt that I was with Amy. It was like, they'd dated a long time, moved in together, and the natural next step was to get married. Without questioning it, or actually thinking about what they wanted, they just settled for the first long-term relationship either of them had found. Amy was right, it was quite sad really.

"Don't you think it's worth doing something, like seeing a marriage therapist?"

"We've been doing that. For the past eight months."

"Really? I had no idea."

"Mel didn't want anyone to know, and to be honest I thought it was a load of crap."

He started peeling the label off his beer.

"Well if you went in thinking it was going to be crap, no wonder it didn't work."

He ignored my comment.

"Do you mind if I just hang out here for a few hours? Don't let me stop you from working, I can just watch some TV."

"Of course that's fine."

"You need to get on with some work?"

"No, I can take a few hours off. Can I be honest with you?"

"I know; I'm an idiot bastard cheat and I deserve to be unhappy."

"Well, that's all true," I said, and he smiled and sighed. "But also...whether you want to win Mel back, or whether you go looking for another woman some day, just remember what a girl likes. Romance and thoughtfulness, not a guy who watches sport all day and never does the laundry."

"I can't change the way I am, Zach."

I shrugged and put the television on. "I better get some work done, actually," I said and left him to it. I realised something; I didn't like Aaron much these days.

Amy

"Hi Amy, it's Mel." I was surprised to hear her voice. She'd never called me at work before.

"Hi Mel. How's everything?"

"Can we meet for lunch?" she asked. I could tell something was wrong from her voice.

I met her in a small restaurant about half way between my office and hers. She smiled but I could see something had changed. She'd aged in just the few days since I'd seen her.

"Aaron is moving out," she said, after we'd ordered our food.

She stared down at the fork, and started twiddling it around slowly.

"Oh Mel, I'm so sorry," I said, unsure how to comfort her or where my loyalties should lie.

"He cheated," she said, her eyes welling up. "And you know what, I'm not even that mad. I was relieved when he told me in a way. Because now I have a good excuse to kick him out."

I squeezed her hand. Despite his immaturity and all their bickering, I didn't expect him to cheat on her.

"But you had such a good time last weekend."

"I know. I thought it might work out. But he felt too guilty I suppose. So he told me, and I got mad, and then I thought – why keep trying?"

"I'm sorry, Mel. I don't know what to say."

"It's okay. It's for the best, really. I just asked you here today because I'd like to keep in touch. I wanted you and Zach to know you'll always be family to me. I don't want Zach to hate me. I really do think of him as a brother." Her eyes welled up and she dabbed them with her napkin.

"Don't be crazy, Zach won't hate you," I told her, patting her hand. "Are you sure this is what you want?"

"Like I said, when he told me, I felt relieved. I told him I want a divorce and he actually had the audacity to start defending himself, saying it was partly my fault! Now I might not have been the easiest person to live with, but I didn't go and sleep with someone else. But you know what, I actually felt elated this morning. I really do think it's the right decision. I'm just emotional, that's all. About the change. I'm not sure how or what to say to the girls."

We changed the subject for a while. Our lunch came and went, and we chat about work and her parents and the children. I left her with a hug and a promise to keep in touch.

Zach

"The truth is," Aaron said after his second beer, "I wasn't ready to settle down, when we got married. I wasn't ready…"

I sighed.

"Aaron, you can be so selfish!"

"I know," he said, shrugging.

My cell rang. It was Amy.

"I just had lunch with Mel," she told me, sounding sad.

"I'm here with Aaron now."

"Okay, I'll let you go. Speak to you later."

"Hold on-" I said, getting up and going into the bedroom. I closed the door behind me and said quietly, "Please, don't let us ever end up like them."

Amy

I smiled. I just expected that we'd be together forever now. That this was it for us.

"We never could," I told him. I meant it at the time.

When I got home from work that evening, Aaron was still there. He looked a mess.

"Can I sleep on the couch tonight?" he asked. "I can't face going back to the house, and I can't move into the new apartment for another two days."

Zach glanced at me and I smiled.

"Of course."

Aaron picked up his phone and wondered into the kitchen area. I heard him telling Mel that he'd stay with us tonight.

"What a day," Zach said, sighing and plonking himself on the sofa.

"It's awful, isn't it?"

"Yes. Very."

"What did Mel say to you?" Aaron asked, coming to join us.

"She just told me what happened, and said she'd like to keep in touch with us."

Aaron nodded.

"I'd like that. I'm hoping we can be friends somehow, when all this calms down."

"Are you sure there's no chance-"

"No. This is it. There's no returning. She had the guts to tell me it was over, and now I need the guts to build a new life."

I patted Aarons hand and offered to make us all something to eat.

"Thank you," he said. "I'm not really hungry."

Zach

I lay in bed that night thinking about my brother, how he'd gone from living with three females, to finding an apartment for one. I tried analysing where they went wrong, when things changed. But it'd happened so slowly I couldn't pinpoint a particular time. Perhaps they were just never in love enough. But how much is enough? They'd been together for years when they got married; surely they knew each other well enough at that point to think they had a good shot at it.

The next morning, Aaron said he had to go home sometime and went off to pack up his things ready to move into his apartment.

"I feel like somebody has died," he said before he left. "Isn't that weird?"

186

"It's your marriage," said Amy. "Your marriage has died."
He nodded his head and gave her a hug.
"Thanks guys."
I shut the door and hugged Amy.
"What a shitty situation," she said, hugging me back.

Chapter Eleven

Amy

The first weekend of March was beautiful, bright and sunny. Zach and I went for a long walk through the park, talking about everything and anything. I think that's what I loved most about our relationship; the talking.

"Spring is almost here," Zach said. "It's good to see the sun again."

"Mmm, it gives you a happy buzz to feel the warmth on your face again."

"What's your favourite spring memory?" I asked him.

Zach

Every April, my grandma and grandpa, my father's parents, used to travel up from Philadelphia for the weekend, and we'd often go out for a picnic.

My grandpa had survived the second world war; he'd only been a child, but as a Jew in Austria, this was quite an achievement. His parents had somehow survived the concentration camp they'd been taken too, but most of their relatives had not. They had nothing left, no money, no home, no friends to speak of. They worked hard for a few years, trying to rebuild their lives, and when my Grandpa was sixteen years old they moved to the US. I remembered his Austrian accent; sometimes it seemed stronger than others and Grandma would have to explain to us what he was telling us as we couldn't quite understand him.

He'd often tell us all about Austria. He'd describe the mountains, telling us they were beautiful, and he'd tell us a bit about Vienna. He said that one day we must go there and see the land of our ancestors, and in particular we must visit the Schönbrunn Palace, where our great Grandfather had worked before the war. He always made it sound like a magical place, and I used to dream of walking over mountains with him, and then seeing a dazzling palace on the horizon where I'd learn about my great Grandfather.

Sometimes, he'd describe being rounded up by the Nazi's, being separated from his parents, and how elated he'd been when they were reunited. He seldom talked about what happened between being rounded up and seeing them again. One day Aaron asked him.

"Grandpa, where did the Nazi's take you?"

"Oh you don't want to know about that. It was very boring."

I have no doubt that it was anything from boring. My father told us after his funeral that my great-grandfather was lucky to survive at all, he'd been days from death of starvation when they found him.

Grandma was also an exceptional lady. She was bought up by a very strict Catholic mother, who she defied when she married a Jewish man. They were very close, holding hands wherever they went, and never arguing. My father said he'd never seen them cross words.

They'd always prepare the picnic, including my grandma's famous fruit cake. We'd sit on a big red checked blanket, and Mom would hand out juice boxes. Sometimes after eating, Grandpa and Aaron would play ball, and Grandma would tell us about her knitting group.

It was just a great family tradition, every year. My grandpa died a few years earlier and Grandma was getting too frail to travel. She was in a home now, and the last time we'd visited, she couldn't remember who any of us were.

"What a great memory. Nice to have a family tradition like that," Amy said, smiling.

"Yes," I said, feeling guilty as I always did when thinking about Grandma. I realised I should go and visit her again soon.

"You miss your grandpa?"

"Yes. But at least he's not here to see me eating bacon. He'd turn in his grave if he knew."

"Sounds like he was a very interesting man."

"We should put Austria on our list," I said.

"Good idea."

"What about you? What's your favourite spring memory?" I asked Amy.

Amy

When we were fourteen, Ed and I decided to run away from home. It was about three months after we had found out that Jack wasn't our real father. I was arguing with Mum a lot, and avoiding Jack somewhat. Ed had just gone into some sort of weird self-protect mode that I'm not sure he has ever come out of. Libby was younger and naïve, and her dad had stuck around, where ours didn't, so we kind of felt she was an outsider.

"I'm leaving," Ed said to me. I'd just had a big screaming match with my mother, where I'd fallen into the typical teenager response of "I hate you" before slamming my bedroom door.

"What are you talking about?"

"I'm fed up with all this. I think we should find our real father."

"How on earth are we going to do that? She won't even tell us his name."

"I don't know. We'll go to America and ask every man there if he's ever met her and, though it might take years, eventually we will meet him."

"What if he's a horrible person?"

"I bet he's not."

I thought for a moment.

"What if he's someone famous, like Bruce Willis, or Mel Gibson?"

"You wish. You can't tell mum where I've gone."

"You're such an idiot. There are about three hundred million people in America. You think you can just wander around for years, speaking to every single man you see?"

Ed gazed into the distance while he thought this through.

"Well, I can't stay here."

"You haven't got any money, anyway."

"I still can't stay here."

"Me either."

"I've got twenty pounds birthday money left. What've you got?"

I found my purse. I had ten.

"That's enough to go to the zoo for the day."

"The zoo? What are you on?"

"If we go to the zoo, they'll never find us. We can find somewhere to hide and stay overnight. It'll send Mum into a panic, and it'll be enough to scare her. Maybe then she'll give you a break, and we could even threaten to do it again if she doesn't tell us our real dad's name."

It all sounded a little crazy, but I loved going to the zoo, and making my mum worry seemed like a good idea.

"When are we going to go?"

"The second day of spring."

"When is that?"

"After the first warm, sunny day of the year, we go the next day. That way it won't be too cold overnight."

This seemed a good an idea as any; we needed it to be reasonably warm after all.

So, the day after the first sunny day of the year, instead of getting a bus to school, we got a bus in the opposite direction

191

and went to Whipsnade, a zoo not far from home. Ed and I wandered around, checking out the various animals. The lions were my favourite. He liked the elephants. We had just enough money to get some lunch. It was a bright, sunny day, very warm for April, and we both caught the sun on our faces.

It was close to closing time when I said we'd better get going.

"We're going to hide and stay here, remember?"

"We can't do that."

"Why not?"

"They'll really, really worry then."

"So what? We don't have the bus fare home anyway."

I hadn't thought of that. It was almost twenty miles away so there was no chance of us walking, either. So, we found a little enclosure. Ed pulled a brown blanket out from his backpack and we pulled it over us. It was growing dark and we figured no one would spot us. Looking back, we must've been crazy.

"I'm starving," I whispered after about ten minutes under the blanket.

"Me too."

Suddenly someone whisked the blanket up from over us. A man in a green uniform towered above us. Within ten minutes, Jack was on his way to pick us up.

Mum was livid. She shouted, she said we were selfish and didn't have any idea how much worry we'd put her through. Even Ed didn't look impressed with himself. The school had called Mum about 11am to find out where we were and they'd been all over Milton Keynes looking for us ever since. We were grounded for two weeks and all pocket money was suspended until further notice.

"I'm still glad we did it," Ed whispered to me a few days later.

"Me too."

I told this story to Zach, who'd been smiling throughout.

"You rebel."

"I know. I think it was the one really disobedient thing I

did."

"Aaron run away once."

"Oh yeah?"

"He turned up a few hours later, hiding up a tree a few blocks down."

"Why did he run away?"

"Because Mom said he needed a haircut. He was frightened, I guess."

We laughed.

Zach

"Hi girls," I said as Sophia and Lucy ran past me, into the apartment, asking where Alvin was.

"He's in the spare room, on the window ledge," I told them.

Aaron looked tired.

"You okay?" I said as he came in.

"Yes. No. I don't know." He sat down on the sofa and put his head in his hands.

Amy had already made coffee and passed him a cup.

"I hate this," he said, gesturing towards the girls who were stroking Alvin in the spare room.

"I'm a part-time dad. This is the first time I've seen them in a week."

"It will get easier," Amy said, although I wondered if she really meant it.

"I miss Mel, too. I'm such a jerk."

"Do you really miss her, or do you just hate being alone?" Amy seemed better equipped to deal with this and I wondered if I could just slip off and play with the girls.

"I hate being alone. I don't miss the fighting, of course, but I miss having someone there to talk to."

"Well, you either give it another go, or you move on. You'll meet someone eventually," I said, feeling pleased I'd finally given out some advice.

193

"Shall I take the girls to the playground. You guys could talk?" Amy said, getting up.

Within a few minutes we were alone and I watched Aaron fall apart the minute the girls were gone. I'd never seen a sensitive side to him, never seen him cry – or at least since I was about eight.

"I just didn't think life would be like this, you know?"

"I know."

"You think, I'll find a girl, settle down, have some kids. I didn't realise it'd be so...hard."

"You bought this on yourself though. You must see that. You're lazy and selfish and trying to live this bachelor life when you're not a bachelor anymore."

"I know. I've realised this. But it's too late."

"Do you love Mel?"

"No. That's the one thing I am pretty sure of. But is love that important? Isn't it all about friendship in the end?"

"That sounds like Mom talking."

"Well, it is, actually."

"Is she a friend? It didn't seem like it towards the end."

"No, I guess not. Ironically, we're getting on quite well now, but I guess that's because we're only discussing the girls. There's no complaining about me working late, or stopping me from watching the game, or nagging me to fix something around the house."

He took a deep breath and then a mouthful of coffee.

"I'm sorry, man. I didn't want to fall apart on you like that."

"No problem. That's what little brother's are for."

Alvin sauntered up and Aaron petted him.

Amy

"Did you know that Mommy and Daddy don't live together anymore?" Sophia asked as Lucy ran ahead and onto the slide.

"Yes. How do you feel about that?"

194

"Well, at first I was sad. But now, I think it's better. They were fighting lots. This way, maybe they will be happier."

"That's very mature Sophia."

"What does mature mean?"

"Grown-up."

She smiled and pushed her chest out slightly with pride.

"You know, my mum and dad don't live together either."

"Really? Do you still see your dad?"

"Yes. All the time."

Okay, so I know I didn't when I was a child, but I'm not going to say that to a little girl whose dad had only just moved out.

Sophia ran off and joined Lucy, who was now on the swings. I went over to push.

Zach

The next day, Mel came over after work. Amy and I had admitted to each other that it felt a little strange and awkward, but we were keen to maintain contact if possible and so Amy had invited her over for a drink.

"How're you doing?" asked Amy as Mel settled down with her mug of camomile tea.

"I'm good, thank you. Things just seem calmer, you know? Now that we've come to this agreement, and there's no more fighting."

"The girls seemed quite happy when we saw them yesterday."

"That's great. I'm so glad you guys could see that. Aaron has done nothing but worry about them, but I think they are handling it well. I told him, plenty of parents get divorced, and I'm sure staying together and fighting all the time would have messed them up more."

We nodded our heads in agreement.

"I should probably tell you," she said, "I'm seeing someone. Only just, but we went on our first date yesterday. I'm not in a

195

hurry to rush into another relationship, it's very casual."

I had no idea how to react to this, it'd only been a few weeks. I gave Amy a look to make sure she knew she would have to respond.

"Okay, well I guess you need to get out there and have some fun, right?" Amy said.

Amy

"Exactly," said Mel. "I just don't know whether to mention it to Aaron, that I'm dating again. Do you think he'd handle it okay?"

Zach hesitated.

"I'm not sure," he said. "It does seem quite soon."

"I know, and like I say, I'm not rushing into anything, I just had one date. I'd just hate to see him out while I am with someone, and he be shocked and freak out."

"Zach will tell him," I said, watching Zach's face turn pale.

"Really?"

"I think that's a bad idea," said Zach.

"No listen," I said, "he'll handle it better coming from you."

"If you don't mind Zach, I would rather avoid another argument."

"I'll think about it."

We talked about the girls, about Mel's job and our work, and she made us promise to keep in touch. As soon as she left Zach pounced on me.

"Why do I have to tell Aaron that she's dating?"

"I just thought it'd be easier for you, than Mel."

I made him call Aaron, to get it out of the way. I heard him say something about "she's moving on, and you need to as well."

I felt bad, then and wished I hadn't said anything or interfered. I told Zach as much when he came back in the room.

"Sorry," I said, pulling my cutest face.

"I forgive you," he said, "but only because you're too cute."

Zach

Amy's cuteness allowed her to get out of lots of things, like cleaning dishes and doing laundry.

Amy

"Hi Libby," I said, getting comfortable on the sofa and turning the TV down.

"Amy?"

"Yes!"

"Oh wow. How are you?"

"I'm good thanks, how are you?"

"Great. Getting excited now."

"I bet you are."

"You're still coming, right?"

"Yes of course, and I'm bringing my boyfriend."

"Okay, cool. Is he American?"

"Yes."

"What's his name?"

"Zach."

"Last name?"

"Why?"

"For the place settings."

"Rosenberg. And it's Zach with an H."

"Right, got it. Thank you. So what's life like in Boston?"

"It's good, work is crazy busy but I enjoy it."

"Tim is coming to Boston just before the wedding actually, but I think you might be on your way here by then."

"I'm looking forward to meeting him. I can't believe you're getting married," I tried to picture her having children and couldn't manage it.

"Me either! Mrs. Libby White. I've been practising my

signature all day today."

"You're not busy at work then?"

"Not really. So would you like to be my bridesmaid?"

I suspected my Mum had put her up to it, but it was nice of her to ask all the same.

"I'd love to. Thank you Libby."

"You will have to match the others, of course. I asked the woman in the shop and she found a stockist for me in Boston. You just have to go in there and give them my name."

"Okay, no problem."

"I'll email you the details. So, I hear you've met your other sister?"

"Yes. She's my dad's daughter. Her name is Jemma."

"What's she like?"

"She's nice. I don't know her that well yet."

"Is she clever, pretty, friendly, what?"

"Yes, all of those things. She's studying to be a doctor." I wondered if she were jealous.

"Well, I'm glad it worked out well with your dad and everything."

"How's Mum?"

"She's okay, working all the time as usual."

"And Dad?"

"He's fine. Look I've got to go but it was nice chatting to you. I'm looking forward to seeing you soon, okay?"

"You too, take care Libby."

"And you, byeeee."

"Bye."

Zach

I was coming out of a flower shop with a large bunch of flowers for Amy when I saw Scarlett's sister, Faith. She caught my eye and smiled.

"Zach, how are you?"

"I'm great, you?"

"Good. Wow, look at these beautiful flowers, who are they for?"

"My girlfriend," I said, feeling very awkward.

"Shame about you and Scarlett," she said, looking away awkwardly.

"Yes, sometimes things don't work out how you expect I guess."

"Well, I think you expected it to end at some point, but Scarlett obviously didn't."

"I didn't intend to hurt her."

"Hmm..."

"I've got to go, nice to see you."

"I'll tell Scarlett you said hello."

"Bloody cheek!" said Amy when I got home, and after she'd whooped over the flowers.

"I know...it's not like I deliberately set out to hurt her, and it's about time they were over it now."

"Seems a bit childish to me." Amy took the flowers and found a vase, which she called a "varse." I still enjoyed looking out for the way we pronounced things differently.

"Did you call Libby?"

"Yes," she said, arranging the flowers, "she said she's looking forward to seeing me soon, and she wants me to be a bridesmaid."

"Well, that's nice, isn't it?"

"I suppose so."

Amy

I was actually quite touched that Libby had asked me, even if it was my mum that put her up to it. I didn't want to admit it though; by allowing everyone to think I didn't care, it was easier to hide my insecurities.

Zach

Towards the end of March my mom called.

"Hi, Mom."

"Hello Zachary."

"I have just been talking to your brother."

"Ah, yes."

"I can't say I'm surprised. You know, I never thought they were good together. And the way he's behaved lately. It's no wonder she got fed up."

"I know." I sighed.

"Still, it's not nice for the girls, is it?"

"No, not at all."

"How's it going with Amy?"

"Great. I'm very happy."

"Good. Aaron tells me she doesn't know about Ellie and-"

I interrupted her.

"No, she doesn't. It doesn't exactly impact my life, and I just haven't found a good time."

"Don't you think she'll be angry with you for keeping it from her? I mean really, it's the sort of thing couples share."

"Yes, I know."

I sighed again. Mom was right. But for some reason, I'd just never bought it up. I hardly ever thought about it, and the longer we were together, the harder it was to mention it.

"I know it's hard. You block it out because it's painful. I do the same thing, to be honest."

"Let's not talk about it anymore, okay?"

"She might be mad, but you really do have to share this, Zach."

"Okay, thanks Mom."

"I'm sorry for moaning at you."

"I know you mean well."

"Just don't want you to throw away the best girl you've ever found over something so silly."

"I got it."

Still, the right time still didn't present itself, and another month passed without Amy any the wiser.

Chapter Twelve

Zach

April. As we drove along, Amy chat about everything and anything. I enjoyed listening to her talk; she always spoke with such passion that she made everything seem interesting. Conversations that morning included those about the present;

"...then Franco came back into the office and said it was all a big mistake, after all that! Would you believe it? So I told Sheryl not to bother."

Those about the past;

"On our eighteenth birthday, my uncle Harry took Ed and I out for drinks. We were both wasted by the end of the evening, and Ed was sick. I've joked ever since that I can handle more alcohol than him, which is so not the case. I was drinking alcopops, he was on heavier stuff."

And those about the future;

"Do you ever think about growing old with me?"

"Yes, all the time."

"Good, me too."

She had been reluctant to do anything for her birthday. She wasn't so thrilled with the prospect of turning thirty. But she had been thrilled when I suggested we go to the zoo. Her passions in life are books, music, and animals. In that order.

Amy

Actually, it's Zach, books, music, and animals. In that order.

Zach

Amy was buzzing when we arrived at the zoo. She couldn't stop smiling, even while we queued to get in. A man was selling candy floss just inside the main gate and I bought her some. We wandered around, hand in hand and I realised something: Amy knew an astonishing amount about animals.

"Deer always seem to be chewing," I observed.

"They are ruminants," she told me, "they have two stomachs. So they swallow their food, and then they bring it up again later to chew it. This means, while chewing, they can keep their heads up, looking out for predators."

"Isn't evolution a wondrous thing?" I said.

"Indeed. They're so cute, aren't they?"

I got the feeling she could stand there forever, watching them.

"Yeah, they are pretty cute."

"I love their spindly legs."

We walked a little further to see the gorillas and she said;

"After chimpanzees, gorillas are our closest living relatives."

"Really? Wow." I looked into the eyes of a gorilla sitting near the edge of the enclosure. It looked kind of sad, but very human-like.

"Yep. They share about ninety-eight per cent of our DNA."

"How do you know this stuff?"

"Sir David Attenborough. He's a wildlife documentary legend."

"I see."

"I love the gorilla's," she said, tilting her head to one side to watch one eating some leaves.

She also loved the zebras, and the tapir, and everything in between.

Amy continued to tell me plenty of facts about the animals we saw, and she took a zillion photos of each and every one. She was happy, and therefore so was I.

"I like watching the people in zoo's as well," she told me as we sat down for lunch. We'd ordered toasted lunchmeat sandwiches and glasses of lemonade.

"Okay, tell me what you see."

"Look around us. There are several different types of people that come to a zoo, and they each have different reasons for being here today."

She'd obviously studied this before.

"Firstly, there are the obvious single dad's. Look, there's one over there."

She pointed subtly at a man with his two children. One, the boy, looked about Lucy's age and was peering at a monkey through the bars. His little girl, only just able to walk by the looks of it, was holding his hand and trying to pull him to the next enclosure.

"It's an ideal place to take the kids out for the day, I guess." Amy smiled.

"Sure, okay I get that," I said, thinking Aaron should bring his girls here sometime.

"What else have you noticed?"

"Well, then there are the people who rarely come to the zoo. They've been dragged along by their kids, or because they feel it's time they had a family day out. That lady we saw at the lion enclosure was one of these people."

I laughed. The woman Amy was referring to had dressed up as if she was going to a party. She wore a lot of jewellery, high heel shoes, a long dress, and smelt very strongly of some designer perfume. Amy had smirked as her son pointed to a lioness and the woman had said "He's big, isn't he?."

"It's a she, actually." Amy had said to the little boy. "The male lions have manes. This one is a lioness."

The boy had grinned at Amy and looked up his mother, who didn't seem impressed.

Amy

"She made me feel underdressed." I said, remembering her Jimmy Choo's and Gucci handbag.

"I think you suit casual trousers and hiking boots much better."

The waitress bought our toasted sandwiches and we each took a bite.

"Go on, next type," Zach said, seeming to enjoy my explanation of the human beings I'd found here as much as the stories I'd told him about the animals.

"Then, of course there are the regulars. Mostly families, the occasional couple or single person. You can tell they are regulars because they know their way around. They never stop to look at signs or the map they give you when you enter. They are genuinely enthusiastic about the animals and you hear them talking about them, sometimes they even remembering seeing those animals as cubs, or whatever."

I looked up from my sandwich and saw Zach watching me, looking at me, smiling. I couldn't help but smile when our eyes met.

"That's you, in that category," he said, taking a mouthful of lemonade.

I smiled. "Finally, you have the photographers. They're easy to spot. Tend to have camera's around their necks, big lenses. They spend ages trying to get the perfect shot."

"There's a photographer over there." Zach nodded towards a guy with a camera, he was sat on a bench, changing his lens. His wife sat beside him, talking about the animals they'd just seen.

"And his wife is a regular. They make a good match."

Zach

"What's your favourite animal?" she asked me.

"Giraffes, actually." I nodded my head towards the next enclosure where I could see two heads walking about.

"Good choice. Why?"

"Well, you know they're just so awesome. Look at them." We looked.

"With their big necks. They're so gentle. Gentle giants, if you will."

She smiled. "I like them too."

"Did you know there's a species of tree called the acacia, which leaves and seeds are eaten by giraffes and other African mammals? They are then carried around, sometimes for miles, before they are deposited in their faeces. So, the giraffes and other animals help to spread the seeds across a wide area. Then of course, those seeds grow into more trees, providing more food."

"Wow. I love that you know all this stuff. That you love animals. It's..."

"It's what?"

"I was going to say cute. But it's more than that. It's adorable."

She kissed me on the cheek and then leaned against the fence, looking up at the "gentle giants."

"I have a book," she said, "on giraffes."

"Cool. I'd like to read it."

She turned to take a photo on her cell phone of a baby giraffe.

"So cute!" she said, turning to me and smiling. Her hair was shining in the low sun and her eyes were bright and excited.

"I've got another birthday surprise for you," I told her.

"As if this and the new time piece isn't enough," she said, glancing at the shiny new watch I'd given her that morning.

"We're going to the Grand Canyon, and Las Vegas."

"Oh wow. Are you serious?" She squealed with delight.

"Of course!"

"That's amazing! Thank you!" She leapt onto me, giving me a big hug.

"When?"

"The third of May."

"I thought we'd have to wait until after Libby's wedding?"

"I decided I'd treat us a little earlier."

"Oh my goodness. Thank you so much!"

We spent the rest of the day at the zoo, I watched Amy be transformed into a little girl again, excited to see the animals and eager to share her enthusiasm with me. I got wrapped up in it, and found myself equally as interested.

We got back to Amy's apartment about six, exhausted. She wanted to stop by and collect any post. She had a handful of birthday cards.

"You know, you could just give people our address."

"I know, I just haven't gotten around to it."

I had planned to take her out someplace nice for dinner but she asked if we could get a takeout instead, and save our legs. I agreed and we ordered some Chinese food to be delivered.

Amy started to play her messages, and came and sat down with me on the couch.

I heard a British voice say "Happy Birthday Amy!"

"That's my brother, I should have called him, really."

"Why?"

"Well, it's his birthday too."

"Of course."

"Oh and that's my aunt..." we listened to the next message.

"And that's Taryn, of course," she commented as different voices came on.

Then one female voice:

"Amy, it's Mum. Happy thirtieth sweetheart. We all miss you."

Amy looked at me sadly, and then down at her hands.

"I hope you're having a good day, whatever you are doing. Maybe you're out with that nice man you told me you've been dating."

Nice man? Dating? Was that all she'd told them about me? That we were dating? We lived together, we hadn't spent a night apart for months and I was just a "nice guy." She didn't even appear to know my name. I was a little hurt.

"Happy birthday darling. Ring me back soon. All our love."

The machine clicked off. Amy looked a little sad.

"You miss them huh?" I asked, attempting to push my slight annoyance to one side.

"Yes. Sometimes. But you know, we're not close like your family."

"Hence why you haven't really told them about me?"

"What makes you think that?"

"What she said: 'that nice man,' she didn't use my name or sound like she knew how serious we are."

She looked nervous for a moment, but then relaxed.

"I just didn't want to tell them over the phone. Like I said, we're not that close, and Mum can be quick to judge situations without knowing the facts. She'd give me a lecture and I'd rather she see for herself how happy we are. So..."

"It's not a big deal," I told her, although I still felt hurt.

"Let's toast. To you, and your thirtieth birthday."

"To us, thank you for an amazing birthday," she said, kissing me on the cheek as we clinked glasses.

Amy

I called Ed the following day.

"Happy belated birthday, thirty year old."

"Thanks Sis, you too. Do anything nice?"

"Went to the zoo. You?"

"Cool. I went out for a meal and drinks with some friends. You know what; I think that was the first of our birthdays where we didn't see each other."

"What about our twentieths? You went to Ibiza with your mates."

"Oh yeah. But we spoke on the phone. We didn't speak yesterday."

"True. Sorry, I should have called."

"No problem, not a big deal, just an observation."

I looked through my birthday cards, and noticed I didn't have one from Libby. I know, I keep stating how we're not close and I hadn't exactly been calling her every day, in fact we'd only spoken a handful of times since I'd been in Boston. But still, I'm her sister. I felt I deserved a card. So I wrote to her.

To: Elizabeth Starling
From: Amy Starling
Subject: Hiya

Hi Libby,
Not long to the wedding now, are you getting excited? We are arrive exactly one week before your big day. What's new with you? I turned thirty yesterday. Getting old now, I am. Ha! Going to get my dress this week.
Speak soon. Love, Amy x

She replied the day before I got my dress.

To: Amy Starling
From: Elizabeth Starling
Subject: Dress

Hello sis!
Oh my god, I didn't send a card! Sorry about that! You know what it's like, busy, busy, busy! I'll make it up to you. I'll buy you a present for when you are here! So, on to more important issues: did you buy the dress I told you to? If so, send pics.
Libby x x

I couldn't be bothered to reply again. I just wanted her to acknowledge that she'd forgotten my birthday which she was obviously happy to do.

Harriet came with me to collect the dress from a bridal chain I'd never heard of. Apparently they had stores all over the world. The dress Libby had picked out was pale yellow-ish gold, strapless and long. It was lovely but not really my sort of thing.

"You look stunning!" Harriet told me as I came out of the dressing room.

"Beautiful!" said the assistant as she started pinning me around the back, pulling it closer around my waist and breasts. "We'll just alter it a little, make it fit better."

"I'm not sure pale yellow is my colour." I told Harriet on our way home.

"You looked amazing. Stop worrying."

"So, Zach is taking me to Las Vegas and the Grand Canyon!" I said.

"Ooh really? How exciting."

"I know, I can't wait."

"He's so sweet."

Zach

Amy smiled at me as we walked down the street, holding hands. I glanced at the time, and realised we were a few minutes late. I quickened our pace.

"What's the hurry?" she said, struggling to keep up.

"I booked a table," I told her. As we reached the restaurant, I peeked inside and saw that Yvonne, Andy and Jemma were already waiting for us.

I opened the door and they stood up to greet us.

"Surprise," I whispered in her ear.

"Happy birthday for last week," Yvonne said, getting up to hug Amy and then me.

"Happy birthday Sis!" Jemma excitedly hugged her tight.

Andy hugged Amy and whispered something in her ear. She smiled and wiped a tear away. We sat and begun a long conversation about how we'd planned this evening without Amy realising. It'd been Yvonne's idea.

Andy had already ordered a bottle of champagne, which he poured out for each of us.

"A toast," he said, raising his glass, "to Amy. Happy birthday sweetheart."

Amy wiped away another tear as we all clinked glasses. I squeezed her hand.

Amy

I was completely overwhelmed. I felt more loved sitting there with my father and Yvonne and Jemma than I'd ever felt before in my life. I knew my mum loved me, in her way, but Andy showed his love. He was encouraging and inspiring and full of hugs and warmth. And then there was Zach by my side, quite literally my other half now. Between the two of them, they made me feel so special.

We drank champagne, we laughed and joked, we ate amazing food and then Jemma gave me a beautiful bracelet, and then Andy passed me a little box which contained a matching necklace and earrings.

"Thank you all so much," I whispered, completely overwhelmed.

Later that night, in bed next to Zach, after an amazing evening with my family, and after amazing drunken birthday sex, Zach asked me what Andy had whispered into my ear to make me shed that first tear.

"He said happy birthday, my dear. I love you and I'm so proud." I wiped away another tear.

"My mum has never said that to me. That she's proud of me."

"But she is," Zach said, squeezing my arm. "She just doesn't show it. You should call her. Just because she doesn't show her love in the same way, doesn't mean you should block her out."

I knew he was right. I told him I'd call her soon.

Zach

I was building a website for a new music store in town. They'd sent me a variety of catalogue images including guitars, flutes, pianos, cellos, drum kits, and a whole host of instruments I didn't even recognise. They sold sheet music, too. I'd always wanted to learn to play something and had spent an inordinate amount of time browsing through the stuff they'd sent me, wondering what might be a good instrument to take up. I wasn't that keen on anything except for the piano, which seemed especially expensive.

Matt called just as I was about to get on with some real work.

"I play air guitar real good," he told me after I explained what I was doing. I laughed.

"How's it going with Harriet?"

"Good. I like her a lot. Thanks for setting that up."

"No problem. You know, it was Amy's idea, really."

"It's always the woman's idea."

"I guess."

"She's got this weird thing though, and I wanted to ask you about it."

"Right," I said, not sure where this was going. "What is it?"

"Have you ever been in bed with a woman, and-"

"Hold on," I said, realising this could be a long conversation.

I got some yoghurt out of the fridge and settled down on my sofa.

"Right, go on."

"Okay. So you're in bed with a woman, you know, fooling around..."

"Yes..."

"And then she sticks her finger, you know, there..."

I laughed.

"Yeah, I quite like that."

"Phew, so it's normal."

"Yup."

"Right. And what about when she wants to tie you up?"

"Well... That's not really that unusual either," I hesitated before continuing. I wasn't sure where this was going but discussing my sex life with Matt wasn't high on my list of good conversation topics.

"Harriet has...well, tools, and costumes, and handcuffs, and a whip."

I tried not to laugh.

"Really?" She seemed so...conservative.

"Do you think that's normal?"

"Who cares about normal? Did you enjoy it?"

"Well...yes."

I laughed again, nearly spilling yoghurt all down me.

"Then relax, Matt. Have fun."

Amy

Zach told me about Matt's call the following Saturday morning.

"I'll never think of Harriet in quite the same way again."

"You can't tell her I told you."

"Of course not. Good for her, anyway. People need to be able to have fun."

I made a mental note to make a little fun of our own at my next opportunity.

"So, are you going to call your mom?" Zach asked. He'd mentioned this every day since we heard my birthday message.

I picked up the phone and went to lie on the sofa. Before she'd even answered, Alvin was walking all over me, finally settling on my lap and purring.

"Hi Mum."

"Amy, how are you?"

"Great, thank you."

Zach settled down on the armchair with a magazine.

"Did you have a nice birthday?"

"Yes, I went out to the zoo with Zach."

He smiled at me, pleased I'd mentioned his name.

"What's he like, then, this Zach?"

"He's sitting right here, I can't really talk about him," I laughed.

"Don't mind me!" Zach said.

"I like his voice, he sounds very American," said Mum.

"Well, he is American."

"Of course." I wondered if she was thinking about my dad.

"So how are you?"

"I'm alright. So the zoo you say? I thought you might have grown out of that by now."

"Nope. Still love the zoo."

I hated the way she always made me feel like I was still a child.

"Well, I'm glad you had a good day. We've been busy with all of Libby's wedding plans, as you can imagine."

"So I hear. Ed emailed me."

"Oh really? He has a nice new girlfriend. Her name is Polly. Let's see if he can keep hold of this one."

"How's Jack?"

"He's fine. How's the weather?"

"It's okay, how's it there?"

"Not bad. Well, I'd better not keep you, I'm sure this is very expensive."

"Okay Mum, speak to you soon."

"Bye dear."

This was a typical conversation with my mum.

"Is that it?" asked Zach, perplexed.

"Yes."

"I talk to my mom for longer than that, and I see her every couple of weeks. You speak to Yvonne for longer than that."

214

"Well, I keep telling you..."

"You're not close, yes, I know. Still, it's a shame, that's all."

"Maybe." I said, picking up my book from the floor and attempting to read it while Alvin rubbed his head on the spine.

Zach

Amy's biggest pet peeve is the sound of people eating. She gets really annoyed, even if someone drinks loudly. She'd mentioned this a few times about people at work, that she couldn't stand the sound of their "munching" as she called it.

So as I sat there, munching on tortilla chips and slurping my coffee, I knew it wouldn't be long before she put her book down, pushed Alvin off her lap and got up to put some music on.

"Chip?" I asked her, holding out the bag.

"No thanks."

"You like my crunching?"

She stuck out her tongue.

"I hate it that you know me so well."

I watched her collect Alvin and her book and settle back down to read some more. The phone rang. It was still beside Amy, who said;

"Oh hi, Yvonne."

She spoke to her for over half an hour.

Amy

I watched Jemma painting my toenails. She was biting her tongue a little in concentration.

"Now this," she said, "is real sister bonding."

I laughed. Libby and I used to do this for each other all the time when we were younger. Spending time with Jemma had been difficult, she was so busy all the time. But we'd slowly been getting to know each other. She was always upbeat, cheerful and

215

happy to see me. I could imagine she had an excellent 'bedside manner' with her patients. When our toes were dry we sat talking for a while, and then the time came and I said "you ready?"

"Yes," she said, taking a deep breath. "I'm not sure why I'm nervous."

We called Zach, who had been working in his office. He set up my laptop and webcam, and we called Ed.

It seemed funny to see his face appear, albeit a little fuzzy. He waved.

"Hello Ed," I said, waving back.

"Hey Ed," said Jemma, waving.

"This is Jemma," I said, grinning and seeing the realisation dawn on his face.

We'd planned this call a few days earlier but he'd had no idea Jemma was joining in. He looked a little taken aback and then he leant forward, studying the screen.

"Wow, hello Jemma!"

I left them alone to talk, and went to make some coffee. I heard Jemma laughing and asking him questions. I wasn't sure he'd be grateful for the surprise, but Jemma was so keen and I knew she'd rub off on him, like she had on me. After she'd gone, I apologised.

"No, it was good. Thank you. You're right, she looks like us," he said, smiling.

"I know. You can do this with Andy, too, if you wanted."

"I want to save Andy for face to face. I'm going to look into coming to visit, later in the year, when I can get some time off work."

"Okay, well, email me soon and I guess I'll see you for Libby's wedding!"

"I'll pick you up at the airport," he said, waving goodbye.

Chapter Thirteen

Zach

"How much stuff do you need to take?" I asked as Amy arrived with a huge suitcase she'd bought over from her apartment.

"Well, I figure I'll want nicer clothes to wear in Vegas, and more practical clothes for the Grand Canyon."

"I guess that's true."

She started putting shoes in the case; at least three pairs went in. I decided not to argue and settled down to read a magazine. Alvin came and curled up on my lap.

Amy popped her head out of the bedroom door.

"I'm so excited!" she said, jumping up and down like a little kid.

"Good," I told her. She carried on packing.

Amy

"Here you go," said Harriet, handing me a large cup of coffee.

"Thanks." I said, burning my tongue on the first sip.

"So are you excited?"

"Yes. Very."

"How's it going with Matt?"

"Good. We're not rushing into anything but I like him a lot and I think he likes me, too."

I held out a key.

"Are you sure you don't mind feeding Alvin while we're

away?"

"Of course not, I'd love to actually." She took the key and put it on the table in front of her.

"Well, remember," she said, "What happens in Vegas, stays in Vegas!"

Zach

I packed about twenty-five per cent of the volume Amy did, zipped up our gigantic case, hauled it off the bed and wheeled it to the front door.

My mobile started vibrating. It was my mother.

"Hi, Mom."

"Hello Zachary."

"We're just getting ready to go to the airport so I can't really speak for long."

"Okay, well have an amazing time."

"Thanks Mom."

"Did you tell Amy yet?"

Amy walked back in.

"Not yet. I gotta go."

Amy

"There's the Stratosphere!" I said, pointing out of the window as we came into land in Las Vegas.

"Wow, look at all those casinos!" Zach said, leaning across me to get a better look.

"I recognise so many of them from different movies."

Soon, we were loading our luggage into a cab and on our way to the Mirage. As the cab pulled up outside, I spotted the replica Eiffel Tower outside the Paris hotel.

"What a bizarre but kind of wonderful place this is," I said, as we checked in.

To get to the elevator, we had to walk across the casino floor.

Despite it being only 5pm, there were plenty of people playing on the slot machines. It was a huge space. We walked past a few of the tables and stopped to check them out.

"It feels like a movie set," Zach said as we reached the elevator.

Zach

We had a partial view of the strip from our hotel window, we could just about see the Eiffel Tower and Caesars Palace.

"I love this room! This is wonderful, thank you!" Amy said, bouncing on the bed. I went over and pushed her down on it, started kissing her neck.

After our "Vegas love making" as Amy called it, we got dressed and went down to the Mirage buffet and helped ourselves to a generous plate of food, plus beer for me and wine for Amy.

"What do you want to do now?" I asked.

"I want to see the Bellagio Fountain."

Amy

I liked Vegas much more than I expected to. There was a certain buzz and atmosphere about the place, and what I'd usually deem tacky had a hint of class. We saw two Elvis impersonators just between the Mirage and the Bellagio, which is only a short walk.

I'd read in the guide book on the way over that the Bellagio fountain performance happened every fifteen minutes during the evenings and that it was a spectacular thing to behold. The writer was right. The music started, the lights came on, and the water danced in front of us. Zach and I stood there in the crowd, silently taking it in.

"Wow," said Zach.

"It's amazing." I said, after a short round of applause.

"Can we stay and watch the next one in another fifteen minutes?"

So, we did. We watched three in total. It was quite romantic, standing there in the warm Las Vegas evening, I leant against the railing and Zach stood behind me with both arms either side of me, his chin resting on my shoulder. We were completely mesmerised. I could have stayed and watched another performance but Zach said;

"Right, shall we have a look around?"

Zach

We wandered into a few different casinos; the Bellagio, Caesar's Palace, and the Venetian. We had a few goes on the slot machines and watched a few of the table games.

"I like Vegas," Amy said when we eventually collapsed back in our hotel room.

"Me too."

The next day, we rented a car and drove to the south rim of the Grand Canyon. Of course, if I'd done my research, I'd have discovered that it's almost six hours worth of driving. Luckily, Amy had bought her iPod so we had some good music to listen to.

"This better be more than a big hole in the ground!" Amy said, as we pulled into the hotel car park.

Amy

After checking in at the hotel, we took the car into the National Park. The ranger gave us a map, showing us where various view points were. We decided to just drive along and stop where we felt seemed a good spot.

We drove through a wooded area, and eventually came to a clearing and pulled up in a parking spot.

We both froze in amazement at the sight before us. The

Grand Canyon. I'd always wanted to see it, and now I was here I almost broke down into tears. It was phenomenal. I cannot put the scope of it into words.

"This is just... Incredible!" I said, leaning against the barrier and taking in the view. Zach stood beside me, and we just looked out at the view for a long time, in silence, listening to others conversations as they passed us by. I wished the moment could last forever. I leaned against Zach.

"Awesome, isn't it?" he whispered. I nodded. Slowly, dragging ourselves away, we went back to the car and drove to other various view points, each one was different and gave us a unique view, each time silencing us with the majesty and size of the whole thing. I read out loud from the leaflet that the Grand Canyon was two hundred and seventy-seven miles wide from east to west.

"Can you imagine someone coming here, hundreds of years ago?" Zach said.

"They wouldn't have known how wide it was, they'd have just seen this huge canyon, and figured they'd walk around it – but what a lot of walking they'd have had to do."

I couldn't even begin to imagine. I tried to count how many colours I could see in the layers of rocks, but gave up. At one point we could see the Colorado river, sweeping through, carving out the canyon. It didn't seem possible that the river could have made this place.

We'd decided to stop at a particular point called Hopi. We settled down on some rocks to watch the sunset. There were a handful of photographers around us, and we all watched the amazing shades of orange and red glow golden as the sun set. The photographers slowly moved off, leaving only Zach and I in the evening dusk.

We were sitting on a ledge, crossed legged, looking out. I leant my head against this shoulder.

"Thank you for bringing me here."

"Marry me," he whispered in my ear.

221

My head spun round to look up at him, elated, surprised and happy at the same time.

"Really?"

"Really. You know I love you. Marry me."

I didn't even have to think about it.

"Yes. Of course I will. And I love you too. Yes!"

We kissed. He wrapped his arms around me and I closed my eyes. It didn't matter where we were, that we were in this incredible place with this amazing view. I felt like we were the only two people on Earth.

After a few minutes, we were both still grinning and I turned back to face the view.

"I'm sorry I don't have a ring or anything," he said, "I didn't plan to ask you today. It just felt like the right moment."

"Don't be silly."

"Let's get one when we're back in Vegas."

The thought hit me at once. Why not get married in Vegas? I didn't say the words but wondered if he'd thought them too. I didn't want to wait, I wanted to be married. I wanted to declare our love to the world. What use is a big fancy wedding? I wanted to be married to him as soon as possible.

Suddenly the amazement of the Grand Canyon wasn't important anymore. I had a more exciting thought on my mind. I wanted to be Zach's wife. Mrs. Rosenberg. Amy Rosenberg.

Zach

I was so psyched as we returned to our hotel room, Amy closed the door and we were all over each other in some sort of romantic, first-sex-as-an-engaged-couple frenzy.

The next day we hiked along the Hermits Rest trail, which is seven miles from the car park, running west along the south rim of the canyon. Each turn of the footpath led to yet another amazing view. We took a lot of photos, and chat to a few other tourists, including a couple from England, who we saw again later at a restaurant near our hotel.

"Do you want to join us?" I offered.

"Thank you! I'm Dan, and this is my wife, Rebecca."

We shook hands.

"Zach," I said, "and this is my fiancée, Amy."

She grinned as I introduced her. Amy and Rebecca fell into easy conversation about where in England they were from, and so on.

"So what brings you to the Grand Canyon?" I asked Dan.

"Well, we decided to try and see all the wonder's of the World. This was the first on our list. Hoping to go to Niagara Falls next year. What about you two?"

"Wow. It was a birthday treat for Amy, she turned thirty last month."

"How wonderful. Where are you from?"

"Boston. Amy is from Milton Keynes."

"Oh yes, I know it, my sister lives there."

"How long have you two been engaged?" Rebecca asked.

"About twenty four hours!" Amy said, still buzzing with excitement.

"Wow, well we need champagne!" Dan called a waiter.

"Congratulations!" said Rebecca.

Amy

Several glasses of champagne later we said goodnight to a giggly Rebecca and a slightly staggering Dan, having exchanged numbers and promising to invite them to our wedding.

"We might see you in Vegas," Rebecca told us. "But if not – at the wedding!" She giggled and turned away.

"I love it here!" I said to Zach as we climbed into bed.

The next morning we had the six hour journey back to Vegas, but between talking about who we'd tell first, what sort of ring I might like, the prospect of seeing the Bellagio fountain again, and remembering the fun we'd had the night before, it passed rather quickly.

Zach

It was gone six pm by the time we dropped the rental car off and got back to the Mirage. I wanted to find the most beautiful ring, and place it on Amy's finger. Then I wanted do a little gambling, just for fun.

Half an hour later, we were out walking down the strip.

"What do you think our wedding will be like?" Amy asked

"I'm not sure. However you want it." I thought she might like to get married in England.

"Would you want a Jewish ceremony?"

"I don't know. I'm not bothered."

"So we could plan any sort of wedding, then," she said, quite quietly.

"Yes. How about something in England?"

She didn't reply. I couldn't tell what she was thinking.

"How about Vegas?" she said, after a couple of minutes.

"What?" I stopped walking and stared at her.

"Are you suggesting we get married tonight?"

She smiled and shrugged her shoulders. "Why not?! Why wait?"

"Wow." I hesitated for a moment, not because I wasn't sure but because it was such a big momentous occasion and I couldn't believe it was quite happening.

"Okay," I said, taking her hand, "Let's do it!"

"Woo-hoo!" She screamed. "We're getting married!"

"Let's find out where the nearest chapel is, and do it proper tacky Vegas style."

My heart was pounding. But I knew it was the right move. We started running to the nearest cab rank, Amy was laughing and her eyes were bright.

Amy

We were standing beneath a bright neon sign flashing the words Wedding Chapel.

"You are sure you want to do this?" Zach said, as we stood outside, looking up at the sign.

"I've never been surer about anything. Are you sure?"

"You bet. But I just want to check. You don't want the big white dress, three hundred guests, the big party?"

"No. I don't. I don't want to have to think about all that. I just want to be married."

"Me too."

"However-" I looked down at my dirty jeans and felt the dampness in my armpits from our day driving through the desert.

"I suppose I wouldn't mind getting showered and changed. Wearing a nice dress. If we get married tomorrow, I could go out and buy something first."

He grinned at me. I grinned back. I could hardly believe we were doing this. Forty-eight hours earlier I'd never have guessed it could happen. Twelve months ago, I'd never have believed I would be married so soon. I wasn't even sure then that I would ever get married.

"Okay, let's come back here tomorrow."

"Let's eat," I said, practically running across the street to a restaurant I'd seen on our way in. We ate pizza, drank wine, and I'd never felt so ecstatically happy in my entire life. We went back to our hotel, gambled a little, and then went up to bed and had the most passionate and incredible sex of my life.

The next morning I woke up, remembered our plan for the day and grinned. I wrapped the white hotel robe around me and stood up to admire the view from the window. This time we were a few stories higher and could see even more of the strip. The sun was rising. Vegas looked very different in the day time to the night. It was almost like a different place. Zach appeared and put his arm around me.

"Good morning, future wife," he said, kissing my neck. It felt good. He slipped the robe off of my shoulder and starting kissing my cold flesh.

"Come back to bed," he said, pulling me back into the room and throwing me on to the bed.

An hour later, I lay in a post-orgasm trance, when I remembered that I didn't really want to get married in my jeans. I jumped out from the bed, and told Zach I was going shopping for something to wear. He persuaded me to wait and have breakfast, which we ordered from room service before getting showered and dressed.

"Shall I meet you at the chapel in a few hours?"

"Okay," he shrugged "but you'll look beautiful whatever you wear."

"Thank you. I'll see you there at 1pm. How does that sound?"

"Perfect."

Zach

I let Amy leave and then decided to do a little shopping of my own. I'd noticed a jewellery store nearby so I went there and had a look around.

I chose quickly. A delicate platinum ring with a single solitaire diamond, and then two platinum wedding bands. I just hoped it'd fit her.

Then I found a store with some men's clothes and bought some smart pants and a new shirt. It wasn't quite the tux I'd imagined wearing on my wedding day, but it looked pretty good on me, even if I say so myself.

As I walked down the strip, I tried to imagine telling everyone; Amy is my wife! We're married! I thought about her finally moving the last of her stuff into my place. About finding a house together. Growing old together. Children and trips to the UK, and a whole life was planned out before me. For once in my life, it didn't scare me one little bit.

Then I had an idea. I called Rebecca and Dan. They answered and said they were staying at the New York, New York.

"You still want to come to our wedding?" I asked.

Amy

I wandered around the Forum Shops at Caesar's Palace and tried a few different dresses on before going back and buying the first one I'd seen.

"You look beautiful," said the sales assistant, watching me turning around in the mirror.

"Thank you," I said. "This is my wedding dress."

I still had about ten minutes to spare, so I called Harriet. She didn't answer. I was bursting at the seams to tell someone; but it'd have to wait.

Zach

I saw Amy arrive at the chapel before I did. She looked stunning. She'd bought a pale green (she later told me it was "teal") dress, which had tiny little straps at her beautiful shoulders, and fell down to her ankles, showing off her curvaceous figure. Her hair was falling all around her, and she smiled at me, a happy, blissful smile which told me she loved me, without saying a word.

"Wow, Amy you look stunning."

"Wow yourself, you look very handsome."

She turned to go in.

"Wait." I took her hand and slipped the engagement ring on her finger.

"Oh Zach, it's beautiful!" she said, kissing me hard on the lips.

"If you don't like it, or it doesn't fit..."

"I love it. I love you. Let's do this!" She walked into the chapel, and I happily followed her in.

The chapel was white and gold.

"How tacky, but perfect!" Amy said, as we walked in.

For a split second, I remembered. I knew. I should have told her before this. Now she surely would be mad when I finally did mention it. But I couldn't tell her now, not on our wedding day, not at the chapel. Was it really a big deal anyway? Not really. So I pushed it to the back of my mind once again and let myself enjoy our wedding.

Rebecca and Dan were standing there, waiting for us. They gave us huge hugs and sat down to watch. The ceremony was short and sweet but kind of romantic too. I didn't take my eyes off of Amy the whole time.

Amy

When Zach looked into my eyes, I melted. I couldn't stop staring into them, watching them look back at me. They looked happy and almost tearful.

I was shocked but impressed with the rings. He'd thought of everything, including inviting our new friends.

Rebecca and Dan had a flight to catch so they gave us more hugs and promised to keep in touch. It felt surreal somehow, that these people who had only met us a few days ago had been our only witnesses.

We left the chapel and walked a good few steps down the street before he turned to me and said;

"I love you, Amy Rosenberg."

"Oh my god, I can't believe we're married!"

He took my hand and we walked slowly back to the hotel, enjoying the warm Vegas sunshine. In the elevator, we started kissing, and he fumbled around for my bra strap. We ran from the elevator to the room, he unlocked the door and picked me up to carry me over the threshold, so-to-speak. I giggled. He threw me on the bed, where we spent the rest of the day. Making love, eating room-service food, drinking champagne, and feeling like the whole world was in perfect harmony.

Zach

Knowing she was my wife – *my wife!* - I felt nothing could come between us. That my whole life I'd been waiting for this moment, and if I died this moment, I didn't care. I had it all now.

If I'd known then, what was to come... If I'd known what a mess we'd be in only a month later...I think I'd have not believed it. I think I would've cried.

Amy

Back in Boston, the telling everyone process began.

To: Taryn Carmichael
From: Amy Starling
Subject: News

Hi Taryn,
I hope you are well and happy.
I've got some news. Zach and I are married! He proposed to me while we were at the Grand Canyon, and we got married in Vegas! Can you believe it? I can hardly believe it myself. It was very romantic and I feel so happy. Please don't tell anyone. I'd like to tell my family in person.
So, what do you think?
Much love,
A xx

My reply came pretty fast.

To: Amy Starling
From: Taryn Carmichael
Subject: Re: News

Amy,
OH MY GOD! I can't believe it. Congratulations! How exciting
and romantic. Don't worry, my lips are sealed. Send photos.
Send more details. What did you wear? Who was there? How
come you decided to do it straight away? How does this affect
your green card application, I take it you will definitely stay
now?!!
Wow.
Love you, Taryn xx

Zach

I saw Matt reading a newspaper, waiting for me. He didn't
look up as I sat down opposite him. Two beers were on the
table.

After saying hello, I decided I might as well just tell him.

"Amy and I got married in Vegas."

He'd been about to take another mouthful of beer, but this
hand stopped midair. His mouth dropped open.

"What?" he said, almost angrily.

"I'm married!" I said again, hardly able to contain my own
excitement.

"Married? Dude!"

It was silent for a moment.

"Were you drunk?"

"No! I asked her to marry me, and she said yes."

"Why?"

"Why what? Why did she say yes?!"

"No, why did you ask her? You've known her for, what, two
weeks?"

"Nearly a year, actually"

"Okay, but still...wow. Sorry. Well, congratulations, man."
He offered his hand. I took it. He smiled.

"So you love her?" he said in an English accent.

"Yes, of course."

"Then I guess we should celebrate. Cheers."

Amy

Harriet whooped and threw her arms around me when I told her. She said she just knew we were destined to be together forever, and she was so, so glad she'd invited us both to the party. Next up, it was Zach's parents. Neither of us was sure how they'd react.

"Dad, Mom?" Zach called out as we passed through the gate into their back yard. Nate was standing at the barbeque, wearing a white chef's hat and a black apron which said "Hunter, Gatherer" in big red letters.

"The kids are here Annie!" Nate came over to us, smiling. He gave Zach a hug, and then to my surprise, hugged me as well. I instantly felt more relaxed. Annie came out, her round hips wobbling underneath her emerald green dress, placed a tray of iced teas on the table and hugged us both. We sat.

I suddenly wished we'd rehearsed this in the car. Thought of a way to tackle it together. I didn't know what Zach was going to say and wondered if it'd been better to tell them without my being there.

"So how's everything going?" Annie said, swishing the ice around in her glass.

Nate bought a plate of chicken wings to the table.

"Help yourself dear," Annie pushed the plate towards me. I felt too nervous to eat and just smiled.

"Dad, can you just sit with us a second, we have some news," Zach began. My heart started to pound. I had visions of them being angry. We hadn't told them in advance, they hadn't attended the wedding, would they feel they'd missed out?

"Nate, get over here," Annie said, grinning.

Nate came and sat at the table, picking up a glass and taking a long mouthful. No one said anything but Annie was looking excited. I took that as a good sign.

"Amy and I got married," Zach said, calmly. He smiled, but I could tell he was a little unsure of their reaction too. Annie's face froze.

He lifted up his left hand and pointed to his ring.

"Married? Don't you mean you're getting married? You're engaged?" she said, looking confused.

"No, Mom, we're married. We got married in Las Vegas at the weekend." Zach started laughing a little hysterically, I wasn't sure if it was out of excitement of the news, or because it wasn't going as he'd expected.

Annie continued to look confused, frowning and looking from to the other of us and back again.

Nate jumped up and came round the table to hug us both.

"Congratulations!"

Zach

"Thanks Dad," I said, grinning. He grabbed his glass.

"A toast!" he said, lifting it up. I glanced at Mom. She wasn't smiling or lifting her glass.

"Wait, just hold on. You got married? In Vegas? You didn't invite us?"

"We didn't invite anyone, I proposed to Amy. She said yes. We decided, why wait?"

"But – it's just – I would have liked to be there, that's all."

"I know, I'm sorry Mom. It was impulsive, but I'm unbelievably happy and-"

My dad, seeing her face still looking shocked and upset, intervened. I could have hugged him for what he did.

"Annie. It's not a big deal. They love each other. Anyone can see that. They got married. Who needs the big fancy schmancy expensive hoo-ha anyhow? Look how happy Zach is. And Amy. Look..."

He gestured to us. I put my arm around Amy, who was looking a little like she might faint. She smiled up at me and looked back at my mom.

"Oh, Zach, my baby is married!" she whooped, jumping up from her seat and hugging us both.

"Welcome to the family Amy!" she said, hugging her tight.

My dad raised his glass again and I picked up mine too. We toasted to us. To me and my wife, who was now hugging my mother with tears in her eyes.

"I'm sorry, I was just shocked. I'm thrilled, really," Mom was saying into her ear.

Aaron turned up a few minutes later and he and the girls joined in the cheer. Later, my mom cornered me and lectured me some more on the importance of informing Amy of my "secret." I told her I really was intending to, very soon.

Amy

The next day I was having lunch with my dad. We'd gone to an Italian restaurant this time. I loved the way he twirled his spaghetti around his fork perfectly. He told me he'd been in touch with Ed, just a few emails but they were friendly and he was hopeful that Ed might come out and visit before long.

"So how was Las Vegas and the Grand Canyon?" he asked, and I almost choked on my food. There was no way of avoiding it any longer. I had no idea what reaction to expect. I'd already put my rings in my purse, to avoid early detection before I could tell him the news.

"The Grand Canyon is amazing," I said, avoiding it just a few more minutes.

"We hiked along the south rim to Hermit's Rest, like you suggested."

"Takes your breath away, doesn't it?"

233

"Zach proposed to me at sunset," I said, smiling and putting down my fork.

"Why didn't you tell me sooner?!" he jumped up, kissed me on the cheek and said "Congratulations."

"He's a great guy. I like him a lot. Of course, you haven't known each other that long, but there's no rush to get married, and I suppose it'll help if you plan to apply for citizenship."

"We got married," I told him "In Vegas."

My dad put down his fork and stared at me.

"What?"

"We're married!" I said, hardly able to contain my excitement, despite the stern look he was giving me.

"Amy, wow, well, congratulations again," he said, but without much enthusiasm.

"You don't seem very happy for me?" I said, searching his face for clues on how this news had affected him.

"I'm sorry, I am happy. I'm very happy and proud to have Zach as a son-in-law. I'm just a little concerned, that's all. I don't have a right to start preaching to you now, or acting like the worried parent. I know I haven't earned that right but I just wonder how well you can know each other. You haven't been dating very long have you?"

"I know him. Really, Dad, I do. We actually have been living together. He's the one for me. Really, he's, I-" I nearly started to cry and he smiled and patted my hand.

"You love him. That's all I need to know. I'm happy. Really. And you know what?"

"What?"

"You just called me 'dad' again."

"Did I?" I felt my face flush a red with embarrassment. I had been trying to avoid saying 'dad' or 'Andy' because neither felt quite right.

"It's okay. I liked it. It's who I am, after all. Even if I haven't behaved like one."

"I think you just did." I smiled. "Thank you for your

concern..."

"So what did your mom say?" he picked up his fork and resumed twirling the spaghetti.

"I haven't told her," I admitted. "I'm going to wait until we go to England, for Libby's wedding."

He frowned and I thought he might say something, advise against waiting to tell her, but decided not to say anything and asked me all about the wedding and our time in Vegas instead.

It occurred to me as I left the restaurant that getting married in Las Vegas may have been the best option for me. I'd have never had been able to chose between a wedding in America or England...never had been able to choose whether Jack or my dad gave me away and I was pretty sure both would have expected to do so. I tried to imagine them all there, Jack and Andy, Yvonne and mum, Libby and Jemma, plus Ed and Zach's family, and all our friends, in one big room while Zach and I had our first dance. I much preferred the reality; just me, Zach, and two almost strangers. None of the family politics.

Jemma called me that evening.

"Dad just told me," she said. "Congratulations!"

"Thank you. I can't quite believe it."

"I'm sure you'll be very happy together."

"Thank you!"

"I want to get you a gift."

"Oh no, you really don't have to."

"Please, let me at least buy you both dinner."

"Seriously Jemma, you don't need to do anything."

"Okay, well how about I give your children free medical exams?"

"Deal," I said, smiling imagining little Zach's running around.

"They'll be my nieces and nephews, after all."

Zach

It was the last good day, before it all started falling apart around us. Of course I didn't know what was about to come, so I was quite happy and content in my ignorance. I got up that morning and went for a run. I came back and watched Amy eating her cereal and watched her go off to work. I sat down and made a few phone calls, did a little work, wasted some time writing my anonymous blog.

I went out at lunch time and bought a pretzel from a street vendor. I ate it quickly as I walked home, thinking about the afternoon's work, which I got on with until about 4pm. Then I stopped to make a salad and steam some fish for our dinner.

Amy came home and we talked about her day, my day. We ate. We both read for a while and talked about our books.

It was just an ordinary day, yet how I'd later wish I could go back to it. How I'd wish I could change it. How I'd wish I'd savoured the happy, loved-up time we shared. Because it was about to come crashing down upon us.

Chapter Fourteen

Amy

I rushed into the apartment and grabbed the phone, thinking it must be Libby. She'd called a couple of times during the week, and left messages to call her back. I eventually emailed her, giving Zach's number. Zach followed behind me.

"If it's for me, tell them I'm out," he said, exhausted.

"Hello," I said into the receiver.

"Hi. I'm sorry, I think I may have the wrong number. Is Zach there?"

Zach had disappeared into the bathroom and I heard the shower turning on.

"You have the right number, but no, I'm sorry, he's not. Can I take a message?"

There seemed to be a slight time delay on the phone, like she was calling from the other side of the world or something.

"Can you tell him Ellie called? We were supposed to chat online but he must have forgotten. Thomas really wanted to speak to him, thank him for the money he sent. Tell him we said hello and if he could call back."

"Sure," I said, wondering who the hell Thomas was and why Zach was sending him money.

"That'd be great thanks. Oh, hang on, sorry, no Thomas, Daddy isn't there. I'm speaking to a friend of his."

I froze. Daddy? *Daddy?*

"Sorry. Thanks, erm, sorry-"

"Amy," I said, and then added: "I'm Zach's wife."

It seemed important. If this boy was my...I couldn't believe

237

it, step-son, I might as well confess it to his mother.

"Oh, wow. Amy. Yes, sorry, he told me about you in an email. Wow, you got married? I'm so happy for you both. Congratulations."

So, it appeared Ellie and Thomas, whoever they were, knew who I was.

"Thank you. I'll give him the message."

Ellie said good bye and I put the phone down and stood, frozen to the spot. I thought I might faint. I heard Zach turning the shower off. I heard my husband, whoever he was – I no longer could be sure, opening the bathroom door and coming out to face me, with a red towel wrapped around his waist.

"What, what's wrong?" he asked, concerned.

"That was Ellie," I said. "Who the hell is Thomas?"

Zach

Okay, I know. I should have mentioned Ellie and Thomas before. Let me tell you, it wasn't something I ever planned to keep from Amy. I mean, she didn't ever ask, did she? She never said "do you have any children?" so I didn't technically lie. It isn't exactly something I tell women on the first date, because it, he – Thomas, doesn't impact my life. Things with Amy went from strength to strength and got serious so fast, and I just didn't find the right moment to tell her. I said all of this, with the water still dripping down my back, whilst Amy stood there, pale, staring at me like I was a stranger who'd walked into the room unexpected. I was suddenly very aware of being naked.

"The right moment? *The right moment?* Oh for fuck's sake Zach! We've only seen each other almost every day for the past eleven months!"

"I'm sorry, I wanted to, it's just that-"

"Before we got married, didn't you think it'd be a good idea then? You know, you'd say "hey, Amy, before I marry you, you should know that I have a son! A son! Who I send money to!"

238

Oh my god, you need to start explaining, right now."

So I did. I told her the story, from the beginning. It goes a little something like this:

Ellie was my girlfriend when I was eighteen. She was president of the Brainiac club and I was the vice president during our senior year in high school. We got it together when the club decided to go out for pizza after a long studying session at the beginning of our senior year. She was pretty and had flirted with me quite a bit, so I just lunged in and we started making out at the back of the pizza parlour. Her mouth tasted of pepperoni and garlic. I spared Amy this detail, of course.

It wasn't ever very serious, we were young, but we went out a couple of times a week, usually to see a movie or get more pizza, or whatever. We started sleeping together one weekend when her parents were out of town. We were friends more than anything. Neither of us ever said I love you or anything like that. It was just as if we were pals who made out occasionally, and then pals who slept together occasionally.

Then, just a month or so before graduation, Ellie told me she was pregnant.

I was sitting in her bedroom at her parent's house, and I just sat down on the bed, stunned, feeling my mouth hanging open. How could this have happened? We'd used protection. We'd been careful. We hadn't even done it that much.

"Sometimes it just happens," she'd said, calmly.

This wasn't how it was supposed to be. I was expecting us to break up before college. Now I pictured me skipping college, going to work at a department store, trying to earn enough money to support Ellie and her baby – our baby.

"I'm keeping it," she said.

I knew that she would. She'd attended some debates about abortion at school and told me how much she detested it. There was no way I'd convince her otherwise.

"Ellie, how is this even going to work?" I said, when I finally got it together to speak.

239

"We'll make it work. You must still go to college. Please don't change your plans. We'll figure something out."

So, that was that. My life changed. That one moment, that one time we'd had sex and hadn't managed to be safe enough had changed everything.

So, we carried on as before. Both of our parents were mad, of course. My mom went on about how stupid I was. My dad just shrugged his shoulders and said something about life throwing obstacles at us and we had to live with our responsibilities. Aaron laughed and said "Whoah, Dude!" Very helpful.

I went off to college, and we wrote to each other, spoke on the telephone, and I came home every couple of weekends. I didn't tell anyone in college what was happening. I said I had a girlfriend back home, but never mentioned the baby. I guess I was embarrassed.

Then, the following spring, Thomas was born. He was so tiny. He had these big eyes, and lots of dark hair. Ellie continued living with her parents, which we all decided was for the best. It was in Ellie's, Thomas', and my best interests for me to finish college and then we'd see about getting a place together.

Thomas was three months old when Ellie told me she was moving to New Zealand. I argued with her. I told her she couldn't do that to me, couldn't take Thomas away from me. What about us? I'd asked her.

"What about us, Zach? Do you love me?"

I looked down at the blue carpet in her bedroom. I couldn't answer that.

"I don't love you either. It's okay. I can't stay here because of you. My dad has a job, he wants to take it, and I'd like to start afresh, you know, go somewhere different and meet people who didn't know me before Thomas. They'll see me as a young mother, instead of the clever girl who got knocked up and didn't go to college."

"You can still go to college," I said.

"I want to go with my family. I need to be with them."

And I didn't argue with her anymore. I know I should have. I know it's terrible. But I was relieved. As much as I loved Thomas, I'd been at college five hundred miles away and only saw him every couple of weeks. I wanted to be young, and free, I didn't want to be, wasn't ready to be a father. Moving to the other side of the world wasn't going to stop me being a father, but it was going to mean I didn't have to act like one. I didn't have to force a relationship with Ellie, and I could get on with my life. I'm not proud of myself for letting her go so easy, but in many, selfish ways, I'm glad that she did.

So, off she went to New Zealand with my son. I was nineteen and I had my freedom back. I haven't seen Thomas since. We talk on the internet, with a webcam, now and then. Usually this had been during the day, when Amy was at work. Ellie sends me photos and I sent Thomas some money now and then. A couple of times I bought him gifts – toys, mostly, or a book here and there. Ellie told me he likes to read. He's twelve now.

Amy

I sat there, listening to Zach's story in disbelief.

"First of all, you don't know what it's like growing up, knowing your father is out there somewhere, but doesn't care about you!" I shouted at him, feeling Thomas' pain.

"Amy, it's not that easy. I send him cards and money. He's not a part of my life but that's not my choosing. He hasn't missed out. Ellie is married, he has a father figure."

"It's not the same!"

"No, it's not the same – you didn't know your father at all. I know Thomas, if only via the webcam. You have to realise, I didn't have a choice."

"How can you say that? You have rights. You could've

stopped her from going!"

"Remember, I was young, and I admit I didn't want the responsibility."

"I can't believe this. You are making someone go through what I went through with my parents!"

"Oh, come on Amy. Listen, you had two parents who loved you, did you not? They might not have been perfect but what I can tell, you had a decent childhood. Your "real" father hardly knew your mother and had a life to get on with. It's the same for me. Blame Ellie, if anyone."

"I do! I blame my mother. I think my father had little choice!"

"Well, then."

Silence.

"But you didn't tell me! How can I trust anything you've said?"

"It's one thing. One thing that doesn't even impact my life much. I'm sorry...I really am."

"I don't know you at all. My father was right."

"What?"

"Andy. He said I should be careful, rushing into marriage."

"You know me, Amy. You've known me longer than him! Come on, Amy. It's me. I'm still me. I understand why you're upset but this shouldn't change anything."

"But it does. It changes everything. You're not who I thought you were..."

"I'm sorry, Amy, really, but it doesn't have to be a big deal."

"Stop saying that, Zach! Oh my god, what have I done? I married someone I don't even know!"

"How can this change everything?"

"Because you've betrayed my trust, Zach!" I got up to leave, I had to get out of there.

"Amy, please, listen, really-"

"No, Zach. You're a different person. I thought we were so close. We knew all there was to know about each other. I don't know you at all."

"You do, come on..."

I got my coat and started heading for the door.

"Amy, please don't walk out, let's talk."

"What if Ellie hadn't called tonight? Would you ever have told me?"

"Yes, of course, I was just waiting for the right time."

"When on earth would be a good time to tell your wife, *your wife*, that you already have a child?"

"I'm sorry, please don't go."

I turned, opened the door. Left the apartment, and walked around for miles and miles. Zach kept calling me so I turned my phone off. I went back to my old apartment, empty but for one mattress on the floor. I still had the lease for another week. I laid down on the mattress, crying and feeling stupid. I'd married someone I didn't even know.

Zach

I know. I should have told her sooner. I don't know what I was thinking. Nothing. I didn't think. That was the problem. It's just that I feel guilty. About Thomas. I tried to forget he existed most of the time. Which might seem harsh, but it's the only way I could deal with the situation. He didn't impact my life that much. I'd only spoken to Thomas a couple of times since we got together, once a month, and then a month ago I'd sent a money transfer and a short letter because it was his birthday. At that point, of course, I did realise that I needed to tell Amy. I just didn't know how to, after all this time.

I called her mobile over and over but she'd switched it off. So I left a message saying I love you and I'm sorry. I knocked on Harriet's door, to see if she knew where she was, trying to sound casual. She said she didn't know.

I called Amy again and reminded her I had to fly to Chicago that night for a meeting with some clients. I said I'd speak to her the next day and we could talk things through, and then get our stuff together for London. Something we'd intended to do that day, before she'd walked out.

Amy

I listened to Zach's message. I didn't want to see him or speak to him, I was so angry. So, while he was in Chicago, I went back to the apartment, packed my things, wrote him a note and tore up his plane ticket. I then told Harriet everything. She just stood there in complete shock. I gave her Zach's passport. I didn't want him following me, but it didn't seem quite right to destroy it, either. She reluctantly promised not to give it back to him until I told her to do so.

I couldn't stand the thought of sleeping in his bed without him, or the thought of him coming back and arguing his excuses some more, so I went to an airport hotel for the night.

Zach

I unlocked the door to my apartment and saw Alvin asleep on the sofa. I called out to Amy, but didn't get a response. Alvin got up, stretched and came over to meow at me. "Amy?" I said again.

Then I saw it. The note on the kitchen counter.

I knew right away what it would say, and felt anger boiling inside of me before I even started to read.

Zach,
I've gone to London alone. I've shredded your ticket. Don't come after me.
This is over, Zach. I thought of you as a person who could never lie to me. Someone who was totally honest and that we were on some sort of parallel together, that we were one unbeatable force, you and me against the world. I thought I knew you. I realise

now I don't know you at all.

We made a mistake in Vegas. It was too soon to get married. I understand why you didn't tell me in the beginning, but by the time we were getting married? So, it's highlighted to me how little we know each other.

I'm not sure what I'm going to do, but please just leave me be and I'll be in touch to get the rest of my stuff when I'm back, after Libby's wedding. I might stay with Andy for a while.

Amy.

Great. Now, I was angry. How could she just walk out like that, tell me it was over via a note? I tried calling her over and over, but her cell phone was turned off.

Amy

I opened my eyes, grimaced at the taste of stale alcohol, and stared up at the white ceiling for several minutes. I tried to remember where I was. A hotel room. Mahogany furniture. Dark blue curtains with golden lining, closed.

Oh, no. No, no, no. Please let me be dreaming. But I wasn't.

I could feel there was someone asleep next to me. I closed my eyes and pinched myself, but I was most definitely awake. The guy in the bar. I didn't even know his name, how shameful. He was facing away from me, towards the hotel room door. All I could see was his blonde hair and the gentle rise and fall of his chest. I moved my hand slowly down underneath the sheets and discovered I was naked.

I guess you want to hear how difficult it was for me to be adulterous. You'd like to hear how I deliberated, or how drunk I was, or how sorry I felt.

The truth was, it was easy. I was a little drunk, but I knew what I was doing. I felt that Zach had betrayed my trust, and so I had a right to betray his. It was revenge. I know, two wrongs don't make a right, and on the grand scheme of things, I guess

245

my wrong was a bigger, more personal betrayal. I didn't think of it like that. I figured that was it, it was over. I was so angry and lost and scared about coming home.

Of course, I would never, ever have slept with him knowing he was who he was. As in, Tim - Libby's fiancé. But I didn't know that, yet.

The truth is, I cannot justify or explain what happened that night with Tim. It was a moment of weakness. I wanted to feel good, to put the horrible past twenty-four hours out of my head, as well as the days that were to come, where I'd have to see my family again.

He'd come and sat next to me at the bar. I'd smiled, hoping he might talk to me. I was glad to discover he was British.

"Can I buy you a drink?"

I told him I'd have a vodka and cranberry juice. Not usually my drink of choice. I wanted to be different that night. Be anybody else, but me. We got to talking. It was nice to flirt a little. I didn't expect to end up in bed. Seriously, I thought it'd be a little harmless conversation. I discovered he worked for some sort of financial company and was in Boston on business. I told him I'd been living there a year, that I worked in public relations. We talked about the differences between the US and UK, and compared words like chips and crisps, pants and trousers, courgette and zucchini.

Before I knew it we were in the lift (elevator), kissing and fumbling around like a pair of sex-starved animals. We made it to the third floor, then to his room, and, well, we did it of course. I'll spare you the details but it wasn't exactly the best ever, due to the alcohol mostly, but, I wondered afterwards, maybe also because we both felt guilty in some way. Like we knew we'd regret this in the morning.

I sat up slowly, not wishing to disturb whoever he was – I had no clue at that point he was about to marry my sister - and slipped out from under the white sheets. My head hurt. A quick look in the mirror revealed what I had suspected: my hair was a mess and I had mascara all over my face. I rubbed it away as best I could with my fingers and started looking for my clothes.

I found my clothes piece by piece, thrown all over the room in the heat of the moment. I felt myself blush. Where was my bra? I looked under the bed and found a shoe. The bra was on the nightstand, beside a condom wrapper. At least there was one thing to be thankful for; we'd used protection. I looked at the blonde guy, and saw he was stirring. I didn't want him to see me naked, so I just stood there, holding my clothes in my arms, trying to cover everything up.

He opened his eyes, blinked a few times, sat up and smiled at me.

"Good morning beautiful," he said, although he looked embarrassed.

"Hi," I said, feeling my face flush red. He rubbed his head and kind of groaned.

"Do you mind if I have a shower?" I asked, mostly because it meant I could get dressed in the bathroom instead of in front of him.

"Of course, but first, I'm sorry, I just...I'm such a shit." He looked down at the bed sheets.

"You have a girlfriend? A wife?"

"Fiancée. I'm sorry."

"It's okay. I'll just jump in the shower, and be on my way." I felt used and stupid. I walked to the bathroom and he blurted out;

"I'm sorry. I just needed one last fling, you know? I've never cheated on her, and I never will again."

"It's okay. I kind of understand." I understood all too well.

"Thank you."

I smiled and shut the door. The bathroom was huge. I threw my clothes in a heap on the floor and shuddered at the blurred reflection of my naked body in the white tiles. I turned the shower on and let the hot water wash away my last ounce of self respect. I borrowed his shower gel, the masculine scent reminding me of Zach and my own betrayal, my own guilt. If only the water could cleanse me of my sins.

I thought about the blonde guy's fiancée at home, waiting for him to return, unknowing. Poor girl. I wondered how he'd think of me in years to come. The last woman he'd slept with before he got married, the one he nearly screwed things up over. For a second or two, I kind of liked the feeling of being a part of his history, whoever he was, and then the shame came back.

I stepped out of the shower and stared at myself in the mirror. I hadn't planned on seeing him again but I still felt used and kind of deflated. At least before I could have imagined that I was irresistible. He wanted one last fling. I was just an easy target. I brushed my teeth, using his toothbrush which looked relatively new, ran my fingers through my wet hair, got dressed and went back into the room to say good bye. He was now up and making coffee. Thankfully, he'd pulled on some jeans.

"Well, it was...nice," I said, feeling my face flush red again.

"Great. It was great. You don't have to go, you know, the least I can do is buy you breakfast."

"Really it's fine. I've got a flight to catch today. So..." I'd never felt so awkward in my life. It was about to get a lot worse.

"Oh, yes, of course. I remember. Me too, actually. Are you flying BA?"

"Virgin," I told him, thankful we weren't on the same flight. I actually had several hours to wait but had no interest in sharing an awkward breakfast.

I smiled and started heading towards the door.

"Thanks for understanding. I am sorry."

"Really, stop apologising. I'm not exactly available myself."

I heard the words coming out of my mouth but didn't quite believe that they were true. If I wasn't exactly available then what was I? Half available? I shuddered.

"Okay, well that makes me feel a little better." He smiled at me.

"It's not a big deal, right?" I said, my hand on the door,

248

ready to escape.

"I doubt Libby would think so. We're getting married next week."

I froze and stared at him. What did he just say? Surely, it couldn't be. I blinked a few times and wondered if I was dreaming.

Please, let it be a dream.

"What? Are you okay? You've gone very pale."

"Is your name Tim White?"

"Yes, but – how do you–"

"I'm Amy Starling," I told him, watching his jaw fall open. "Your future sister-in-law."

On the plane, something changed in me. The realisation of how immature, and selfish, and stupid I'd been hit me somewhere at about 35,000 feet. What was I doing, cutting Zach out like this? Running away at the first sign of trouble? Was what he'd done really worth ending our relationship over without at least hearing him out a bit more? Hadn't the happiest months of my life just been spent with Zach? I didn't know how to get that back. I thought about Tim and shuddered with shame. I wasn't sure who I was more angry with, Zach, or myself.

Zach

"Harriet, please just let me explain," I said quickly, seeing the anger on her face.

"Okay, you've got five minutes," she said, opening the door wide enough to let me in.

"I'm stupid. Very stupid."

"Well, I agree on that point."

"I should have told Amy, a long, long time ago."

"Yes."

"But no matter how stupid I am, I do love her. We can be

happy together, you know that, right? You've seen us. So I just need her to calm down, listen to me, and I think in time, she could maybe forgive me. You've got to help me."

"I'm not sure I can help."

"Please Harriet," I said, my voice cracking in desperation, "I love her so much."

Her face softened.

"Okay, sit down."

"I don't know where she is. She's not at her apartment. Our flight is at 3pm. She shredded my ticket."

"Go to the airport for three."

"You think I'll be able to find her in the crowds?"

"Ring the airline, explain your ticket has been destroyed, and you can just get on the plane with her. You'll see her at the gate, surely."

"I called the airline. They need the credit card number which booked the ticket. Amy booked it."

"Okay..."

"I don't know what to do." I felt my eyes well up.

"Oh Zach," she said, "it will be okay. She'll calm down."

"How can I even speak to her?"

"Can't you get another flight?"

"I guess I'll have to."

I went back to my apartment. Amy had taken all of my stuff out of our luggage and left it on the bed. I threw it all into another case and looked for my passport. I couldn't find it anywhere. The phone rang.

"Hello?" I said, hoping it was her.

"Hi Zach," said Ellie.

"Oh, hi Ellie."

"Sorry to call you again. We were going to talk on the webcam but you didn't turn up. So I called yesterday, spoke to Amy. Just wondering if everything is okay?"

"It's fine, I'm sorry, so very sorry. I can't talk now. I'll email you in a few days, is that okay?"

250

"Yes of course. Can you just say hello to Thomas?"

"Sure."

"Hi Dad."

"Hi Thomas."

It felt weird, having him call me that, when he didn't even remember me, to him dad was just a guy he saw on the computer screen once a month. Ellie's husband was much more qualified for the dad title.

"How are you?"

"I'm fine. Thank you for the money."

"You're welcome, what did you spend it on?"

"Star Wars stuff."

"Wow, I didn't know you liked Star Wars."

I didn't know anything…I thought about how Amy felt, not knowing her biological father and felt like a big, heavy guilty weight had been put on me. As we were talking I was looking around everywhere for my passport. I couldn't imagine where it could possibly be. Had Amy taken it with her?

"Hey, Thomas, I'm thinking I might come and visit you guys sometime. I think we should spend some time together. I like Star Wars too, you know. We could watch them together…and…stuff. What do you reckon?"

"Really?"

"Yes, really."

"Cool."

Darn it, still no passport.

There was a knock on the door. I opened it. Harriet was standing there, holding it up.

"Thomas, I'll send you a long email later, okay? I've got to go."

"Okay, bye."

"Bye."

I hugged Harriet.

"Thank you."

Chapter Fifteen

Amy

So, as you heard at the beginning, I returned home. And Zach turned up. And he told my family, just like that, right out of the blue. I watched each member of my family's jaws drop as Zach said the words:

"Actually, I'm her husband."

Zach

"What the hell did you have to say that for?" Amy half shouted as soon as we got into the back yard.

"Well, it's the truth, isn't it?"

"That's not how I wanted them to find out. You know that. Plus, I left."

I felt a moment of regret, but then remembered how I'd felt, being married to Amy without her parents knowing. She'd said over and over again that she wanted to tell them in person, but the truth was, I felt like I'd been a big, hidden secret.

"Your note doesn't make our marriage null and void Amy!" I said, sitting down on a wooden bench. She sighed and came and sat next to me.

The yard was well tendered and full of color, but smaller than I'd imagined. Amy had told me stories of her youth, how her parents weren't there much, but her step-father grew fruit and vegetables and herbs, and her mom planted flowers and shrubs. She'd talked of playing with her siblings, snow ball fights in winter and water fights in summer. Now that I was here, I could really picture her, with pigtails and a little dress on, running around, laughing, creating these memories which she'd later share.

In fact, the house was smaller than I'd imagined as well. Amy had told me that houses in England were typically smaller but I hadn't imagined they'd be so close to together. It was cute, though. It had character and charm and if the circumstances had been different, I'd have enjoyed coming here and meeting her family. But it hadn't quite worked out the way we'd planned it.

We sat in silence for a few minutes. All the speeches I'd prepared on the drive to the house had somehow been wiped from my brain and I couldn't think where to even start.

"I guess I should apologize for leaving the way I did," she said, quietly.

"Yes. You should. It was pretty harsh."

"I'm sorry. I needed to get out, get away as quickly as possible."

"I thought we were closer than that. I thought we'd talk," I said, wishing I didn't sound as hurt as I felt.

"It's not like that Zach," she said, sighing, getting impatient.

"Then tell me what it is like, because I haven't got a clue."

She sighed again.

"You were the one who lied-" she began but didn't finish.

"I know, and I'll spend the rest of my life making that up to you. I'm still the same person, Amy. It doesn't change who I am."

"I'm sorry, it's not really the place to discuss it," she said.

"I can't keep apologising Amy." If only I could go back and make things different.

I looked at her for a few moments. At the face I'd fallen in love with. The hair I'd run my hands through, the body I'd kissed and caressed all over, and I wanted to grab her. To tell her how stupid and hurtful and crazy this all was. I wanted to beg her to think about what she was doing. But instead I got up. I told her I'd find a local hotel and suggested she call me on my mobile in the morning.

"I'm sorry for barging in and telling your parents like that," I added. "It wasn't the right way to go, and this isn't the best place to talk. But we must talk, surely you know that?"

She nodded and agreed she'd call me in the morning after she'd had some time to explain to her family and then think a little. Then she gave me some rough directions to the nearest hotel.

It hadn't gone as I'd planned. I had some sort of deluded fantasy that she'd be glad to see me. That my coming here would prove my love, rekindle whatever had been lost, make up for my deceit, and she'd throw herself into my arms, forgive me, and everything would be fine. But she'd been cold, distant, and distracted somehow.

I drove slowly to the hotel, got a room, and sat up half the night, cursing the time difference and falling in and out of sleep. I kept dreaming that Amy was lying next to me, and everything was as it should be. But then I'd wake up and realise, of course, that it wasn't.

Amy

After Zach left I went back into the house. My family were all talking quietly in the living room, and as I walked in they fell silent. I went over to the sofa and sat next to Ed.

Everyone looked at me, waiting for an explanation. I didn't know where to start.

"Well?" Libby said eventually.

"What do you want to know?" I said, a little coldly.

"Let's start with who Zach really is?" Jack said, smiling, but looking concerned.

"You heard him," I said. "He's my husband."

"Since when?" Ed chimed in. I imagined all the jokes he'd be coming up with about me and my secret marriage.

"Two weeks ago," I told them, looking down at my hands.

This wasn't how I'd planned it. We were supposed to arrive together. I was going to introduce them all to him. I was going to say: "This is my husband!" and they'd be shocked, maybe even a little upset that they'd missed the event, but they'd be pleased. Zach would charm them all and they'd welcome him into the family.

I then thought about Zach's family. They were thrilled. They'd whooped and screamed and hugged us both tight and said we were perfect together. His mum had asked me if I'd consider converting to Judaism, and Zach had told her to "leave Amy alone." His dad went out and bought champagne and I remembered looking at Zach across the table, thinking I'd never been so happy.

My eyes filled up with tears and Ed put his arm around me. I swallowed a few times and looked up to see my entire family sitting there in shock, not sure what to ask me next.

"How long have you known him?" Mum finally asked

"A year. I have mentioned a guy I was seeing in my emails? And I did tell you I was bringing a guest."

They all nodded, and someone said something about not realising it was serious.

"Well, it was," I told them. In a weird way, I was kind of enjoying the attention.

"How come you didn't tell us?" Ed asked, looking hurt.

"I just...I wanted to tell you in person. To introduce him and, well it all went wrong."

I started crying more heavily and felt like a little girl again. As it turned out, I didn't want the attention. I just wanted it to be normal, the way it should have been. I glanced at Tim. He was staring at the carpet. Ed put his arm around me.

"And what's going on now?" Jack asked.

"We had a big fight, that's all."

"Are you sure know him that well?" asked mum, as I knew

she would.

"Yes. Everyone in Boston thinks we're great together. Really, I don't regret marrying him." I was starting to feel defensive, even though I knew she was right, in a way.

"Everyone, like who? There's this whole new world you have and you haven't shared it with us."

Mum came over to the other side, and put her arm around me. I felt stupid for ever thinking my family wouldn't be there for me when I needed them. Their faces of concern all showed me now that they cared, while being sensitive enough not to ask why Zach and I had fallen out.

"Everyone. Like my friend, Harriet. Taryn, when she came to visit. My dad."

"Your dad?" asked Mum. I glanced at Jack. He smiled at me.

"Yes. I see him regularly. He loves Zach."

"Then I'm sure we all will, when this spat is sorted out," said Jack.

"Where did you get married?" Mum asked, after a long silence.

"Vegas," I told them, sniffing. "We got married in Las Vegas."

Zach

I awoke the next morning to the sound of the phone ringing. It was Amy.

"I'm sorry, did I wake you?"

"It's okay." I couldn't be angry with her. I was just so glad she'd called.

"Can we talk? Can I come to the hotel?"

"Of course. I'll buy you breakfast."

"I think the least I can do is buy you breakfast," she said, and sounded as if she were smiling. This seemed a good sign.

I pulled myself out of the bed and into the shower. A thousand thoughts were running through my head. I got dressed quickly, and sat down on the uncomfortable bed. I followed the swirls in the pattern on the carpet with my eyes. Finally, a knock came on the door.

"Hey," I said as Amy came into my room and sat down on a chair in the corner. I perched on the bed and we smiled at each other. For the first time, I felt uncomfortable with her.

"Did you sleep well?" she asked politely.

"Not really, just a few hours. Your family are great. I know I only saw them for a few minutes, but I knew who was who straight away."

She smiled sadly.

"You want to get out, go for a walk?"

"Sure."

Amy

It felt strange to be driving with Zach in the passenger seat. I hadn't driven at all in America, he'd taken us everywhere. He'd never seen me drive. It'd never occurred to me before how strange that was, although oddly enough we were still on the same sides of the car; me on the right, him on the left. It was only the position of the steering wheel that had changed.

I drove him to Willen Lake; and told him how Ed, Libby and I had each learned to ride our bikes there. We'd had family picnics, with ham sandwiches, Mr. Kipling's cakes, pork pies, crisps, and orange squash. We'd climbed all over the children's playground beside the lake until Jack had shouted at us that it was time to leave. I don't know why I was taking Zach there. I just wanted him to see it; a place that was in my history.

We pulled up in a car park close to the Peace Pagoda; a small Buddhist temple which has always been a place of wonder to me. As a child, I loved to climb the steps to the beautiful white building, staring up at the golden Buddha and take a moment to admire the calmness of the place, before running off, playing tag with Libby and or Ed, and listening to stories from Jack about how the pagoda was built and why.

Zach and I got out of the car and walked slowly towards the peace pagoda in silence.

"Wow, what's this?" Zach said as soon as his eyes fell upon it.

I told him what little I knew of the place, and shared some of my memories. We continued to walk around the lake, passing the hospice where my grandmother had died. I put a few coins in the charity bucket outside and we talked for a while about her.

"My Nana was a great lady," I told him. "Taught me everything I know about birds."

"I didn't know you knew that much about birds!" Zach smiled.

"That, over there," I said, pointing to a flutter of wings on the lake, "is a duck."

"Wow, you're so clever," he said, smiling.

We walked in silence for a few minutes. I had a feeling of dread. I knew the time had come to talk it out, except I wasn't ready. I started babbling on about having a boring flight, and the man who sat next to me, and Zach just blurted out;

"We need to talk, Amy, don't we?"

We were approaching a bench. We sat on it. I stared at the ground and took a deep breath.

Zach

"I can't even begin to explain myself," she said, with tears in her eyes. I felt relief flood through me.

"I was scared," she continued. "Scared and stupid. It all happened so quickly. I just felt like I didn't know you at all, you'd kept this big, huge thing from me, and it was like it suddenly hit me that maybe this had moved too fast. I felt I didn't know you at all."

"Well, I should have told you from the beginning. But it doesn't change who I am, Amy, you know me. You know me better than anyone else. And yes, we moved fast. It was pretty impulsive, getting married, but I still believe it was the right thing to do."

"What about your parents, and Aaron – no one ever mentioned it."

"We never do, I know that seems crazy but my parents were pretty upset with Ellie at the time, and they've kind of learnt to accept it by forgetting that he exists. I believe my mom sends him birthday cards but they don't have much other contact."

"Did they know that I didn't know?"

"Yes. Aaron and Mom told me over and over again to fill you in."

"Well, I guess at least I know now." She sighed.

"I realise it was stupid of me, and I will keep saying sorry until you forgive me."

"What about the boy, Thomas. Don't you think you're missing out? Don't you think he needs you?"

"We do speak now and then. On web cams. We email. But yes, I suppose I am missing something. I would like to visit him. It's just...alien to me I guess. I know that sounds cold."

"When did you speak to him? When I was out?"

"At work, yes. The time difference makes it difficult. We only do it once a month. We send a few emails too. He seems a happy kid, and Ellie and Jonathan – that's her husband – they have other kids now and I guess I've always felt he's better off there, with them."

Amy sighed. "I get that. I guess."

"You know you didn't have to leave like that. Hiding my passport with Harriet."

"I'm sorry. It was pretty immature."

"Well," I said, unable to resist her beautiful face. "I'm here now. Can't we carry on as before? Like we planned? I'm sorry. I'll always be sorry. I love you."

"I love you too." She lent her head on my shoulder and wiped a tear from her cheek.

"I think we can work this out."

"Good." I felt elated. We grinned stupidly at each other.

Amy

I know, I should have told him about Tim. I almost did, but something stopped me. I didn't want to lose him, and I felt I needed him there with me during these few days. I wasn't sure I'd get through all the family stuff without him. So, just as Tim and I had promised each other, I forgot about it, pushed it to the furthest corner of my mind, and kept it there.

We had walked the entire circumference of the lake, got back in the car and I said I'd introduce him to my family properly.

"Are you nervous?" I asked as we pulled up in my parent's street.

"Not as much as you were, meeting my parents."

"That seems a long time ago."

"We'll need to talk more, about Ellie and Thomas," I said.

"Yes. I know. We will, and I am sorry, again."

"You can stop saying sorry now," I said, squeezing his arm.

We got out of the car and walked up to the front door. As I rung the door bell, I realised I was rather nervous myself.

"Hi Amy," Mum said, giving me a brief hug, as if she hadn't already seen me that morning.

"Mum, this is Zach," I said, "my husband."

"Lovely to meet you Zach," she said, shaking his hand.

We went through to the living room and I introduced him to everyone. He shook their hands and we all sat down.

"So, what do you do Zach?" asked Ed.

And so the questioning began. We told them about our apartment, about Alvin and our jobs. We told them about the Grand Canyon, and Vegas and our wedding. We told them a little about Zach's family. It was like filling them in on a whole years worth of news. They seemed genuinely interested – even Libby and Mum, and I wondered why I hadn't made more effort to stay in touch.

It was just after lunch, and everyone was milling about in the garden. Zach was chatting to Ed, Tim and Libby and Jack was finding some furniture to sit on in the garage.

"You get on well with your father, then?" Mum asked me.

"Yes, I do." I wasn't sure what to expect from her.

"Good, I'm glad. I was only trying to protect you before because I wasn't sure how he'd react."

"Well, he was pleased to hear from me. He wants to meet Ed, too. He's been very welcoming."

"How is he, anyway?"

"He's good. He's married, and has a daughter, Jemma."

"You have another sister, that's nice."

I smiled. She was different, somehow. She looked a little older. Maybe I'd just seen past the stupid jealously and resentment of the importance of her work, and was now better able to have a decent relationship with her.

"So are you going to live in Boston for good, then?"

"Yes. I'm going to ask Ed to sell my house for me once the current tenants lease has run out."

"Right. I hate to see you leave again."

I was too surprised to reply so I just I gave her a little squeeze.

"Well, we should keep in touch better. Zach set me up with a webcam to chat to Taryn, we can use that, and you could come visit."

"I would like to visit Boston again, actually."

"We're not far from New York, either. I haven't been but Zach and I have talked about it a few times. We could give you a little tour, it'd be nice."

Mum smiled and somehow, I felt glad I'd come home after all.

Zach

"Have you ever been to London?" Libby asked me.

"No, I've only seen Heathrow airport," I told her.

"Well, you and Amy should come down one day in the week. You can do some sightseeing, and come to our place for dinner."

"That would be great, thank you."

"I still can't believe you're married," she said, taking a seat that Jack had put out. I sat down next to her.

"I know, it all happened pretty quick."

"How did you and Amy meet?"

Amy

"So, Andy is a nice guy, huh?" Ed asked me the moment we were on our own.

"Yes. You'll really like him. Yvonne and Jemma too."

"I was thinking about planning a trip some time, perhaps I could stay with you and Zach?"

"Of course."

I watched my family gathering around, and felt more comfortable with them. They were all making an effort to get to know Zach, and they all seemed to have genuinely missed me. I felt a pang of guilt as I watched Libby and Zach listen to Tim talk about his recent trip to Boston.

The next day, Ed, Libby and Tim all returned to London, and Zach and I went to stay with Taryn, Josh, and Emma, who were now living in Oxford.

Zach

"Ooh look, it's the newlyweds!" Taryn called from her front door as we walked up the steps.

She hugged Amy tight and winked at me over her shoulder.

After all the hello's, we went through to their living room.

They had blue suede sofas which you kind of sunk into as you sat. Emma was climbing all over Amy and Josh bought us in cups of tea and cakes.

"So, Las Vegas."

"Yes," said Amy, sighing happily and looking at me.

We told the story all over again, with Taryn asking for every detail and Josh telling us a few things about his own trip to Vegas for his bachelor party. A small black and white cat walked in and sniffed Amy's toes.

"Oh, Austen," she said, picking him up, "how I've missed you."

I watched her making a fuss and realised this was the cat Taryn had taken from Amy when she moved away. She gave him a cuddle and I wondered how Alvin was doing.

"Zach, you want to come out and play a few games of pool with me while the girls talk?"

"Love to."

"Great. Let me get my shoes, buddy."

Amy

I loved Taryn and Josh's house. It had floor to ceiling windows facing out across their immaculate garden, bringing in lots of light. We sat facing out, watching the rain drip down the windows, while Emma played on the floor in front of us.

"So, how did your family react to the news?" Taryn asked, tucking her feet underneath her on the sofa.

"Well, Zach and I had a bit of a fight and we arrived separately," I admitted.

"Oh, no. What about?"

"He has a son. In New Zealand."

"What? You never told me that before."

"I didn't know before! Thomas has such little impact on Zach that he just managed to forget to tell me. Then it seemed too late, so he didn't. So I was ignorant, for all that time. I got

263

so angry. He said he never found the right moment to tell me."

"Oh my god, that's awful! No wonder you fell out. You must have been so angry!"

"I was." I bit my lip. So angry that I went out and betrayed him myself.

"So does he see the kid?"

"No, not since he was a baby. He's twelve now."

"Wow, I really am shocked."

The guilt was brimming up inside me, and I wasn't sure I could keep it in any longer. I didn't respond, and swallowed hard to stop myself from crying.

"Seriously, Amy, you need to punish him for this," she laughed. "He owes you some grovelling."

I burst into tears.

Zach

Josh ordered us a pint of Guinness each and we went and sat at a table.

"Have you ever been to Ireland?" Josh asked.

"No, I'd love to though. This is my first trip to Europe."

"Dublin is fantastic," he said, "you can visit the Guinness Storehouse, and there's plenty of other cool things to do. I think you'd like it there."

"I'll add it to my list," I told him.

"You have a list huh?"

"Yes, Amy and I have literally written down all the places we'd like to travel. South America, Japan, Africa...maybe New Zealand."

"That's cool. Taryn and I were going to travel as well, see the world, but then Emma came along and everything changed. Don't rush into children, is my advice. They are a joy, but there's no hurry."

The pool table became free.

"Ready for a game?"

"Sure."

Amy

"What's wrong?" asked a horrified Taryn.

"Oh god Taryn, I've betrayed him, far worse than that, and he doesn't even know," I sobbed.

She passed me a tissue and I blew my nose.

"Right, come on, out with it."

I took a deep breath.

"After I discovered all this, I booked myself into a hotel for one night. I wanted to be alone, and I didn't think he would find me there. I was so angry, I just wanted it to be over."

"Right.. so you're in the hotel..."

"And this guy started talking to me at the bar, buying me drinks..."

"Oh Amy, you didn't?"

"I did." I started crying again and she put her arms around me.

"You were angry and upset. I think if you explain that to Zach, he'll forgive you. You have forgiven him, haven't you? So just calm down."

"It gets worse," I said, taking another deep breath before telling her just how much worse.

"Okay, continue...you're not pregnant are you?"

"No! It only happened a few days ago."

"Right. So, how does it get worse?"

"I didn't know who this guy was...but I discovered in the morning it was Tim."

"Tim who?"

"Libby's fiancé." I said, and started sobbing again.

"Oh my god! You mean of all the men, in all the bars, you managed to find your sister's fiancé?"

"Yes."

"What a shocking coincidence."

"Yes."

"If it wasn't for the circumstances, it'd almost be funny."

"But it's not funny, is it?"

"So what happened next?"

"Well, I was calmer, I didn't know what was going to happen with Zach but I didn't want him to find out. Tim insisted he'd never cheated before and never would again. So we made a pact to forget it ever happened, never speak of it again, and keep it a secret." A fresh round of tears started.

"Oh, Amy."

"I know."

"You need to tell Zach. You can't have this hanging over you."

"How can I tell him? What if he wants to divorce me?"

"He loves you so much, he'll understand that you were hurting and angry. He might not be happy about it, but I bet that doesn't mean it's over."

I took another deep breath.

"Okay, I know you're right. I will tell him."

"Good girl."

"Thanks Taryn."

"You need to tell Libby as well."

"Oh no, I can't...it's only six days until her wedding."

"Just think about it. Wouldn't you want her to tell you?"

I didn't reply. I knew she was right.

"Right, now let's fix your face so that the boys don't know you've been crying."

"Taryn," I said as she was about to leave the room.

"Yes?"

"I love you, thank you."

"Love you too babes."

Zach

I beat Josh at pool. I'd never beat Aaron so I was quite proud

266

of myself. We walked back to their house, and found the girls setting up the table for dinner.

"Smells good," I said, wrapping my arms around Amy's shoulders.

Taryn smiled kind of sadly. I wondered if she knew about Ellie and Thomas, then realised of course she did. Amy told her everything.

"Everything okay?" Josh asked.

"Everything's great," Taryn said, producing a pasta dish from the oven, I noticed she winked at Amy, who just smiled at her.

The following morning, I went out for a run. I hadn't been for the past few days and it felt good to be out and about. I liked the village Taryn and Josh lived in, it was very English-looking, with cottages and rose bushes and green fields in the distance. When I got back, Taryn was sitting in the kitchen reading a newspaper with a cup of tea.

"Good morning, I didn't know you were up," Taryn smiled, getting up to pour me a coffee.

"Yeah, I took the keys hanging up in the hall and went running."

"No worries, couldn't you sleep?"

"I always get up at this sort of time."

"Oh, okay," she said, "I'm just up early because of Emma. She was crying about an hour ago, but she's fast asleep now."

"The joys of parenthood," I sat down opposite her.

"Amy told me about your son."

"I thought she might have."

"She's forgiven you. Many wouldn't have."

I wondered if she included herself in this "many."

"I know it seems pretty ridiculous, but at least it's all out there now."

"I just hope you're as forgiving, if it ever comes to it," she said, getting up.

"What do you mean?"

"Nothing. I better go get showered."

I frowned as she walked away, having no clue what she was talking about. Did Amy have her own surprising confession? At least that would even up the score a little.

I thought about Thomas again, tried to imagine meeting him, taking Amy with me. I was sure she'd want to come. I was sure she'd push me to book the flights as soon as I told her I wanted to go. I thought about Andy then, and hoped I could be as welcoming to Thomas, as he had been to Amy.

Amy

We spent a few hours that morning with them, before heading off back to Milton Keynes. We parked the car at Milton Keynes station. We were going down to stay with Libby and Tim for a night, have dinner with them, and spend the day in London tomorrow.

"You're quiet." Zach said as we got on the train.

"Am I? Sorry."

"Is something wrong?"

"No, I'm just tired."

I'd been going over and over in my head how I was going to tell Zach about Tim. There was no way I was telling Libby. What was the point? Did I really want to ruin their wedding plans? Was it really anything to do with me? If Tim hadn't met me in Boston, it would have been some other girl, some stranger that he'd never see again, and she'd never know then, would she?

Zach pulled out a book he'd been reading and I put my earphones on. I hated being cold towards him, but I didn't know how else to be until I found a way to tell him.

First, I had to deal with seeing Libby and Tim.

Zach

We came out of the underground station and my first real

sight of London was the Thames, with Big Ben and the Houses of Parliament across the water.

"Wow," I'd said, "Big Ben is smaller than I thought."

Amy linked her arm in mine and we walked along, eventually finding Libby and Tim's building. Libby gave Amy and I both big hugs and Tim kind of nodded his head.

"Wow," I said again as I walked into their place. They had large windows with an amazing view. Libby gave us a short tour, including an expensive looking bathroom, an amazing kitchen, and a huge bedroom.

"I love this place." I told them.

"You can buy it if you're interested, we're going to be moving to Kensington, buying a house, after the wedding of course."

"We're going to be staying in the US," Amy said quickly. I was getting the impression she didn't like Tim.

Amy

"That'd be a bit weird, anyway, wouldn't it?" Libby said. "Living in the house your sister lived in."

I thought I might be sick.

The oven beeped and they dished up what looked like Marks and Spencer food from plastic containers. It tasted wonderful though.

I managed to forget, just as Tim had asked me to, and just the opposite of what Taryn had told me to do. We had some wine, and I realised Tim wasn't that bad. He was funny now and then, reasonably intelligent, and he obviously adored Libby.

They pulled out a sofa bed for us in the spare room and we crashed out, tired from the travelling and several late nights.

The following morning, we said our goodbyes and headed out towards Big Ben, Zach taking plenty of photos. We then walked through St. James Park and up to Buckingham Palace, chatting about Libby and Tim and the wedding. It was like old times, times in Boston and I felt rather happy.

"Let's go to Covent Garden," I said, "for lunch."

"I'm glad we're okay," he said, squeezing my hand tight.

"Me too," I said, wondering how I'd ever get up the courage to tell him, and more so, realising why he'd found it so hard to tell me about Ellie. Talking about something that might ruin our relationship was pretty much impossible to spit out.

"Complete honesty from now on, yeah?"

"Yes," I said. It was now or never.

Chapter Sixteen

Zach

It was quite busy on the underground, so we were kind of separated. I watched Amy's face to see when she signalled me that it was time to get off. She looked nervous.

When we reached Covent Garden, I could see her comparison with Faneuil Hall. There were lots of little stores, and street entertainers. The smell of coffee and market stalls. We wandered around for a bit, I bought a couple of souvenirs for my parents, Sophia and Lucy and Amy got something for Harriet. It started to rain so we stole away in a café and ordered some lunch.

"Are you okay? You don't seem yourself," I said.

"I'm fine, it's nothing." She didn't look at me as she spoke, but down at her place mat.

"Listen Amy. From now on, it's brutal honesty, and open communication. What do you say to that?"

She nodded, but her face turned to white and her eyes filled with tears again. She sat up and started moving her hands on the table in a circular motion. She didn't look at me as she began talking again.

"I have to tell you something. Before we can start afresh."

"Okay." I felt nervous, she seemed pretty serious.

"I slept with Tim."

What? I couldn't quite believe what I was hearing and just stared at her for a few moments.

Silence.

"Say something Zach."

"When?"

"In Boston."

"What?"

"In Boston."

"When?"

"The night I left. I checked into a hotel at the airport."

"What the-"

"I didn't know who he was," she started talking quickly, "I was drunk."

"Do you have feelings for him?"

"No! Not at all. I don't even know him. It was a one-time thing. I didn't even know who he was until the next day and-"

"Have you told Libby?"

Her sister, for goodness' sake.

"No, I agreed not to. I don't want to hurt her and-"

I got up and walked out into the street. She followed me. It was raining heavily and we got soaked within seconds.

"Why? Why did you do this?" My voice was starting to get louder but I couldn't remain calm. I wanted to hit him. I wanted to hit the wall. I wanted to drive in the stupid fucking rental car with the driving seat on the wrong side, and smash it in to a tree.

"I don't know. To feel good I guess. I was lonely."

"To feel good? What the fuck, so you are going to cheat on me every time we argue?"

"I thought it was over. I considered us broken up."

"How? You left a note! A note! We didn't even talk through anything. You can't just leave a note and think that's it. You must have known I'd call or something."

"I was sad and alone and felt you had betrayed me."

"So, it's my fault, is it? Two wrongs don't make a right, and I didn't cheat on you, it's not the same thing."

"I'm sorry Zach. It's not your fault. I'm so bloody stupid!"

She burst into tears and tried to hug me. I pulled away.

I began pacing around, consumed with some sort of rage I'd

never felt before. She just stood there. Finally I stopped and looked at her, rain dripping off her hair and nose and her eyes red with tears. For a second I wanted to hug her but then I visualised her naked, in bed, with Tim, and the anger returned.

"I can't believe you did this, and you're going to let your sister marry him."

"I was all alone, and I was depressed."

"For fuck's sake Amy!" She seemed shocked at my cursing.

"How many excuses are you going to give? How *selfish* are you? How did you think I was feeling, all on my own, with nothing but a note. A stupid, child-like note."

"I don't know. I didn't think."

"Oh, well that's alright then. You didn't think."

"I didn't really consider it cheating, because I'd left you and-"

"Yes. You left. Then the exact same night, you just do it with a random person - or not so random as it turns out!"

Tears were streaming down her cheeks. I watched her getting hysterical and I almost went and comforted her, I wanted to hold her and tell her it'd be okay. But I couldn't. I looked at her hard and I suddenly hated her. At that moment I had never hated anyone more. For putting me through this. After almost a year of feeling amazing, I now felt the lowest I'd ever been. I started walking away, not aware in which direction. I just wanted to be away from her. She started following me, pleading and begging, crying hard and almost shouting. "I'm sorry Zach. Please don't leave. I'll never, ever hurt you again, I'm so sorry. What else can I say?"

We passed a couple running to get out of the rain.

I stopped, turning to face her. I didn't dare look her in the eyes, so I just stared at her feet.

She was wearing the sneakers she'd bought when we went to look for a present to buy my parents for their wedding anniversary.

"You're not the person I thought you were."

Funny, she'd said the same thing to me. Right before she

273

went out and screwed another man.

"Yes, yes I am, just like you're the same person despite keeping Thomas from me. If you could just give me a chance to-"

"No, you're not. You haven't even told your sister what you've done! To treat me like this, when you thought we were going to break up anyway, is one thing. But your sister! You're covering up for a person who was prepared to cheat just one week before his wedding! How could do that?"

"You know what it's like with my family. I don't want to cause problems."

"Listen to yourself, you're being so selfish, Amy!"

She looked shocked.

"I promised Tim."

"Well he's obviously more important to you than your sister."

"It's not like that. Please, Zach just let me-"

"There's nothing to explain Amy. There's nothing you could possibly say that will justify what you've done."

"Please, you know I'm not close to Libby, that I have problems with my family-"

"Your family could not have been nicer to me the past few days. What is your problem with them? Are you jealous of Libby? Grow up and get over it."

"Okay, but still-"

"Maybe you were right. Maybe we rushed into this too fast. I guess I should be grateful that you've made me realise so soon, before I wasted half my life trying to make this work. The Amy I thought I knew and loved would have gone to her sister immediately and confessed. I don't even know you at all."

Again, I echoed the words she'd said to me before during our fight. The fight that broke us up. The fight that drove her to sleep with Tim. I suddenly realised this was all my own fault, after all.

"I'm going home. It's over."

"No, please don't say that," she started crying hysterically again.

I had to get away. I kept picturing her, naked with Tim. I could see her all over him. Hear her groan as he screwed her. It made me want to vomit. I had to get away from her.

"I'm going home." I starting to walk faster towards the building.

"I'm sorry for coming here."

"I made a mistake, Zach. A mistake, please, you can't leave!"

I spun around to face her.

"We both made a mistake. In Vegas."

"Don't say that!"

"Why not?"

"Because I've been so stupid but I don't want to lose you. I love you, I've always loved you."

"Why didn't that cross your mind when you were writing me the note, or seducing your sister's fiancé?"

"I realise now I was just stupid and scared. You hurt me too, remember."

"Well. It's too late now. It's over." I didn't want to see her ever again.

"Zach, come on, we can talk about this. You just need to calm down."

I turned around to face her again and she took a step back as if she was frightened. I wasn't even sure where we were now, but we were soaked through.

"Okay. Let's talk. Did you enjoy it?"

"No, it was awful and I felt disgusting afterwards."

"Did you orgasm?"

"What?"

"It's a simple question. You wanted to talk about it. When you screwed Tim. Did he make you come?"

"No, I didn't. It was over very quickly, if you must know."

Somehow, I got some sort of consolation from that, although it might not be true, of course. I still wanted to leave.

I started to sprint away, knowing she couldn't keep up with me.

"No, please Zach!" she screamed.

"Amy," I said, turning and running backwards. "Let it go. It's over. View it for what it was: an amazing year. That's it."

I ran. Amy was shouting after me, but I just kept running. I ran as fast as my legs would take me and when I knew she was out of site, I went into a hotel and asked the receptionist to call me a cab.

An amazing year. Now what?

Amy

So that is how I came to be soaking wet and standing, in the middle of Covent Garden, with the sun coming out and a bright, clear rainbow above my head, crying as if I'd lost everything.

I called his mobile phone, he didn't answer. His words stung: "Take it for what it was, an amazing year." I did all I could to find him again. Eventually, I made my way back to Milton Keynes. The rental car was gone. I called his mobile again, and still no answer.

No one was home when I arrived back at my parents. I called Harriet and told her everything through broken sobbing and begged her to get him to call me the minute he got home.

"Email him," she said after getting me to calm down.

"What?"

"He's always checking his email on that iPhone of his. Write a long email, telling him everything you want to say. I bet you he'll read it before he finds a flight out of there."

That was actually a good idea.

"Thank you Harriet."

Next, I called Libby and asked her if she was free to meet me at a pub in Dunstable for lunch. She agreed, although she sounded suspicious.

276

I opened my laptop and began typing.

To: Zach Rosenberg
From: Amy Rosenberg
Subject: Please, please, please read this.

Zach,
Before you delete this email, please, please hear me out. Give me a chance to explain a few things. I beg you to at least read this. First, with regards to my family... Yes, I need to stop acting like a child and just be happy for Libby, and stop carrying all these issues around. I'd come to that conclusion over the past few days. I've let go of a lot of hang-up's. Just wanted you to know that.

I'm also sorry for leaving the way I did. That was an awful, heartless thing to do. I guess I just freaked out. You shocked me with this whole Thomas thing but I should have done this in a different way and again, I'm sorry.

I have no excuses about Tim. It was a stupid, terrible thing that I did and I am so, so sorry. I felt it was over between us and I guess it was a way to try and get over you. I felt betrayed and it was almost like revenge. But it didn't work, Zach. I'll never be over you, whatever happens. I love you. I always will.

I've been a coward and I realise that now. I'm going to tell Libby today. I've arranged to meet her at a pub half way between Milton Keynes and her place in London. I'm scared, and I don't want to hurt her, but she needs and deserves to know the truth. So. I just thought you should know that I'm going to tell her. Not because you told me to, but because it's the right thing to do.

I don't expect you to forgive me right away, or at all even, or to even want to talk to me. But please, Zach, whatever happens, know that you are an amazing person whom I am desperately in love with, and I will do anything to prove that to you. Please just give me that chance.

I love you.

Amy.

With tears in my eyes, I sent the email, borrowed Jack's car keys, and headed out to meet Libby.

Zach

I took out my iPhone in the airport, intending to email Thomas. I was about to delete Amy's email, but feeling a little calmer now, I decided to read it. I was going to have to wait at least twenty-four hours for a flight home.

I read it, and forwarded it to Aaron. I called him and told him to read it right away.

"Well. What do you think?"

"Does she know about Ellie and Thomas?"

"Well. I told her, just before she left. Just before she slept with Tim."

"You didn't tell the woman you loved, the woman you married, about something as big as that? I'm not saying she's justified for cheating. But just think about how honest you've actually been."

"I know, I should have told her. It's just that the story somehow always makes me look bad. Because I haven't made much effort, you know, to be in touch with them regularly or anything."

"It's not exactly as if he's around the corner."

I knew I should have told Amy. I read her email again. Half of me wanted so much to call her, and the other half wanted to never speak to her again. The latter half kept thinking about her naked with Tim. I wasn't sure I could ever get over that.

Amy

"Hi sweetie." Libby greeted me with a kiss on each cheek. She'd become so...fashionable.

We found a table outside and ordered some food. I decided to get it over with right away.

"Libby. I have to tell you something."

"Okay." She shrugged, obviously unaware of what was about to befall her.

"In Boston. Well...I slept with Tim."

There, it was. Simple as that. Just a few words really. I watched her face and she stared at me blankly for a few seconds before saying;

"Well, I suspected. I wasn't one hundred per cent sure, but thanks for confirming it to me. I wondered if you would."

"You know?" I almost shouted at her. Had Tim actually told her?

"Well, I knew he'd cheated. He told me when he got back. You should have seen him Amy. He was in tears, telling me he loved me and he'd never do it again and he needed one last fling. I was mad at first. But...well, I still really want to be married to him. You saw his apartment over the Thames, Amy, it's amazing."

I couldn't believe what I was hearing.

"You what?"

"You heard me. So he confessed, I got angry, and then it was fine. I only figured out it was you yesterday."

"How?!"

"Well, you just acted so strange around him. And when I introduced you, you didn't look at him. In fact you've kind of avoided him ...so I put that together with you falling out with Zach. So..."

"I'm so sorry Libby. I had no idea at the time who he was. It was a freakish coincidence and I feel awful for not telling you sooner."

"It's fine, really. I'm not sure I'd have the guts to tell you, if I'd, you know, slept with Zach or something."

My heart skipped a beat at the sound of his name. I imagined him in bed with Libby and thought I might pass out with the pain of it. I realised what it must be like for Zach, thinking of Tim and I. The memory was pretty awful. His imagination of it was probably even worse.

"Well, thank you for...understanding," I said, still hardly believing what had happened.

Our lunch arrived. We'd both ordered chicken and bacon salads. I wasn't very hungry and only picked at mine.

"So, what's happened with Zach?" she asked, putting a forkful of lettuce into her mouth.

I felt my eyes fill up with tears.

"I screwed it up. He can't forgive me for what happened with Tim."

She leant forward and put her hand on mine. In some strange way, for the first time in my life, I felt close to her.

"You really love him, huh?"

I ended up telling her everything, repeating some of the stuff I'd told everyone a few days ago at my mum's house. I told her about how we met, and meeting his family, and all the time we spent together, how he made me feel, about him proposing and the wedding and the day we spent in bed in the Vegas hotel room. Then I told her about Thomas. How I'd left.

"But he's everything to me," I said, sighing. "I'm not sure what to do now, if he won't forgive me."

"Wow. Amy, listen to me. You love each other. He just needs to calm down, and then he'll realise he can get past this. You'll be fine. Call him now, I bet he's already thawing out."

"I wrote him an email."

"Good. What did it say?"

"I just explained a few things. Apologised over and over. Told him I love him."

"Well, good luck," she said, smiling sympathetically. And there it was, the moment of closeness was gone.

"So, I've been wearing my wedding shoes around the house,

to, you know, wear them in before the big day. It was Mary's suggestion actually. Did I tell you that I asked Ed to do a reading? I found this poem..."

So there I sat, with this woman – my sister – a person I barely knew anymore, or maybe I never did, and listened to her harp on about her wedding to her rich man, who had cheated on her, realising that she loved his money and status mostly, realising that she hadn't the passion and intensity and pure love that I felt for Zach. I listened to her and felt my heart breaking, realising that Zach was probably on his way home. Thousands of miles away already.

Zach

I looked at my phone again. I had another two emails from Amy. And with surprise, I realised I also had one from Libby.

To: Zach Rosenberg
From: Amy Rosenberg
Subject: Important stuff you should know

Hi Zach
I just wanted you to know that I told Libby. She already knew. Can you believe that? She knew and she doesn't care. I don't think she has much feeling for Tim at all. She's marrying him for the money, the status, and the lifestyle he'll give her.
Yet, here I am, perhaps the exact opposite to my sister, married to the man I am in love with...and I messed it all up. Please Zach. You said: communication is the key. Please call me or email me as soon as you get home. Even if only to yell at me. Please.
Amy

I opened the next one.

To: Zach Rosenberg
From: Amy Rosenberg
Subject: A-Z

Hi Zach,

This might seem corny. But I was thinking about the A to Z thing, that Sophia said once. Do you remember? She said we were like the alphabet: From Aay to Zee. So, for lack of going crazy wanting to talk to you, I wrote this for you:

Why I love you, from A to Z (Amy to Zach):
A – Alvin.
How much you love Alvin. You're so cute together. I love the way you feed him before you feed yourself. The fact that you adopted him when he had nowhere else to go. That you love cats as much as I do.

B - Body.
I love the way you press your body up to mine in bed. The way your skin smells right after you've had a shower.

C – Common interests.
We like the same movies and books and music. I love talking to you after we see a movie for the first time, or read the same book. We like doing the same things, like walking in the park, eating good food, reading, idling time away on our computers, sex! How could I ever find another man who shares these things with me? How could I enjoy any of these things again without you?

D – Dan and Rebecca
Rebecca text me today, asking if we'd like to come for dinner before we leave. They stood there with us on that happy day. How can I tell them I messed it up? Let's go see them together,

show them that what they witnessed was real.

E - Exceptionally good taste.
In clothes. Music. Movies. Everything. I love that you always look good, smell good, and have all these great opinions.

F – Family.
Firstly, you are my family. I want to make a family with you. I also love your family. I miss them.

G - Giraffes
The way you love them. The way you read about them. Talk to them at the zoo. You're so sweet...I love that about you.

H - Hair.
I love the way it's messed up each morning. The way you spend ages styling it. The way it feels when I run my fingers through it.

I - Intellectual.
You're smart, intelligent...you carry all this knowledge in your head. I love the geek in you.

J – Jokes.
You're so funny...you make me laugh every day.

K - Kiss.
The feel of your lips on mine. Or on any part of my body. Your smooth, sweet, pink lips. Sometimes I think we could make out all day. It's like we're teenagers again.

L – Love.
What is love? It's a feeling, an emotion. But it's more than that. It means that I care about you, I want to be with you every minute of every day. I want to grow old with you. I want to share my life with you. If you'll let me.

M – Marriage.
Okay, so we haven't been married long. But just think how we felt that day in Vegas. Zach, I'd marry you a thousand times over. We can build a great, happy marriage. Just let me prove it to you.

N - Natasha.
The name of our future daughter. I've dreamt about her. She'll have cute little pigtails and she'll adore you. You'll be this wonderful father and if it's possible, I'll love you even more for it.

O - Oregano.
I love the way you put some in everything you cook.

P – People skills.
I love the way you fall into easy conversation with everyone you meet.

Q – Queen.
I love that you're always singing Queen songs. Especially in the shower!

R - Rosenberg's.
That's us. Mr. & Mrs. Rosenberg. I'd love to keep that name. I want to be your wife.

S - Sex.
From the first time, you knew exactly how to make me feel amazing. The thought of never making love to you again is just unbearable.

T – Tea.
You always know when I need a cup of tea. We're on the same wavelength, you and me. We just got thrown off course because

we both made silly mistakes.

U – Umm...
Okay, I can't think of anything for U :o)

V – Vegas.
I don't think I've ever been so happy as when we were in Vegas. Have you? When I think of how in love we were – how in love I still am...

W - Waking up with you every morning.
Opening my eyes and seeing you there, either sleeping with this cute look on your face, or seeing you looking at me, smiling. Each time it filled me up with love, and warmth and excitement.

X - Xtremely (I'm sorry that's the best I can do)
I'm extremely sorry, Zach. What can I do or say?

Y - Yellow.
Yellow reminds of waking up in our bedroom, seeing the sunlight pouring through. Lying together under the covers.

Z – Zach, please call me. Please. I love you.

Amy.

I couldn't help but smile as I read each one and pictured each memory. I opened the next email with extreme curiosity.

To: Zach Rosenberg
From: Elizabeth Starling
Subject: You and Amy

Hello Zach,

I hope you don't mind me interfering. Amy told me all about what's happened with you two, and I wanted to do something. Help in some way if I could. After all, it's partly Tim's fault that you are in this mess.

First, Amy adores you. Before she left for Boston, she was always the quiet one. She only ever seemed happy if her head was in a book. But she's different since she met you. You made her happy. She is so very much in love with you. So much so, I'm jealous because I've never felt that way about anyone, even though I'm days away from getting married! So if you feel that way too, Zach, then you ought to forgive her. Because that kind of love, that kind of passion for another person, it doesn't come along every day.

Second, I know you must be agonising about Tim. But, while it might seem an insufficient reason to you, she was lost and lonely and hurt and made a stupid, drunken mistake.
I don't know you at all Zach, and I have no idea if this email will mean anything to you, or if you will read it in time, or if it'll be too late. But I will tell you this. I'd like to see you at my wedding tomorrow, and the details are in the attached files. Come, please. I'd like to get to know my brother-in-law, and I'd like to see my sister happy again.

She has forgiven you. Now give Amy a chance to make it up to you. Please.
Libby.

I re-read all three emails several times. I looked at a photo on my phone of me and Amy in Vegas, taken by Dan at the wedding chapel. We looked so happy. Man, I wanted that back. I wanted to hold her again. I closed my eyes and yet again saw the painful imagine of her with Tim. I still wasn't sure I'd ever be able to get that image out of my brain.

Chapter Seventeen

Amy

I sat in the hotel suite, fiddling with my bouquet, staring at the yellow roses. They looked like they were made of velvet. I leant my head down and breathed in the sweet scent.

"Don't yellow roses mean friendship, rather than love?" one of the bridesmaids asked Libby.

"Yes. But I like them."

How different my wedding to Zach had been.

Libby and Tim had planned a very fancy, no expense-spared wedding. It must have cost them a fortune. Three hundred guests were attending the ceremony at the hotel. The cake alone cost more than five thousand pounds. There was a photographer, videographer, vintage cars, hundreds of flowers, champagne, balloons, a four course banquet. There was even going to be a fireworks display that night.

I was one of eight bridesmaids. I had my yellow dress on, and watched the other girls rally around, all wearing the same matching dresses. My hair was pinned up and my make-up had been done professionally. I was the first one ready and while the others got their hair, makeup and nails done, I sat there poking the flowers, wishing I was in Boston, snuggled up in bed with Zach.

I made small talk with some of Libby's friends, chat to my mum a little about her retirement, and gave Libby a pep talk when she started getting exceptionally nervous. I moved around as if in a dream, it was all very surreal. I kept checking my email on my phone, still no reply from Zach and no text message from Harriet who was to contact me as soon as he got home.

Soon, we were all being carted out of the hotel suite and downstairs to the lobby. I was carried along with the others, not really caring much about what was going on. Jack and Libby linked arms and I smiled at them. I couldn't imagine getting married and having Andy give me away, not with Jack standing there watching. He'd raised me, after all. But I couldn't imagine Jack giving me away, either, while Andy looked on. So, really, it was better. Marrying in Vegas had been a good way to avoid all that. Not that it mattered much now.

Then I saw him, standing at the entrance to the great room the wedding was to take place in. He was chatting to Ed, and he looked up at me, smiled and then winked. It was going to be okay.

Zach

I stood outside the ceremony room, waiting, hoping I'd get at least a few minutes with Amy before she had to go in.

"I thought you had to go home urgently for work?" Ed said, coming to stand beside me.

"Change of plan," I told him. "I got someone else to take care of it."

"Great."

"You look a lot like your dad," I told him.

"Really?"

"Yes. He can't wait to meet you."

Ed nodded.

"I wouldn't have ever have looked for him," he said, "but I'm glad that Amy did."

"Amy was compelled to," I said. "Like I said, he's a nice guy."

"That's good. I'm glad he didn't turn her away. I'm glad they get on well, and that she has family over there now too."

"She misses you, though." I wasn't sure Amy would appreciate me telling him, but I was sure it would help if I did.

"I should call her more often."

"Yes, you should. Come and stay with us over the summer."

"Thanks, I will."

"You don't get old buildings like this in the US, do you?" said Tim, walking up and tapping me on the shoulder.

The hotel looked more like a manor house from a seventeenth century novel than a modern hotel. It was quite something. But still, I didn't respond, I had nothing to say to him. He shrugged his shoulders and begun a conversation with Ed.

And then, there she was. Walking down the grand staircase with a bunch of giggly bridesmaids. She looked as beautiful as ever and she was already looking at me, nervous and expectant. I smiled and winked, to let her know it was all fine. Everything would be fine.

She walked quickly ahead of the others and stood in front of me. Ed and Tim had moved off into the ceremony.

"Zach," she said. "I'm sorry, I-" her eyes welled up with water.

"Stop," I said, putting my fingers to her lips. "I love you Amy, simple as that. It's not okay, and it'll take some time, but I forgive you and I hope you can also forgive me."

A tear ran down her face.

"I love you too."

"Complete one hundred per cent honesty from here on out, right? I mean it," I said, putting my hand beneath her chin.

"Right."

She fell into my arms and I held her there.

"I liked your email, from A to Z."

"Zed, not zee," she said, laughing a little and wiping away a few more tears.

"Have I smeared my make up?" she asked. I laughed. "No."

"Well hello Zach," Libby said, grinning widely. "I'm so glad you came."

"Libby emailed me," I explained.

289

"You did?" Amy seemed surprised.

"Stole his email address from your phone while you were peeing. I felt you maybe needed some help."

"Well, I was likely to come back anyway, Amy sent me some pretty nice emails herself," I admitted.

"Still...Libby...that's the nicest thing you've ever done for me," Amy said, hugging her.

"And now you're going to do something for me in return. Get the bridesmaids lined up, will you." Libby winked at me and I told her good luck before slipping past them to find a seat besides Ed for the ceremony.

Amy

I was grateful to Libby for trying to help me fix things with Zach. I realised something as we were walking down the aisle; we were different, so different. She would never have become my friend if we'd known each other at work or whatever. Yes, I admitted to myself, I'd been jealous on occasion; she was the baby who was pampered, I was the eldest who had to be responsible. She was my sister. Not my friend, but that was okay. I didn't need to be concerned that she didn't call or take any interest. It didn't matter. She loved me, and I loved her. That didn't mean we had to like each other all that much or talk every day.

The wedding was something out of this world. The whole day was a whirl, like something out of a Disney film. We watched them get married. Zach squeezed my hand tight throughout the ceremony. We had photos and speeches and then a reception dinner. We went from glass to glass of champagne. I took Zach and introduced him to my aunts, uncles, and cousins, as my husband. My Aunt Erica was the most shocked.

"My god Amy! When did you get married?"

"In Vegas," I told her, "we didn't want a big fuss."

"Well, I'm so happy to meet you Zach," she said, shaking his hand.

"He's quite a catch Amy, handsome, American, charming."

Zach laughed modestly.

"I know," I said, "I'm very lucky."

The firework display must have cost thousands. Zach and I stood a little further back from everyone else. They all ooh-ed and aah-ed and I rolled my eyes at Zach.

"You wouldn't have wanted all this," he said, gesturing his hand over the crowd of people "for our wedding?"

"Ha! No way. Our day was perfect the way it was. It's just a shame I screwed everything up so soon afterwards."

"Don't Amy. I had just as big a part to play. Let's have a fresh start. Deal?"

I nodded my head and looked up at the different lights in the sky.

"Do you think, maybe, later this year, we could plan a trip to New Zealand?" he asked after a few minutes silence.

"Of course." I squeezed his hand and leaned into his chest. "I'd love to."

We watched the continuing display.

"It's like taking a couple of thousand bucks, and setting light to it, isn't it?" I said.

"Yup." He laughed.

"You want to stay here, in England? Live here I mean? If you want me to move..."

"No. I want to be in Boston. That's our home." He nodded and smiled.

"So you want to...stay here until the end, or?"

THE END

Fantastic Books
Great Authors

Meet our authors and discover our exciting range:

- Gripping Thrillers
- Cosy Mysteries
- Romantic Chick-Lit
- Fascinating Historicals
- Exciting Fantasy
- Young Adult and Children's Adventures

Visit us at:
www.crookedcatbooks.com

Join us on facebook:
www.facebook.com/crookedcatpublishing

Lightning Source UK Ltd.
Milton Keynes UK
UKOW05f1014290614

234246UK00001B/19/P